A Woman's Touch

Part one of A Woman's Touch series

Liz!
Save this one
for the spank
bank

Delaney

Dusty
the Mullie
UK
i. Spent

By Delaney Foster

CHAPTER ONE
Heidi

Monday, May 19

Some women have life by the balls. You know the type. Dropping the kids off at private school in messy buns and yoga pants. Soccer moms with a Louis. If that's you, please don't be offended. Seriously, I applaud you. Some of my best friends are you. I used to *be* you. Different time. Different place. However today, life hasn't let me anywhere near its balls. Hell, I can't even get it to buy me a drink. It flirts and teases and then slaps me in the face. Hard. The sprinkle of hope that it can't hold out on me forever gets me through the day. My Tuesday nights are currently spent with four of my closest friends and a really hot kickboxing instructor we like to call "Hot Alex". Creative bunch aren't we? I go to Target when I need to, rather than when I want to. I've estimated this saves me a good two hundred dollars a week. Do the math. That's over 10,000 a year. I am a baseball mom and my son does go to private school (paid for because I've learned to stay away from Target). I also happen to carry a Louis. But you can bet your sweet ass I worked my butt off for it. Every other Saturday night you'll find me and my kickboxing crew at Jackson Street Pub doing things we probably shouldn't talk about here. And there's hell to pay if any pictures of such unspoken incidents end up on Facebook or Instagram. I'm in a good place right now. It hasn't always been that way.

I stand here now, looking around my office, amazed actually. Amazed at how far I have come and at the same time, waiting for the alarm to sound to wake me from this impossible dream. Something that started as a hobby has now become a full blown successful business. Friends and neighbors used to always ask for my "help" planning parties and weddings, decorating this room or that one, and getting their out of control closets back under control. It came to my attention I had a knack for this sort of thing. So I took a few classes and here I am. Okay, yea, maybe it wasn't that simple. Let me just say, when you go out on your own with a business like mine, wear your big girl panties because there will be disappointment. Stand up straight, paint on your best smile, and try again. *And again.* Fake it til you make it, baby.

Today is my one year anniversary as a storefront business. The past year has definitely been a learning experience. I've fought the good fight and now am able to put the first year notch in my belt. If I had parents who gave a shit, they would be proud. Now as I walk out of my office and down the short hall into the front of the store, I take in a deep breath and smile. Big. The outside walls are a combination of exposed brick and plaster. Lining them on opposite sides of the store are crisp white shelving units displaying tubs, baskets, and crates varying in style and color to be used for organizing. Sleek chrome track lighting on the ceiling accentuates the walls of shelves. The front of the store is entirely made of glass. In fact, if it weren't for the matching chrome handles on the doors, you wouldn't even know they were there. Taking center stage, console tables and shelves made of reclaimed wood, hold an assortment of decorative accent pieces. Upside down whiskey barrels are sprinkled throughout, exhibiting wrought iron lanterns, boxwoods in clay pots, and the most delicious smelling candles ever. Overall, I'd say if modern and rustic ever had a baby, this space would be it.

Did I mention that on the rear wall next to Shelly's desk there's an Otis Spunkmeyer oven? *"Why cookies?"* you ask. *"Why not cookies?"* I say. I feel like any time a person spends money they should have cookies. Or wine. Wine is good too. I suppose now would be a good time to introduce you to Shelly. She stands about 5'3", shoulder length red hair, and beautiful baby blue eyes. She is my administrative assistant. She also happens to be my very best friend and has been since we were five years old. Yes, we're the same age. She'll tell you I'm older because she counts months. I don't.

But if I want to stalk the good looking guy I saw last Monday at the grocery store and write my number on his windshield in lipstick, she's there. Driving. Afterwards when he calls to tell me he has a boyfriend, she's there. With a chick flick and a fresh batch of brownies.

If I want to start a business on nothing but a hope and a prayer, she's there. Leaving behind the classroom of three year olds she teaches every year to answer my phone and file my papers. Most importantly, when I wake up feeling like I want to hide under the covers and never come out again, she's there. Telling me to suck it up and get my act together.

   As I round the corner I catch her grabbing a cookie from the tray on her desk. I put on my best possible *"I mean business"* face and stare her down. "I'm not paying you to eat cookies all day."

"True. You're paying me to answer the phone and look pretty. Since, the phone isn't ringing and well, it doesn't get any prettier than this-" She

5

breaks off into a pause and tilts her head from shoulder to shoulder as if contemplating the best of two options- "I figured I should take a crack at the cookies."

If Shelly isn't being sarcastic, she's sick. At the precise moment she chose to shove the entire chocolate chip cookie into her mouth, the phone rings. Of course. I purse my lips and narrow my eyes at her before answering. She draws an imaginary halo above her head and commences chewing, closing her eyes and making sounds I could closely associate with someone having sex, and takes her seat at her desk. I jot down a name, number, and date on scrap paper and end the call. She can add it to my calendar after her little cookie-gasm.

"I'll be in my office getting ready for my appointments. You should really try one of those cookies. They smell delicious." I say over my shoulder as I walk back down the hall to my office and I'm almost positive she's flipping me off right now.

The cookies really did smell amazing and I can almost taste their warm chocolatey goodness. But rightnow is not the time for cookies. Right now I have things to do and money to make. Here's where I tell you what exactly it is that I do. *A Woman's Touch.* That's the name of my business. That's also what we do. Get your head in the game perverts. You've heard the saying something bland or unappealing could use "a woman's touch." Well, that's what we do. Whether it be decorating a home, organizing a kitchen pantry, or planning a wedding, we do what you either can't find the creativity or just simply don't have the time to do. I, Heidi Lemaire, head the operation, working closely with four of my very best friends. Each of us has our own little niche that we excel at. Last May, I decided to take a leap of faith and expand my office beyond the little sunroom in my apartment, resolving that having an actual physical place for clients to make purchases as well as schedule appointments for our services, would make me a double threat. Two birds. You know the rest.

I call to confirm my afternoon consultation appointments, then I go over the day's schedule with the other girls, hop in my Jeep, and head out. Five hours and a slowly progressing migraine later I'm pulling into a downtown parking garage not far from the federal courthouse. The bride I just left has mentally drained me, New Orleans traffic has me losing my religion, and now I'm here. Dealing with some completely ridiculous letter I got in the mail last week. Apparently someone has decided my property was up for grabs and didn't think I should have a say in the matter. I walk a few blocks over until I reach the tall glass building on the corner. The first floor is a bank. All of the upper floors are leased to private businesses for office space. I am here because I followed the address on my letter of eviction to some overpaid lawyer's office. I check the directory near the elevators for the location of their suite then make my way to the eleventh floor. The doors open into a grand lobby featuring rich mahogany floors, Persian rugs, and 17th century inspired furnishings, complete with old English leather sofas with wood frames, matching leather chairs, and mahogany tables. I marvel at the truly beautiful space for a second. *And why didn't I go to law school?* Then I remember why I'm here and my blood pressure begins to rise again. So much for the beauty. Time to face the beast. The law offices of Alexander, Strauss, and Morrow notified me I have ninety days to relocate my business before they resort to further legal action. Mr. Alexander's secretary doesn't seem to appreciate my stopping by unannounced. Well maybe if he'd returned my phone calls....

"Ms. Lemaire, I told you Mr. Alexander isn't in at the moment. If you'd like me to leave a note that you stopped by," she starts.

I'm sure the petite little brunette means no harm, but I'm not interested in anything she has to say. I cut in before she has a chance to finish. "No. No notes. No messages. No voicemails. You either send me in that office or I find a way to teach Mr. Alexander some manners."

The woman closes her eyes and lets out a long gush of air through her nose as she stands to lead me into his office. "Follow me," she offers. Well piss. She was right. He's not here. Not that I thought the woman was lying...I just feel defeated. I feel angry. I feel bad for being angry with her. It's not her fault. I feel like tacking every little post it note in that stupid bright yellow note pad on his desk all over his office to remind him he needs to return my calls. Or maybe I should plop myself in his big leather chair and wait for him to get back. Or maybe I just need wine. And a bubble bath. Maybe some cheesecake. I apologize to the woman and make my way back to my Jeep.

"So what are you going to do now?" Shelly questions when I get back to the store that afternoon.

"I dunno. Write a letter?" I guess. Isn't that what people usually do when something pisses them off? I can't afford my own attorney so I'm not really sure what to do in this situation. What I do know is that I have come way too far and fought way too hard to have it all taken away because some d-bag with more money than sense saw something he wanted and decided just to take it. The letter doesn't state who wants my store. Or why. But I get the strange feeling I'm playing the role of David and the mystery shopper is Goliath. Normal people don't just go around kicking business owners out of their businesses.

"Girl," she says, pressing her lips together and widening her eyes for dramatic effect, "nobody reads those letters. Why do you think politicians hire assistants?" She pauses as if waiting for me to answer, even though I know she isn't. "Uh, so *they* can read the letters. Duh."

I stare blankly at her logic. She is obviously growing impatient with my silence. "Heidi, why would you write a letter to a man you can just drive down the street and see?"

She's right. It happens occasionally. I take out my cell phone and make an appointment with United States Senator, Nick Knight. And then I decide it's been a long enough day and that bottle of Moscato isn't going to drink itself.

"Mom, can I have a BoomCo?"

I'm in the kitchen watching Hudson watch television. I monitor his viewing choices from behind the bar that separates the living room from the kitchen in my apartment. He sometimes tries to sneak in shows he has no business watching. *Kids*. Commercials make toys look so cool. And when you buy them, they last about a minute and either break or get boring. And then we go buy them something else. Just like the toymakers knew we would. Genius.

"What's a BoomCo?" I ask him while draining the hamburger meat.

"It's really cool! The bullets really stick. And when I say stick, I mean stick. You have to work really hard to get those things off!" He's obviously excited about whatever it is. He's six. It doesn't take much to excite him. "Oh, and can you buy two of them? Pleeeeeease? So me and the kid next door can shoot each other?"

I give him an amused look. "Why in the world would you want to shoot someone with a bullet you have to work reeeeally hard to unstick?" That just sounds painful to me.

He looks at me like I have three heads. "Mom, it's Nerf. It doesn't hurt." He says this as if it's something every person should already know.

"I'll think about it."

"You always have to think about it." He looks defeated. I laugh.

He's right. It's my go-to mom response when I don't want to say yes right away. Even though chances are I'll buy him the toy tomorrow.

I chop the lettuce and tomato and construct our taco dinners. We talk about our day during our meal then Hudson has his bath and gets ready for bed.

"Wanna hear my new song?" he asks as I tuck him in.

It's part of our nightly routine. He sings me one of his Hudson originals. I tell him a bedtime story and rub his hair until he falls asleep.

Hudson sits up and grabs his mini acoustic guitar. He has absolutely no idea how to play but that doesn't deter him one bit.

He strums, "I've got a chicken. I've got a chicken. I've got a chicken and his name is Peck. Peck. Ohhhhhh Peck. You are my chicken and your name is Peck."

"Did you like it?" he asks when he's finished.

His little voice is music to my ears. I smile and kiss his forehead. "I loved it."

I tell him a story of a man with magic shoes and it isn't long until he's sound asleep. The six year-old boy that owns my heart.

CHAPTER TWO
Heidi

Tuesday, May 20

It's 10:30 in the morning and I'm standing in awe of an immense combination of black glass and steel. The building stands five stories high and has a slight "S" curve on the side that bears a logo which informs visitors they are, indeed, in the state of Louisiana. In front of the structure is a pond with a large metal globe sculpture located in the center. Four water sprays frame the globe, creating an almost peaceful environment. I called earlier to confirm the appointment. Not out of insecurity. Out of habit. Do you have any idea how frustrating it is to show up at a client's house only to have to wait in the driveway for forty-five minutes because they forgot you were coming and went grocery shopping?

I channel my inner confident business woman as I step through the revolving door, shoulders back and head high. Don't get the wrong idea here. I am confident in my professional ability. I *appear* confident in everything else. In my line of work, appearances are everything. You have to look the part, dress the part, and act the part. Give me a home that hasn't been updated since 1972 and I'll make it look like it was newly constructed. Put me alone in a room with a man who sets the budget for an entire country and I'm completely out of my element. That's what Shelly is for. She's my brains. *Maybe I should have brought her with me.* Confident designer? Absolutely. Confident business woman? Work in progress.

I make my way through the security station at the entrance and am directed to another wing of the complex. A long, wide hallway, one right turn, and a sharp left later, I reach a large open lobby I assume to be the entrance to where all the politicians hang out. A red head behind a large crescent shape desk smiles as she greets me. "Good afternoon. How may I assist you?" *She's friendly.*
"I have an appointment with Mr. Knight."
Her smile instantly disappears, replaced with stone cold incredulity. "Yes. Of course you do." *Or not.*
I wait.
Tick-tock.

A few uncomfortable silent moments pass. I glance around the lobby and tap my foot a couple of times, waiting for- oh, I don't know- her to send me in, send him out, something. What I get is a whole bunch of nothing. Decisively, I approach the desk. "Is there somewhere I should be going to meet with him? Or will he be coming out?"

"Your name?" She doesn't even bother looking up from her computer. *What a bitch.*

"Heidi Lemaire." I don't know why I thought the mention of my name would make her drop everything and suddenly become helpful, but I said it with the confidence that suggested she should do just that.

My confidence doesn't affect her, however.

She types something on her attention consuming computer and picks at her fingernails until she hears the faint sound of a water droplet. Her eyes never leaving the screen, she bitterly says, "Fourth floor. Go left out of the elevator. His office is at the end of the hall."

"Thank you. It was a pleasure." *It was so* not *a pleasure.* I make sure to give her a cheeky smile before I head to the elevators.

I get the same warm welcome when I approach the area outside the office at the end of the hall. Thing One and Thing Two have obviously rallied together to make this meeting completely awkward from the jump. This one has long blonde hair, fair skin, bright red lipstick, and a smaller desk.

"Ms. Lemaire?" she questions. I nod once. Politely of course. I do have manners you know.

"Have a seat. He'll call for you when he's ready." Thing Two points to a leather settee settled against the wall to her right. To her left is a set of glass paned double doors that I assume lead to his office. I cock my head and ponder for a moment. Hmm. I guess I was expecting something resembling the entrance into a bank vault. You know, with key pads and retina exams.

I sit. I sigh. *"He'll call for you when he's ready."* Seriously? I find myself rolling my eyes and pulling out my phone. Just as I'm texting Shelly how excited I am that his majesty the politician has made time to meet with the likes of me, the French doors leading into his office open simultaneously.

My breath catches. There, in that doorway, stands sex on legs. This man is the epitome of tall, dark, and handsome. Life has given me the gift of eternal male objectification all wrapped up in a sleek silver suit with a crisp white oxford and a dark gray silk tie. His hair is somewhere in between chestnut brown and copper. His jaw is chiseled and he sports a

11

two-day stubble. I'm guessing he's done this on purpose to add to his overt sex appeal. Or he may have just forgotten to shave. The messy hair and stubble are a stark contrast to the rest of him. His olive skin is flawless. His eyes are golden. No, maybe they're green. Okay they're gold with green flecks. Well, they're indescribable but beautiful nonetheless. Don't even get me started on those lips. Perfectly plump with a very lickable cupid's bow. Great. He's not smiling. Why isn't he smiling? Am I drooling? I press my lips together to make sure I'm not and then I stand. I flash him my beauty queen smile. Not that I've ever been a beauty queen, but I have seen them smile and I can fake smile with the best of them. He reciprocates. And the heavens open up and the angels sing and all is right in the world again! This man. If they could bottle him, I would drink him.

"Ms. Lemaire," he says as he gestures toward the inside of his office. He's still smiling. I'm still staring.

I have abruptly lost the confident business woman I channeled earlier. I'm yelling and searching everywhere for her but apparently she's hiding under the bed like a three year old afraid of a thunderstorm. *Chicken.* I guess I'm on my own. All of a sudden, I feel underdressed and entirely self-conscious in my ivory shift dress and wedge sandals.

He sits in his black leather executive chair behind his grand desk of two-toned golden burl and dark walnut wood. *Nice.* He's got good taste.

"Please. Have a seat." There goes the smile. Maybe he doesn't like being gawked at? Who am I kidding? How could he look like that and not know it? Either way, I look away and drag the confident business woman from under the bed by her hair.

Being that the only other furniture in the office suited for seating are the two chairs in front of his desk, I choose the closest one and sit gracefully. I feel like I'm about to enter a spelling bee but I've forgotten the alphabet.

"It is *Ms.* Lemaire, isn't it?" He places heavy emphasis on the zz in Ms. *Is he fishing?*

"Actually, it's Heidi. Just Heidi." *Well played.* I draw an imaginary tick mark on an imaginary chalk board under "Team Heidi."

"Heidi," he repeats as if he's contemplating some deep hidden meaning in my name, "I hope you didn't have any trouble contacting me."

*Now that you mention it...*I force a smile and make light of my experience with his catty assistants. "Actually making the appointment was no problem at all. Getting into your office took an act of Congress though." I quietly laugh at my own little joke. Get it? He's a senator...Okay it's funny to me.

One corner of his mouth twitches. He wants to laugh. I know it. But he doesn't. "Well I'm disappointed to hear that. I'll make sure your next visit is a more pleasurable one," he states.

The way he says *"pleasurable"* has the word wrapping around my body like a silk robe after a hot bath. Little plastic party horns are going off in my head at the indication that I'll be visiting him again. I catch myself staring at him and realize I should probably say something in response. Crap. I thought only guys zoned out like this. What the hell? "Oh, it was actually a joke. It's no big deal. Really." *Your receptionist is a twit.*

"I train them to be selective," he explains. Shit, is he reading my mind? He continues, "I'm sure you can imagine the amount of people that walk through those doors without appointments."

It's apparent I'm not catching on so he elaborates. "People wanting charity, jobs, tickets fixed," he pauses to think before continuing, "among other things."

Awww just can't get the panty droppers to leave you alone huh big guy? *Must be rough.*

"No, it's fine. I understand. You're important. I didn't expect it to be easy," I reassure him. I make sure and look him in the eye to convince him that I'm serious.

"Easy is never worth much in my opinion anyway." His tone is matter-of-fact and his intense gaze is boring into me until my mouth goes dry and I have to lick my lips. His eyes drop to my mouth as I do this. It's suddenly very hot in this room. I watch as his Adam's apple shifts slightly in his throat. I don't respond. I couldn't if I wanted to.

The silence only lasts a few seconds but it feels like it's been an eternity when he breaks it. "I don't have a lot of time so we should get right to it." He pauses a moment before smiling again. This one is different. It's tilted more toward one corner of his mouth. And he has one brow slightly arched as if challenging me to say something.

Under normal circumstances I would accept his challenge and tell him a few of the many, many things I'm thinking we could *get right to*, but we can all agree these are not normal circumstances and I am utterly speechless. He's eyeing me for the second time in our brief acquaintance. I must look like the village idiot. Where in the world is Shelly when I need her? *Come on, Lemaire. Get it together.* Focus. Focus. I pull my eyes away from his glorious face to find my portfolio. I pull out the letter and plop it on the desk in front of him. "I think we have a miscommunication here," I inform him.

He narrows his eyes and I see a slight twitch in his lips as I cross my legs and prop the folder back on my lap. I'm nervous but I refuse to let him know that. His eyes briefly scan the paper. He leans back and props his elbows up on the arms of his chair, locking his long fingers in front of him. "Oh? And why is that?" he asks.

You obviously don't have to be smart to be in politics. "Because my business is not for sale," I sternly inform him, "and this," I emphasize my meaning by waving my hand in circles over the paper in front of him, "is bullying."

He chuckles. I don't remember saying anything funny. "What is it that you do, Heidi?" he inquires.

The impatient section of my brain wants to say, *"What the hell does it matter? Can you fix it or not?"* But the logical section wins out and instead I reply, "Design. Event planning. Organization. In short, I make things pretty."

The senator ponders my answer for a brief moment before responding. "A Woman's Touch?" He's holding back a smile as he emphasizes the word *touch.*

So that's what this is about? My business name? I guess he was hoping for a different profession. *Politicians.* I'm sure he can hear my jaw clench. Typical man. Out of the many responses running through my mind right now, I look him dead in the eye and choose the simple and polite one. "It's a figure of speech. A saying."

He nods once in acknowledgement, stands, walks around to the space in front of me, and leans his cute little behind against his desk. He stuffs his hands into his pockets and crosses his legs at the ankle. His presence is intoxicating. He's so close. So. Very. Beautiful. I almost forget why I'm here. He looks down at me and questions, "So, Heidi, what makes you think there's anything I can do?"

I'm looking up at him, my eyes pleading with him to do something. Anything. He appears so powerful. I feel meek. I don't like it. But then again I kind of do. I want him to fix this. I want him to lean down and tell me not to worry. I want to put it in his large, strong hands and not think of it again. I'm suddenly tired. So tired. Tired of carrying the weight of the world on my shoulders. Tired of always being the one everyone looks to for answers. He can't write me off. He can't send me away without even trying. I manage to quickly shut down the pity party, and square up my shoulders. I take in a deep breath and give him an answer, praying it's the one he needs to hear. "Hope."

CHAPTER THREE

Nick

Note to self: Save the Sazerac for weekends. Stick with Johnnie Walker on weeknights.

I pop two ibuprofens and down half a pot of coffee. I could use a trip to Waffle House right about now. Greasy eggs and bacon is always a great hangover cure. I hadn't planned on going out. I knew I had a meeting this morning with an unhappy business owner and the last thing I wanted was to be hung over having to listen to that shit. Occupational hazard I suppose.

I had to get out of the house, though. Elise has been blowing up my phone for the past three days. Regardless of what her messages say, I know she doesn't want to *talk*. We never were good at talking. As a matter of fact, there is only one thing that we were good at, and that's not happening at any point in our future. What is it with women and their ex's? Why do you assume the fact that we used to sleep together gives you a free pass to call us every time you need a consolation lay? You're baggage now. Maybe that makes me an ass. So make me a name tag and call me an ass.

Okay, so maybe it's not that cut and dry with Elise. The back story: We dated for six years. Then, I proposed. Six months later I bought us her dream home. Two months after that I caught her with her hand in the cookie jar. It didn't end well. There is something to be said about the ending of a bad relationship. It breaks the heart but mends the eyes. You begin to see things that weren't there before. You begin to realize that comfort doesn't equal love. I can't tell you exactly what *love* is, but I can tell you what we had wasn't it. I'll spare you the gory details of my post-Elise revelations. What I will tell you though, is that Johnnie Walker and I became real close friends. That was four years ago. I haven't spoken to Elise since the day she cussed me out for donating all her things to Salvation Army. Don't look at me like that. I had to hit her where it hurt. Maybe if she'd have kept her clothes on then, well, she could have kept her clothes. That chapter of my life is over. The book is closed and on the top shelf collecting dust.

Hangover aside, the night did have its advantages. Tall, long black hair, leggy. I think she said her name was Autumn. Some judge's granddaughter. I got her number during a private cocktail party last month at the very same place we met last night. The evening ended with her little purple dress hiked up around her waist, ass out, watching me fuck her from behind in the bathroom mirror. All in all it was a decent night, though I can't say I'll be calling her again.

Now back to my morning. Typical morning at the office- emails, conference calls, meetings. Here's your basic introduction to my life: I used to be a criminal law attorney. Now I am a United States senator. I make laws. People follow them. Sure there's a lot more to my job than just that, but it doesn't add to the story right now and that's all you need to know to keep reading. But you can imagine I am an extremely busy man. So when I get a message that a disgruntled business owner I'm meeting with is calling to confirm her 10:30 appointment, you can guarantee I forward it to Candace. First of all, if we have an appointment, you're there at 10:30 or I'm coming to whip the piss out of you. I'm not calling to confirm. Get a personal assistant for that shit.

An hour later, at exactly 10:25, I receive the email from MacKenzie, in downstairs reception, that my appointment is here. I'm on the phone with Columbia so she'll have to wait. I'm not being an asshole. I told you, I'm a busy man. And she's early. I've still got five minutes to finish my phone call.

When I was first elected, I practiced an open door policy at my office. Whenever I was in town, constituents of all occupations and backgrounds were welcome to walk right in and let me hear it. But for the past year or so I've found I need to be a little more selective. Don't get me wrong, I have my fair share of little old ladies or pissed off old men complaining about noisy neighbors or bad water. I get farmers, bankers, and school board officials. But as the visits from the girl from the cocktail party or the waitress at the restaurant became more and more frequent, I had to coach Candace and MacKenzie to screen my visitors a little more carefully. So lately it's been business as usual. Stuffed suits and grandmas. I listen to their concerns, tell them lunch is on me, and promise to bring up their problem during the next session. Well you can imagine my surprise when I open the doors to my office to find her. *What.The.Fuck.* She stashes her phone away and stands. Maybe I should start taking appointments more often. This woman is approximately 5'8"-5'9" in her heels so I'm gauging 5'5" barefoot. Her long hair is pulled to one side and draped over one shoulder so that her curls fall loosely over her breast. Her golden brown hair is highlighted with subtle blonde streaks. She's tan, but I'm betting it's not her natural skin tone because her eyes are light. Her dress. Holy shit. The bottom layer reminds me of a silk slip nightgown a woman would wear to bed. It hugs her curves and stops just above her knees. The outer layer is a loose, thin, sheer material. She's staring at me with these beautiful, bright, emerald green eyes. And then, she smiles. It's forced, I'm sure of it, but contagious. I have no choice but to smile back. I am trying too hard to match her false enthusiasm and I feel as though I look like a psychopath. *Okay Norman, stop staring and invite her inside.*

I recall the name from my calendar reminder and repeat it for confirmation. She sure doesn't look like anyone I've met at a cocktail party. I would definitely remember that face. And I would have most definitely had her naked before now. I try to pinpoint where I would know her from. Nope. I got nothing. But hell, if she's here for a date, count me in. *No such luck.* The woman in my office is Heidi Lemaire. The business owner here to grab me by the balls and insist I put on my armor, hop on my horse, and come to her rescue. I start the meeting off with the usual small talk. I don't really care if she had trouble contacting me or not. She's here now so who gives a rat's ass? I expect the usual "No problem at all" bullshit when she cracks some lame joke about an act of Congress. And then laughs at herself. *Charming.* But I bet I make her stop laughing in..five..four..three..two..Bingo. No more laughing. She's trapped in my gaze. Her lips are slightly parted and she's holding her breath. She quickly regains her composure and dismisses her treatment downstairs as no big deal. I'm not sure why I feel the need to explain my professional tactics to her but I do. And she continues to shrug it off. She's either putting up a really good front or she just really doesn't care. Finally, I catch a tiny glint of seriousness in her eyes and fight to hold it. Hold it. *Right there. Don't lose her.* Seconds later her tongue snakes out to wet her lips. The movement is slow and cautious but I doubt it's done this way on purpose. I'm now hypnotized by her perfect little mouth. *This isn't a fucking date Nick. Quit thinking with your dick.*

I quickly switch gears and remind us both why she's actually in my office in the first place. I expect passionate ranting or hysterical crying when she presents her complaint. She doesn't do either. She just pulls out a sheet of paper and mentions something about a misunderstanding. I scan the document and try to decipher the purpose for her visit. My brain is on Red Bull and Viagra. I'm trying to focus but I can't seem to take my eyes off of the exposed flesh at bottom of her thigh. I don't think she's aware her dress has inched up beneath her legs as she shifts uncomfortably in her chair. She pulls to adjust the material over the top of her thigh as she crosses her legs, but she would have to stand to do anything about the bottom. Lucky for me she has opted not to.

She mentions something about bullying as she motions towards the letter and I can't help but laugh. I stop myself when I realize she's serious. I don't want to insult her. *Bullying.* That's cute. My mind flashes back to the address on the letter. *A Woman's Touch.* Maybe this is my lucky day after all. There are only a limited number of things that name can ensue and my mind is hard-wired to go straight for the filthy stuff. I'm not a shy guy so I ask her directly what it is that she does. What I want to ask is what it is that she touches. But I am feeling rather gentlemanly this morning so I don't. Her answer throws me a curve ball. Didn't see that coming. She's a designer. Damn. There goes my happy ending massage.

She wants to tear into me. Curse me for judging her. I can see it in her eyes. But she bites her tongue and remains polite. *Interesting.* If she thinks she's intimidating me she's wrong. I am a master of intimidation and Heidi Lemaire is about to find that out. I move to stand directly in front of her, not leaving any room for her to move or stand. She has no choice but to look at me. To look *up* at me. Her expression changes slightly. It softens a little. It's subtle but I catch it. I like it. I ask her what makes her think I can help. She looks up at me with those hypnotizing eyes. She doesn't even have to answer the question. I'm going to help her. I just can't let her know it yet. Like I said, she doesn't have to answer, but when she does her answer is unlike any I've ever heard in my two years in office. *"Hope."* Fucking hope. Like I'm her savior. Her hero. Newsflash: I'm not the hero in this story. I'm the villain.

I move toward the door hoping she'll take the hint and leave before she screws with my head any more. "Leave the letter here and give my assistant your number. I'll see what I can do," I tell her. She extends her hand to shake mine as she makes her way out of my office.

"Thank you Mr. Knight," she says.

"Nick. Just Nick," I tell her with a smirk, mimicking her response to me earlier.

She gives me an acknowledging nod, releases my hand and stops in the doorway on her way out. "If you ever decide you want some help with this office, I happen to know a great designer," she declares. And then there's that smile again. It continues all the way up to her eyes. This time I notice her dimples. This smile is sincere. And it's breathtaking. Then she winks at me. Fucking winks. At me. Little Red Riding Hood has no clue she is messing with the Big Bad Wolf.

I simply smile back and reply, "I'll keep that in mind."

"What the hell is wrong with my office?" I think as I take a seat behind my desk and look around. I decide she must have been kidding. There's nothing wrong with my office. Then I open my Mac book and do something no man with a functioning penis should ever do. I google Heidi Lemaire.

CHAPTER FOUR
Heidi

"So he's attractive?" Shelly eyes me over the rim of her glass of iced tea.

"Very."

"Rich and powerful?" It's not really a question though she phrases it as such.

"Obviously," I answer anyway.

"Lots of sexual tension?" Another statement/question. She does this a lot.

"There is."

"So, you're complaining about having to deal with him. Why?" She takes a big gulp of tea before setting the glass down.

It's late May and we're having lunch outside at our favorite Italian bistro. It's a small local place off Decatur. I've heard in whispers that the family who owns it is old Italian mafia. But you can't believe everything you hear. One thing I have learned since living here is the shadier the place looks on the outside, the better the food tastes. Suppato's is packed today. It just finished raining so the humidity is thick. Shelly is on her third glass of tea. She'll be cursing me later when she can't stay out of the bathroom.

"I'm not complaining. I'm contemplating."

"That's an awful big word there, tiger" Shelly teases. "What is it you're con-tem-pla-ting?" She carefully enunciates each syllable to highlight her use of the word.

"Stabbing you with my fork." I stab my tortellini with my fork as a warning.

She eyes me carefully. "Ma'am, I'm gonna have to ask you to put the fork down and step away from the pasta," she says before adding, "You know, that's really just your subconscious saying you want to be stabbed....by a hot sexy senator." She stuffs a piece of garlic bread in her mouth.

I snort. Hey, it happens. This makes her laugh with me, almost choking on her food.

"Oh. My. Gosh. You are ridiculous," I tell her when I stop laughing.

"Actually, my subconscious wants the sexy senator to tell all his golfing buddies they need to back off my business." Unfortunately, my hormones and my subconscious aren't seeing eye-to-eye right now.

"How can I possibly take this whole thing seriously when all I can do now is picture him naked? Who knows? Maybe a little desk sex will get this thing rolling a little faster."

20

We stop laughing so Shelly can give me a taste of her infinite wisdom. "Okay. You have to focus on the big picture here. He's probably passed your letter off to some attorney friend of his and you will most likely never see him again. Once all this blows over, then you can hop on over to his office and personally thank him." She wiggles her eyebrows and puckers her lips.

"Shelly, I can't *actually* sleep with him. I was kidding. The list of things that could go wrong is a mile long. Remember Monica Whats-Her-Name?"

She bursts into a fit of laughter. "He's not the president, Heidi. And that was a completely different situation," she informs me. "You are damn good at what you do. This guy is gonna fight for you because you deserve it. Not because you gave him the good-good. Take your sexual frustrations out on Alex. I seriously doubt he'll mind."

She gives me a wink and I reach over and steal a bite of her risotto. Just like that, I feel better. *Yeah. I've got this.*

Shelly is right. I can't screw my way out of this. I spend the rest of my afternoon being a talented designer and stop worrying about things I have no control over. She knows me better than anyone. Even the things I don't say out loud don't get past her. When I'm feeling insecure about a particular thing, I tend to drift toward the one thing I am secure in. She's known me long enough to notice. And she always steers me right back on track. If I were a lesbian, she'd be my soul mate.

I haven't had the best track record with relationships. So, I just don't do relationships. I do sex. Very selectively of course. The bar is set pretty high. I don't just drop the panties for anyone. I've always been told, *"Stick with what you know."* What I know is that love has been a disappointment. So here I am. I have no expectations from the men I see. No expectations. No disappointments. That's my motto.

It started in high school with Trey. I loved Trey. He was your typical all American high school guy. Football. Grades. Friends. He had it all. We dated five years. He was my first. I can't tell you it was romantic. As a matter of fact, I can't tell you anything about it at all. He got me drunk when my mom was out of town. Totally ruined my de-flowering. But because we had been dating over a year it wasn't supposed to be a big deal. Well, it was to me. After that, Trey just took what he wanted, when

21

he wanted it. I was young and in love so I didn't know any better. I thought that's just how it was.

I suppose he got bored with me because he soon moved on to Amy. Then Chandra. And April. He even took Madison to senior prom, leaving me at home. Alone. He came over afterward though so that makes it okay right? Not quite.

I quickly figured out that I had a gift. Wrapped in a pretty pink package and called a vagina. Everything he threw at me, I threw right back at him. He flirted with my friends. I started flirting with his friends. Innocently of course. And they seemed to like it. He didn't. That's when things got physical.

Trey would tell me no one wanted me. That I was all used up. That if he left me I would be alone because nobody wanted someone else's leftovers. He told me I was needy and that's why he cheated. He told me it was my fault. Then he slammed me against the door of his apartment and choked me until I cried.

I had to prove him wrong. To prove someone *would* want me. Then one night at the local Blockbuster I met a guy named Chris. Chris wanted me and it didn't take much persuasion. I was actually impressed with how easy it was. My one night stand with the local video clerk did wonders for my confidence. The "power of the V" was now in full effect. I became a master in the art of flirtation. Trey soon became putty in my hands. He never found out about my night with Chris. I guess I was better at keeping secrets than he was. He had spent five years breaking me down and murdering my self-worth. My confidence was a distant memory. But there was one thing. One thing I figured out I was good at. One thing I couldn't mess up. The art of seduction. And I practiced that art frequently with Trey. Until I became a novice at a game he taught me to play. Then I left him. The last time I saw him was at a New Year's Eve party a few months later. He followed me to my car and stomped my head into the pavement with his steel toed boots. The following day, after I checked out of the ER with a concussion, I packed up my crap and got the hell out of dodge.

A couple of years after I left Trey, I met Cole. Cole seemed perfect. Cole should have been an actor. Cole and I spent ten years together in a marriage that neither one of us had the guts to admit was bad. Today, men are only good for one thing to me. A means to an end. A fulfillment to a need. Don't go jumping to conclusions. I'm not some man hating she-woman. I like men. I just don't *need* one. I can change my own light bulbs and take out my own trash. I make my own money and pay my own way. So there you have it. There is reason number one: why I don't date.

CHAPTER FIVE
Heidi

After work, I drop Hudson off with his dad at baseball practice and head to the gym for our Tuesday night kick boxing class. Shelly, Hannah, Meghan, and Ashton are helping each other with hand wraps when I walk in. The class has been part of our work-out regimen for six weeks now. After the first time, I was almost positive I would have to chop my legs off and never step foot back in that gym. Ever. Now, we're all addicted. I get all wrapped up and select my bag. It's the same one as always. Right in the middle. Next to our instructor. I unknowingly chose this bag our first class. It didn't take long to figure out why this one was unoccupied. Hot Alex felt the need to use my bag, and my inexperience, to demonstrate proper technique. Much to his surprise, I'm not the type to embarrass easily so I played it up. I remember him grabbing my leg when I attempted my first high kick. He held my ankle and guided my leg further up the bag. *"Do you think you can handle it?"* he had asked. His British accent was an immediate turn on.
I moved my leg up further without his assistance and arched an eyebrow at him.
"Well it is my first time. So be gentle."

Tonight's work out is unusually intense. Intense is pretty normal but tonight is crazy. Alex is on fiya and my body is screaming at me by the time class is over. You'll get no complaints from me though. Beating the crap out of that bag is something I look forward to every week. It helps relieve pent up frustration. And my frustration-o-meter is through the roof this week.
The other girls always head next door to La Comida for two dollar margaritas afterwards. Tequila and I are not friends so I usually just go home alone. Don't feel bad for me. I don't stay that way for long.
As we were leaving our second kick boxing class, four weeks ago, Alex approached me.
"It's nice to see you came back for more." He's wiping the sweat from his body with a towel. I wish he'd just let me do that for him. I could do a much better job.
"Yea, I tend to know a good thing when I see it." Yes, I was openly flirting with the kick boxing instructor. He's hot and I'm single. It's not illegal.

Alex ended up joining us that night for margaritas and later on, I ended up back at the gym naked and panting in the boxing ring. Check that one off the fuck-it list.

I don't normally like to let the men I see double dip. It helps keep things uncomplicated. But I make an exception with Alex. There's no way I can watch him hot, sweaty, and half naked for an hour every week and not give him the business. Needless to say, we've been doing our little post-workout mattress dancing for about four weeks now. However, after the first time in the boxing ring, we moved it to my apartment.

I shower as soon as I get home and put on my usual t-shirt and panty pajama combo. I don't see how people sleep with pants on. I feel tangled and trapped. And hot. As it is, I'm usually kicking one leg out from under the comforter to find the blissful coolness of the top. Then I get too cold and snuggle back underneath. It's a nightly pattern. Hot. Cold. Hot. Cold. Somebody please tell me I'm not the only one who does this. Okay, focus. Back to the story.

Here I am in my PJ's waiting for Alex. Waiting. And waiting. I wish he would hurry. Baseball practice is over at 7:30 and Cole will be dropping Hudson off soon.

A knock. *Finally.* I open the door a bit to make sure it's him. It is. I scowl. "Took you long enough." I reach around the door and grab his shirt to pull him inside.

Alex's grin resembles that of the Cheshire cat. Slow and wide. "So you missed me?"

"Parts of you," I reply.

He inches closer so that there are just a few inches between our bodies and wiggles his eyebrows.

"Oh? Which parts in particular?"

My hand slides down his chest, over his abdomen, finally skimming over his crotch. I stop there for a brief second before making my way around to his perfectly toned backside. All the while, my eyes never leave his. He still bears that ridiculous grin but his eyes are dark and salacious.

Alex is absolutely adorable. His body should be on an infomercial. People would definitely buy what he's drinking. His face has boyish features that any woman would find attractive. He is tall. I would say 6'4" at least. His smile is radiant and when he shows it, which is quite often, his eyes sparkle. He has dark brown curly hair. And don't forget the accent. The accent alone is enough to soak the panties.

"Oh you know, just the important ones," I couple his grin with one of my own.

He wraps his arms around my body, placing his strong hands directly below my behind and scoops me up. I hook my legs together around his waist and loop my arms around his neck. He smells like aftershave and soap. Manly and clean. He carries me to the small round dining table and sets me on top of it. I curl my fingers up in the hair at his nape and pull his head to mine. He licks his lips and leans forward. He is so close now. I can feel his breath on my face. His forehead touches mine. I close my eyes, part my lips and hold my breath as I wait. In the stark silence all I can hear is his breathing and my own pulse beating in my ears. Then, I feel his smooth, soft lips touch mine. I let him linger there for a moment before I twirl my fingers tighter in his soft curls and pull him closer, forcing him to kiss me harder. I can feel him smile against my lips. Just as he begins to pull away, I lightly scrape my teeth over his plump bottom lip. It pleases me to open my eyes and find his are still closed. He's enjoying this. I run my tongue across the spot I just skimmed with my teeth and gently suck his lip between mine. Softly, I press my lips against his as I bring my hands around to cup his cheeks. His freshly shaved jaw is silky smooth. I open my eyes and pull away. I'm done wasting time so I grab his t-shirt and pull it over his head. I toss it to the side and reach for the hem of my own shirt. I have it halfway off when Alex places his hands, palms down, on the table next to my legs. His thumbs stroke the outside of my thighs as he leans in close enough that our noses are almost touching. He looks like he's about to tell me he's dying. It bothers me a little. I let go of my shirt and give him my full attention.

"I'm going to need you to quit coming to class wearing nothing but those tight pants and a sports bra. It's a bit distracting."
I pull my head back to get a better look at his face. He can't be serious. *You're going to need me to do what? When did you start paying my bills?* I laugh. "Two things: One, it's a tank top. Two, I thought you enjoyed my distractions." *Well that's a relief.* I thought he was about to tell me something deep. I'm not ready for deep. I prefer to splash around here in the shallow end.
As I say this, I wrap my legs tighter around his waist, pulling myself to the edge of the table. He stands up straight, causing my legs to unlock and fall to his sides. I let out a disappointed huff.
"I do enjoy them," he gives a slight roll of his hips, grazing the inside of my leg with his rock solid arousal, "Obviously."

26

"What I don't enjoy is walking the room during a water break and hearing Dax and Todd having a full blown debate of who gets to *tap your ass* first."

Wait. Is he jealous? Jealous is never good. Jealous leads to angry. Angry leads to having your head slammed against the bathroom mirror. No, jealous is not good at all.

"So, you're upset that someone likes my ass?" My eyes pop open wide as I feign shock.

"Yes. I covered that already. What the hell, Heidi? Are you trying to piss me off?"

Uh no. Why would I do that on purpose? I inch all the way to the edge of the table and lean forward so that my breasts are pressed tightly against his chest. I bring my arm around his body and softly trace my index finger up and down his spine. I feel him shiver. I inhale his fresh, clean scent and speak quietly into his neck, allowing him to feel my breath on his skin, "What I'm trying to say is you should be proud that your classes are paying off. Isn't that a good thing?" Distraction by flattery. His body reacts and his hands find their way under my shirt to my back. His head falls forward and I can feel his breathing increase in speed against my chest. I can sense that physically, I am soothing him, but his mind is still not in a good place right now. I place quick, light kisses along his neck. He slowly lifts his head again in a move to halt my actions. His hands come up and cup my face, forcing me to look at him.

"Normally yes, I'd be flattered. But since I don't normally go around fucking the women I train it puts me in an awkward place. I figured there were two ways for me to react tonight. I chose the one that wouldn't get me fired."

Realization hits me. "So that's why you were so intense? Kicking and punching the shit out of everything. Because you were upset about my wardrobe?"

I give him a reassuring smile and place my hands on top of his. He doesn't answer but I see his jaw twitch so I gather I'm right. "Fine. Baggy tees and sweatpants from now on. Good?"

His expression remains stern which is unusual for him. He's contemplating something. It's always been so easy with Alex. We laugh. We flirt. We tease. We have sex. He leaves. We don't contact each other during the week. We haven't exchanged phone numbers. Hell, we don't even know each other's last name. He is Hot Alex and I'm Heidi. We made the agreement before he ever came to my apartment. It keeps things simple. Uncomplicated. I don't have time for complicated.

27

"Are you fucking other men?" Annnd now we're swimming to the deep end. I have to stop this before I drown.

Of course I'm not. I like sex. Diseases? Not so much. I told you, I'm selective. I'm a woman with assets and I've learned how to use them. I flirt with several men. I've only slept with a select few.

"No." My answer is immediate and firm. I need him to believe me. I'm not sure why it matters that he does, but it matters. "Are *you* fucking other men?"

I don't ask if he's sleeping with other women. Partly because I'm trying not to care and partly because I don't want to know. Ignorance is bliss. And also because I am a half-naked woman alone with a half-naked man and having this conversation isn't exactly what I had in mind for the evening.

His features soften and finally give way to my favorite smile. "Okay, now you're just being ridiculous," he says.

I pull my shirt over my head and let it fall on the floor next to his. His tongue slides out slowly to wet his lips at the sight of my now exposed breasts. He watches as I lie back on the table and pull my legs up, bending my knees. I raise my arms above my head and grab hold of the edge of the table, causing my chest to poke out at him.

"That's enough with the crazy talk, Alex. Time to do what you came here to do."

In one swift movement he's got his hands under my butt, lifting me off the table so he can grab my panties and pull them off. I lift my bottom up to assist. He grabs my hips and slides me to the end of the table. I can feel his hardness through the fabric of his athletic pants. He starts grinding against me. It's driving me crazy. He leans on top of me and teases my left nipple with the tip of his tongue, circling the hard peak once before taking it into his warm mouth. He never stops grinding against me even as he seems entirely focused on my breasts. He repeats the process on my right nipple, gently biting this one before he moves his mouth away. His actions are so tender and slow. "Is this what you want, love?" My hands find their way into his hair, twisting and pulling at his curls. I arch my back, silently begging him for more. I feel my body start to tremble and I know I can't wait much longer. "Yes Alex, please."

He lifts his head to look at me. He smirks. It's a cocky, confident smirk. He knows he's got me close. So close. "You're fucking sexy when you beg." He pulls away from me and I immediately feel the loss. He reaches in his pocket for a condom before pulling his pants off. My insides clench at the sight of him. He is gloriously made. Long and thick. And just the sight of it has me moving my hips in anticipation. He finishes rolling the condom on and guides himself inside, only giving me the head at first. My body is greedy so instinctively I move myself further down to fill myself with more of him. He responds to my enthusiasm by pressing himself deeper inside of me until I'm completely full. The motion is achingly slow yet wonderful at the same time. He holds himself there for a moment, letting me take in the feel of him. His hands firmly run over the tops of my thighs, his fingertips digging into my flesh, stopping just close enough for him to graze his thumbs over the top of my sensitive mound. His touch there is feather light.

My insides are throbbing. I want more. I need more. I urge him to give me more with the rise and fall of my hips. Coming away from him and then slowly sliding back onto his full length. His hips begin to thrust in sync with mine. Slowly at first and then rapidly picking up pace. His hands have moved to my hips now, using them to pull my body into his. His thrusts are becoming harder, faster, more urgent, hitting the exact same spot inside of me every time, causing little ripples of pleasure, each one more intense than the last. Alex is grunting now. I know this as a sign that he'll be coming soon. My breasts feel heavy, bouncing each time he pounds into me. He lets go of my hips and takes one of them into his hand, roughly squeezing and kneading it. I wrap my legs around his waist and grab hold of the edge of the table at my sides for leverage. The waves are getting more and more intense. It starts in my toes and works its way over my entire body until finally I'm arching my back and crying out.

I close my eyes as the orgasm washes over me. My breath is slow and hard. My mouth is dry and I feel my body going limp. I lick my lips and open my eyes to see Alex watching me. His expression is impassioned but he still manages a quick smile. He slows his thrusts as I come down from my high, allowing me to catch my breath before speeding back up so he can finish. His face turns serious again as he pumps in and out of me, searching for his release. I sit up and wrap my arms around his neck. My bare breasts rub his chests as he moves. I run my tongue up the side of his neck and then back down, stopping right above his collarbone to nibble and suck. He fists his hand in my hair and pulls me into a desperate kiss. As our tongues find each other, I begin sucking on his. He tightens his grip in my hair and pounds me harder. He pulls his mouth from mine and throws his head back and lets out a loud groan. Once he's finished, he rests his forehead against mine, waiting for his pulse and breathing to return to normal. We stay there like that, eyes closed, breathing each other in, for what seems like eternity before he pulls himself out. Neither one of us speaks a word as he walks past the living room and down the hall to the bathroom. That's nothing out of the ordinary though. We usually don't.

I put my t-shirt back on and go to my bedroom for fresh panties and pajama bottoms. As I'm pulling up my pants I turn to see Alex leaning against the doorway fully dressed. His curls are wild and sticking out from my pulling on them and he's grinning. He has the cutest dimples.
"What?"
He shakes his head once. Still smiling, he says, "Nothing."
"Uh uh. Something. Tell me."
I walk over to him and wrap my arms around his waist, resting my cheek against the center of his chest. He props his chin on top of my head and inhales a deep breath through his nose. He moves to hold me close.
"There's something I want to ask you, but considering we've been romping around for the past month it seems a little out of place."
"Ask anyway." I probably don't really want him to, but I'm curious. I'm not jumping to any conclusions. It may not be anything personal.
"May I have your phone number?" I feel his chest jump as he chuckles at his question.
"You may not." There, that wasn't so hard.
Alex grabs me by the biceps and holds me away from him. The adoring smile is gone, replaced by a look I'm not sure I've ever seen on his beautiful face. He's angry. Or disappointed maybe? I can't tell.
"Are you pissing around, Heidi? I'm asking for your number. Not your hand."
"Well I'm not sure what that means really, but I am pretty sure I'm not doing it. Alex, we have a good thing here. Please don't do this."
"Don't do what exactly?"
"This. Make things complicated."
"How fucking complicated is a phone number? Ten digits Heidi. People exchange them all the time."
He lets go of my arms and takes a step back, raking agitated fingers through his hair.
"We had an agreement. You like sex. I like sex. We like sex with each other. We don't need to talk about our day or go out to dinner, or for that matter, even have anything else in common. We fuck. See? It's simple."
"No one ever actually sticks to those agreements, love. It's a crock of shit people make up when they haven't decided whether they really like each

other or not. Is that what this is? You don't know whether or not you like me?"

He walks over to the sofa and plops down, his elbows resting on his knees and his head in his hands. He's looking at the floor and running his fingers back and forth through his hair. I move to stand in front of him. He senses my presence and looks up at me with big brown eyes. I take his hands and move them from his knees so I can straddle his lap. I run my fingertip along the side of his face, and then over his outer ear and back down his neck, and press my lips gently against his forehead. I hold my mouth there for a bit then tilt my head back so I can see his face.

"Alex, I need you to hear me right now. I know this is going to sound incredibly cliché, but I swear it's the truth. This has nothing to do with you. I'm sure you're a really great guy. Just from the little I do know of you, I do like you. This is all me. I'm completely wrapped up in my own stuff and I just don't have room for anything else right now. And I'm not just talking about time. Mentally. I just can't."

He pauses a minute before responding. "I thought I could do this. I honestly thought I had hit the jackpot with you. I mean, what man wouldn't want a beautiful woman who wants absolutely nothing from him but his stiffy? But I can't. I tried. My reaction to knowing those guys at the gym wanted from you what I want from you proved I'm not in this for the same reasons anymore. The game has changed for me. I can't play your way anymore."

"Are you breaking up with my vagina?"

He lifts me off his lap and sets me on the sofa next to him. *I guess so.*

"Are you capable of a serious conversation?"

"This is a serious conversation."

He stands and smiles a weak smile as he shakes his head. "No, Heidi. I am not breaking up with your vagina. But if in the future your vagina wants to see me, she'll have to come find me."

I shrug and smile. "Fair enough."

And just like that he turns and walks out the door. I don't stand. I don't follow. I don't walk him out.

CHAPTER SIX
Heidi

Wednesday, May 21

I have three appointments today and I'm running on four hours sleep.
Hudson wasn't feeling well when Cole dropped him off. It was a rough
night so I don't make it in to work until 9:00. I wish I could have slept 'til
noon. Shelly eyes me as I walk past her desk and head toward my office.
"Spill," she demands.

"Nothing to spill. Hudson was sick."

"Liar," she mumbles as she follows me down the hall.

"I heard that. And I'm not lying. It was a bad night. He had it coming out
both ends."

"Didn't need to hear that, but thanks. Want a cookie?"

"No thanks," I sigh and take my seat behind my desk. "We're probably
going to have to switch to Zumba on Tuesdays."

"Tell me you didn't break up with Hot Alex." She sits in the chair across
from me.

"I didn't break up with Hot Alex."

"Then what's the problem?"

"You can't break up with someone you're not dating."

She looks puzzled so I decide to cut to the chase. "Hot Alex decided he
didn't want to *not* date me anymore."

"He broke up with you?"

"He broke up with my vagina. Well...He says he didn't but it felt like he
did. So, I don't know. It's complicated."

"I thought you didn't do complicated."

"Exactly. Which is why he broke up with her."

"Are you seriously speaking about your lady parts in the third person?"

"Shut up. It makes it less about me that way. I have work to do," I say,
hoping she takes the hint to leave. She does. I don't really want to talk
about Alex any more than I already have. When it comes to feelings I'm
not much of a talker. Actually, when it comes to feelings I'm still not sure
how I even feel about that whole situation yet. I get together everything I
need for the day and head out.

Thursday, May 22

Last night was movie night. Hudson and I watched Frozen. He loves watching the little snowman. I love watching him. Naturally, he got the BoomCo he asked for. I'm a sucker. Sue me. Needless to say at the end of the movie when the villain is revealed, Hudson decides to make use of his new toy. He shoots the television screen and it takes us a solid two minutes to pull that thing off. He wasn't kidding. It really sticks. Once the bullet is removed and the victim is rendered in good condition, the victim being my television, I scold him.

"Hudson, you know you're not allowed to shoot that in the house."

He looks up at me through innocent eyes, "But mom, he's a bad guy. You're supposed to shoot bad guys."

What am I supposed to say to that? "Let the cops shoot the bad guys. And let little boys hug their mommies."

He climbs up onto my lap and wraps his little arms around my body as much as he can and tells me, "I will take care of you, mommy. I won't let the bad guys hurt you." His compassion melts my heart. I make it my personal mission to ensure his heart remains untainted and that he grows into a man who knows how to cherish and respect a woman.

"And I promise to take care of you too my little man," I say, pulling him further up on my lap and squeezing him tight. Hudson falls asleep curled up against my chest while watching another movie. He stays snuggled close all night and we both sleep peacefully. Movie nights are my favorite.

Tuesday, May 27

I wrap up what I like to call a 'furniture facelift' project I've been working on and hand the other two I have going to Meghan. The girls decided to go to kickboxing class tonight and I have a few errands to run before we meet.

Once we're all wrapped up and ready to go, I occupy my usual spot and wait for Alex to come in. It's been a week since our little heart-to-heart and I'm kind of nervous about seeing him. He starts our warm up before he even gets to his bag. The music is louder than usual and I notice he's keeping his shirt on. He never keeps his shirt on. In the middle of our arm stretch exercise he approaches my bag, stopping just in front of it. His eyes run up and down my body and I catch a hint of amusement in his smile.

"Nice outfit," he observes.

I am wearing a light pink ¾ sleeve sweatshirt that falls off one shoulder and a pair of black cropped leggings. The sweatshirt is loose and hangs well below my butt. "I'm glad you think so. I wore it just for you," I inform him.

He eyes me suspiciously. "Okay I lied. I like it when you look at my butt. So no. I didn't wear this for you," I admit.

"I really need to start the class."

"I say you fake a stomach ache and we skip the class and go to my place," I tease.

"It's not Biology, Heidi. These people are paying me."

"So that's what it will take then? I can pay you."

Alex pulls his shirt over his head and tosses it aside, delivering a wink in my direction just before he takes to his own bag and begins tonight's workout.

Class ends and he makes a bee line for the back of the gym. Do not pass Go. Do not collect two hundred dollars. Throughout class he didn't stop and talk to me like he normally does. I'm thinking maybe it's because the music was so loud tonight. Or maybe the music was so loud so he wouldn't talk to me. I brush off the thought and grab my gym bag. The girls opt for frozen yogurt in place of margaritas but I decide to skip this one and head home. Shelly relays a message that Senator Knight's secretary called to set up an appointment for me to come in and discuss my situation. It looks like I'll be seeing him again after all. Friday morning at 9:30.

When I get home I go through the usual motions of showering and getting in my pajamas and wait for the knock on the door. One hour and two episodes of that show where four friends play practical jokes on strangers later, Alex still hasn't showed. This is the first time in over a month he hasn't come over after class. I miss him. Hey, I said I don't date. That doesn't mean I don't feel. I power up the Kindle and read until Hudson gets home from baseball practice.

Friday, May 30

The plan for the day is to drop Hudson off at his grandmother's, attend my meeting with the senator, and then go in to work. Only, I don't feel much like dealing with the big business bullies or figuring out how to

34

make deer heads and dead fish look like they belong on a living room wall. I overslept and now I don't have time for Starbucks. Damn.

Once Hudson is settled I call to confirm my appointment. I never spoke with the woman who set the appointment personally and I don't want to make an unnecessary trip. I also don't want to show up unannounced and embarrass myself. Shelly can sometimes get carried away playing matchmaker so I want to be sure the meeting is legit. The last two times I've called his office have been miserable. You'd think I was trying to sell him life insurance or something by the way he avoids me. And his staff, cute as they are, are not the most agreeable bunch. So I am pleasantly surprised to not only be transferred directly to his office, but to hear his own sexy voice on the other end of the line. So smooth. Like those commercials with the chocolate and red silk. Yum.

"Good morning Heidi. What can I do for you?" he says.

Since I was fully expecting Thing Two to pick up, I don't have anything prepared to say to him. Why am I calling again? Oh. Right. The meeting.

"Good morning Mr. Knight. I was just calling to confirm our meeting," I manage.

"Nick. Please. And there's no need for you to call and confirm your appointments with me, Heidi. If I ask you to meet me, I'm going to be here."

Well don't I feel like a child scolded. "I'm sorry. I just wanted to make sure...Since I didn't actually take down the appointment myself...That the message was relayed correctly...Really. I apologize." I sound like an idiot, pausing between each explanation. Why does this man make me so nervous?

"Don't. I appreciate the professionalism. Just know it's unnecessary with me. I'll see you at 9:30," he states. I think I hear a lightness in his tone. Maybe he's smiling? I can't be sure.

"9:30. Thanks." I reply simply. He ends the call without another word. I continue through traffic until I'm once again at his office.

Thing One smiles as I approach her desk and sends me right up. She must be having a better day today. Thank goodness. I don't feel like putting up with her crap. I receive a similar response from Thing Two. She informs me Nick is in a meeting that has run over and apologizes and lets me know he'll be out soon. It's really not a big deal since I am ten minutes early. You never can tell about traffic, you know. She also offers me water while I wait. I decline. The last thing I need right now is to have to pee. Approximately seven minutes later, two well-dressed men with black leather planners walk out of Nick's office. Once they move past me I spot

Nick in the doorway. His bright, sky blue shirt is a stark contrast to the black suit and tie he is wearing. His hands are in his pockets and he's smiling. Either his meeting went well or he's glad to see me.

CHAPTER SEVEN
Nick

Eminent Domain. When the government wants to take something that belongs to someone else and use it for something they feel works better for them. That's what Heidi is up against. I made a few phone calls, the first of them to one of the attorneys listed on her letter who, coincidentally, used to be my partner when I practiced law. He is now my best friend and currently not much help in this situation. I also brought it up at a luncheon with a few other officials and got the same response. The state wants to delegate Heidi's property to a third party who in turn wants to build a casino in its place. Everyone I've spoken with tells me it's for "the betterment of the community." It's "economically beneficial" they say. I can't say I disagree. Hell, I probably even voted for it. But I can't tell her that.

I spent most of Thursday afternoon researching eminent domain cases and trying to decide the best route to take. My next step is to find out what investment firm is kicking her out and deal with them directly. I haven't spent enough time with Heidi to understand what she is hoping to accomplish from this so I had Candace, my assistant, call and set up another appointment for her to come in. Then I politely inform both her and MacKenzie, who works in the downstairs lobby, Ms. Lemaire is to be treated with nothing but respect from this moment on.

Since the moment that woman walked into my office last Tuesday, I have done nothing but think about her. Even spending the past few days in Washington didn't get her off my mind. I discovered through Google that she owns her own business. *No shit.* Thanks Google. You've been loads of help. She is thirty-two years old, although she doesn't look a minute over twenty-five. And she went to school in Austin, Texas. How she ended up here is anybody's guess. I'd sure like to know. All of the above was freely given in her biography on her company's website. Aside from that, there's nothing. No pictures. No Facebook profile. No Twitter. Zip. Nada. Nothing. So there I sit for over a week wondering about a woman I have no business wondering about.

On Friday morning I'm sitting at my desk going over competitive education proposals when Candace informs me that Heidi is on line three. I don't have to pick up to know what the call is about. She's calling to confirm our appointment. I should forward it to my assistant again but instead, I pick up. I confirm our meeting and prepare for a different one I have coming up in about ten minutes. This first meeting is with a couple of city engineers about a project proposal for an extension on a state highway. Boring shit. Thirty minutes later I walk the men in black to the door and spot Heidi waiting on the settee. Instinctively I smile. I nod towards my office, silently inviting her in. She receives the gesture and stands. I watch every move as she walks past. She smells incredible. Like vanilla and amber. Soft and sweet. Like a gentle breeze. Her long, strapless, black dress highlights her bare shoulders. Her hair is pulled into a ponytail high on top of her head and her long dangly earrings draw attention to her neck. I want to touch her there. Taste her there.

She sits in the same spot as last time. Her expression is different today. Almost solemn. And I catch myself wanting to know why. Seriously Nick, who cares? It's her shit, let her deal with it. I shake the thought, opting to offer her some coffee instead. She didn't come here for me to play counselor.

"Coffee?" I propose as I walk to the machine on the wall behind her. I think she thinks I am no longer looking at her because she closes her eyes and rolls her neck from side to side. Like someone doing warm up exercises before a work out. My fingers twitch. I want to walk right over there and work her out. What I do, however, is grab two mugs and the cream and sugar. I'm assuming she'll say yes.

"That would be heaven," she replies. If she's talking about the massage I'm mentally giving her, then she's right, it would. The coffee doesn't deserve that much credit though.

Before I can ask what she takes in her coffee she is standing right next to me. Her hand cups the top of one of my hands, silently offering to take the mug from my grasp. I turn my head to protest but forget what it was I wanted to say when I realize how close she is. She's looking up at me. I can see the pulse quickening in her throat. Hear the soft gust of air as she exhales. Smell her incredible scent. "Tell me how you like it." I'm not even sure I'm talking about the coffee anymore.

She releases my hand and looks away. Her eyes close for just a moment before she answers with a smile, "Three creams. Four sugars."

"Are you sure you want coffee? I could just bring you a cow with a side of diabetes."

She laughs. It's angelic. I'm pathetic. "Actually, I hate the taste of coffee. I drink it for the caffeine mostly, and the warmth," she explains.

I hand her the mug and take my seat behind my desk. I watch as she places her chin against the rim and softly blows into the cup. Her full lips form a seductive little "o". She has no idea what her mouth does to me. Instinctively, I lick my lips, although I'd rather be licking hers. She's watching me now. I wish I knew what she was thinking. I find myself tracing circles around the brim of my coffee mug with my middle finger as I study her. I must be making her uncomfortable because she sets the mug down without taking a sip and clears her throat. *Fuck.*

I lean forward, placing my elbows on my desk and smile. It's a bit overdone but I'm hoping to relax her a little. "What do you want first? The good news or the bad?" I ask.

She takes her coffee and holds it close to her chest with both hands. The gesture reminds me of a child with a blanket, like the mug will protect her from the bad news. She takes a sip then answers, "Bad. Then good. Do it fast. Like a Band Aid." She speaks the words quickly as if prompting me to do the same. I feel the corner of my mouth turn up. Seeing her nervous intrigues me. She tries so hard not to let it show but I've spent the last ten years of my life in courtrooms so I've pretty much got the body language thing down to a science. She doesn't like being manipulated. That much I can tell. What I want to know is why. Why she feels like she has to be in control. Why she wears this mask all the time. The fact that I even give a shit just pisses me off. I should just tell her there's nothing I can do to save her little business, fuck her senseless, and go on about my way. That's what I should do.

"You're not fighting an easy battle. And I haven't had much luck so far," I tell her.

She processes the information. She's calm. This is good. "That's the bad news?" she half questions, half declares.

I nod. "So it looks like you and I will be spending a little more time together." I don't fight the boyish grin consuming my face. I lean back in my chair and wait for her response.

She returns my smile. "And this is the good news I assume?"

I chuckle. "Well I guess that's a matter of perspective."

She takes another sip of her coffee then sets the mug back on the table beside her. There goes the security blanket. I guess she's feeling comfortable now. She sits up straight and squares her shoulders. She takes a deep breath before responding. "I haven't busted my ass working seven days a week for the past four years to give up now. This is my dream. And you don't give up on your dreams Senator. A life with no dreams is just….well, a nightmare."

39

She reaches for her purse then stands to leave. As she's walking towards the door she looks over her shoulder at me and says with a shrug, "Besides, I can think of worse things than having to spend a little more time with you." She's flirting with me. Fucking flirting. Wait. Why is she leaving? As if she is reading my mind, she says as she walks toward the door, "I have to go. I have another meeting. Thank you for your help." "My pleasure Ms. Lemaire. Be back here Monday morning so we can go over what you need to do next." My tone and my expression are both serious now. She's flirting with fire. I'm about thirty seconds away from bending her ass over this desk.

She gives a slight nod and replies, "Yes, sir."

"I promise Heidi, I will do everything I can to make sure you don't walk away from this thing a victim," I assure her. And I'm almost convinced I mean it. *That's a first.* Please tell me I'm not turning soft. She gives me a sweet smile and walks out the door. I grab my crotch just to make sure I'm not growing a vagina. Nope, all good. I need scotch. And sex. Soon.

Once Heidi is gone, I make plans to meet friends for a drink this weekend. Then I reject some idiot's amendment proposal that we give animals the right to vote. He's your dog. Feed him, bathe him, love him, and he could give a shit less who is the next president. Saturday night can't come fast enough.

CHAPTER EIGHT
Heidi

The meeting didn't go as well as I had hoped. Although, I do believe Nick when he tells me he's going to do everything he can. Maybe it's because of who he is. Or maybe it's something else I haven't quite figured out yet, but I feel...taken care of with him. I'm drawn to him. Like a moth to a flame. I'll probably end up getting burned. As if it is ever even going to get that point. I doubt if he's even single. Why would he be? Unless he's a complete ass and I just can't see it. Or maybe I don't have the right parts. Why am I spending so much time worrying about it?

In other news: I am in desperate need of some retail therapy today. Shelly and I swap going to the office for a day at the mall. Shopping is great but it's not much fun alone. She's concerned about missing work so I tell her I happen to know the boss so I'm sure it's okay. We try on dresses we know we'll never buy, as well as a few that we just can't do without. We leave The Shops with a bag full of sexy underwear and a couple of new dresses. While walking along the river we hear a musician playing his saxophone under a nearby pavilion so we sit in the grass and listen for a minute. I drop Shelly off back at the store, pop in to check my messages, and then go home to get Hudson's bag packed. This is his weekend to spend with his dad. I enjoy the time to myself. Or the time with my girls. Depending on what we have planned. But I miss my little man when he's gone. It's been the just two of us for two years now. I've become accustomed to our nightly routines. The apartment is so quiet when he's not there singing, or reading out loud, or pretending to fight ninjas or drive fire trucks.

By six o'clock Hudson is with his dad and I'm opening the refrigerator, digging in the cabinets, and reopening the fridge, trying to find something I'm hungry for. I finally decide on leftover pizza, run my bath water, and pour a glass of Sangria. About five chapters into *Wuthering Heights* my glass is empty and the water is getting cold. The hot bubble bath relaxed my muscles. *Or maybe it's the wine.* It's probably the wine. I need more wine.

The sexy underwear serves its purpose. I smile proudly at my self-administered mani-pedi and new navy blue lace bra and panties. Every girl should pamper herself once in a while. My skin is silky smooth, my nails are a cheerful shade of hot pink to match my toes, and the lace makes me feel pretty. Time to curl up under the blanket with another glass of wine and catch up on recorded episodes of television shows I don't like to watch when Hudson is around. Me time.

Saturday, May 31

I've been awake a whopping forty-five minutes when Shelly calls.
"Hey bitch we're going out tonight. Wear that cute little blue dress you bought yesterday and meet us at Social at eight."
Is she serious? It's eight o'clock in the morning. I haven't even had two cups of coffee yet. "Us?" I inquire.
"Yes. Us. Me, Hannah, Meghan, Ashton, Emmett. And maybe one other guy. I don't know yet."
She is not trying to set me up with one of her boyfriend's friends again. This never works out. It usually goes something like this: Shelly meets one of Emmett's motocross buddies. She thinks he's hot and wants me to sleep with him so she can hear the gory details. My best friend tries to pimp me out on a regular basis for her own twisted fantasies. I'm a little offended. I have never done it. I will never do it. If she wants to know what's under the tree she'll have to unwrap the package herself.
"Drinks, yes. Other guy, absolutely not."
"Come on Heidi. All you have to do is talk to him. One day you're going to meet one you can't resist."
"Introduce him to Ashton. He has a better chance of sleeping with her than me."
"Ashton is a vegetarian," Shelly reminds me. This is our way of saying she doesn't like "meat." You connect the dots.
"Exactly. I'll see you later." It's my polite way of saying this conversation is over. I am not some desperate old maid who needs to be set up. It's embarrassing. I have no trouble finding men. And it's my decision not to date. I wish she would stop already. One day I'm going to do like they do on those movies and hire a man to pretend to be madly in love with me. And just for fun I'll make sure he's about ten years younger and utterly clueless.

At eight o'clock on the dot I'm walking out the door. I wear the dark blue peasant dress Shelly suggested. It hits mid-thigh and comes off the shoulders. It has long sleeves but is light and flowy. If that wasn't a word before, it is now. I pair my new dress with some really cute cowboy boots that go up just past my calves. I leave my hair down but dress it up with a waterfall braid around the crown. It's casual but flirty so I'm good with it. The girls are already at the bar when I arrive. I don't like being first because I never know if I should wait to order or screw it and say every man for himself. So, I just try not to be first. They're about two martinis in so I need to catch up. I order a lemon drop shot followed by a second and a third. Then I get to the martinis. The bartender is either amused by us or making a helluva commission off our tab because he keeps mixing drinks and making us his test dummies. There was one with jalapenos that almost made me lose it. A *hot n dirty* I think he called it. I recommend you stay clear of that one. By the time we were ready to go to Jackson Street we were all feeling no pain. Bartender: one. Party girls: zero.

We take our favorite spot at the end of the bar. Thank goodness for Emmett and friend for being the evening's designated drivers. We would have had to eat ourselves into a coma to sober up enough to drive otherwise. The DJ plays a few songs I know but nothing I love so I stay at the bar and people watch. Emmett's friend, who I now know is called Drew, strikes up conversation but I'm not really interested. I really just want to dance. Man I wish he would play better music. Then I hear it. *The bass.* And I'm gone. Yep. That's me out there. Backing that ass up. Soon I'm joined by my girls and we are probably attracting more attention than we should but we have beer so who gives a shit. I love to dance. I have been dancing since I was ten years old. Jazz, tap, ballet. And in my early twenties, booty. Tonight we're going with booty. I love dancing. What I hate is trying to dance and having some chemically imbalanced horn dog rubbing his goods all up on my backside. Seriously guys. Back up. It's not sexy. I ease away from horn dog and try to finish the song. Now it's just ruined. I need another beer. The song ends and I go back to my corner and resume people watching. Then I see *him.* At the other side of the bar with his arm around a blonde. She's laughing. Of course she is. He's funny. He's buying her a drink. I freeze. I slowly stand and keep watching Alex and his new friend. Damn, that wasn't even a rebound. That's more like an alley-oop. The ball didn't even bounce off the rim yet and he's already dunking it. The music changes. It's slow. I hear piano keys. It's familiar. *Somo.* The song gives me motivation. Or it could be the alcohol. Who knows. I move towards him. The sexy lyrics saturate the air between us. I hear the mention of candles dripping on bodies. Drunk or not, this is definitely sex music. He's still talking to her. His hand is rubbing her back. I should leave him alone. He doesn't belong to me and I have no intentions on taking this thing anywhere outside the bedroom. I should just let him go. I don't know if it's the alcohol or the hormones but I place my hand on top of his arm, halting his movement. He turns to look at me.

"Alex." It's all that I can manage right now. The song keeps playing. He drops his arm and stares at me. Silence.

"Dance with me." My voice is bold and determined. I move closer to him and grab his shirt. Super tramp is eyeing us closely. Okay so she may not actually be a tramp. She's probably a very nice girl. But she's a nice girl trying to take something I want. Alex still doesn't move but his eyes never leave mine.

Just like the song mentions, there is definitely some freaking heat between us two. I begin to dance in front of him. Slowly. Rolling my hips. Sliding one hand around his neck. Never breaking eye contact. He stands. I take him by the shirt again and lead him onto the dance floor. Poor super tramp. She never had a chance. I wrap one arm around his neck and twist my hand in his curls. My other hand rubs his chest. Alex strokes my back as our hips move back and forth together with the music. His hands slide around to my hips so he can guide my movements. One hand moves further down, grabbing my thigh and sliding it up his leg. He slips his hand under my dress, skimming my behind before moving lower. I tighten my grip in his hair and pull him into an intense kiss. He slowly releases my thigh and my leg falls back down. Our hips continue moving together in figure eights and he takes a handful of my hair, pulling me deeper into the kiss. We pull away and I feel the instant swell of my lips. He looks down at me and smiles as he takes his thumb and runs it over his bottom lip. "Time to go, Heidi," he commands.

All I can do is nod. Alex takes my hand and leads me through the crowded dance floor toward the bar. My other senses catch up with me before we get to the door. "I need to tell Shelly so she doesn't worry. I'll be right back."

He nods and orders a beer while he waits. I find my friend outside talking up some people she went to school with. With the way Jackson Street is set up it's easy to go from one establishment to another. Situated within a courtyard type circle in the center of a city block is a number of businesses, including the Pub, California Pizza Kitchen, another locally owned restaurant, a sunglasses boutique, a candy store, and a daiquiri stand. Across the street is a movie theatre. It's all very convenient. They even have valet parking if you're feeling spoiled. In the center of the circle is a gazebo where local bands play live music on the weekends. It's like a block party. Not far from this gazebo is where I find Shelly. She could strike up a conversation with a brick wall. I tap her on the shoulder.

"Hey I found a ride home."

She dismisses her other friends and turns to face me. "You dirty little whore," she accuses.

"Alex is here," I clarify. As if that makes a difference to her.

"So I take it you two kissed and made up?"

"We're working on that part," I quip.

"You're still a whore."

"Haters gonna hate," I retort.

She shoulder bumps me, shoving me backwards. "Whatever."

I stumble and bump into something tall. And hard. I turn to find out what or who has awakened my senses so delightfully and find myself grabbing onto a firm bicep.

"Ohmigosh I'm so sorry. My friend..." I begin but abruptly stop speaking as he turns around.

"Holy shit." I'm sure my mouth is hanging open and there's a good chance I'm drooling.

"Nick Knight." It's a statement meant more for my own reassurance rather than to define the man in front of me.

The corners of his mouth turn upwards, slowly revealing his perfect white teeth and he nods. "Heidi."

"Wow," I spit out as my eyes roam over his casually dressed body. The man is definitely wearing those jeans. They hang low on his hips and are baggy for the most part but appear a little snug at the tops of his thighs. I can just imagine what his ass looks like. *Turn around. Turn around. Pleeeease turn around.*

Just the front part of his dark gray tee shirt is tucked in, revealing a silver belt buckle and black leather belt. "You look hot." There goes the alcohol induced word vomit. That's when I notice the gorgeous blonde who has now hooked her arm through the arm I'm not currently touching.

I backtrack, "I mean the whole suit and tie thing really works for you too but the jeans. The jeans are just...wow..and," I squeeze the arm I'm still holding on to, "holy biceps Batman." No filter.

He flexes. Strictly for my entertainment I'm sure. The corner of his mouth twitches and he looks away. *Shit.* Did I embarrass him? He looks at Shelly, paying no attention to Blonde Bombshell.

"How much has she had to drink?"

"Too much," she answers immediately. I roll my eyes at them both. I've been worse off. It's not that bad.

Nick grabs me at the elbow on the arm that's holding his and holds me steady. Once he's confident I'm not going anywhere, his hand moves from there to my waist. "She needs someone to feed her. Or pour a pot of coffee down her throat," he teases.

Shelly grabs my hand and tugs. "I'll be sure to take care of that."

"Make sure it's sweet. She likes it sweet," he says with a wink. This man is adorable.

"Ohmigosh you remember how I like my coffee?" I croon. I'm probably inching a little too close to him at the moment. Blonde Bombshell looks like she's ready to claw my eyeballs out. I can't help it. He smells so good. His dimples are perfect. His eyes are burning into me. I really want to kiss him. Not a good idea. You shouldn't mix alcohol with hormones. People get naked. Bad things happen. Or good things. Depends on how you look at it.

"Heidi, we should go," Shelly insists. I don't want to go but she urges me on with wide eyes and a slight nod towards the Pub. Alex. *Crap.* I have to go. I back away from Nick and bring my hand to my mouth as the realization hits me.

"I'm sorry. I have to go. There's some..." I begin to explain when Shelly cuts me off.

"We have people in there waiting on us. We probably shouldn't be rude," she interrupts.

"Right," Nick replies. "I wouldn't want you disappointing anyone. I'll see you Monday Heidi. It was very nice meeting you Shelly," he tells us while reaching out to shake Shelly's hand.

"Yes!" I exclaim. "We have a meeting," I advise him. As if it were a new bit of information he is just becoming privy to.

"We do," he confirms.

Shelly pulls me away. I turn and smile and wave like an idiot. Nick chuckles.

Shelly leans in close to me while we walk back to the bar where Alex is waiting. "You said he was hot. You didn't mention he was scientifically created in a lab. No man is *that* perfect."

I laugh and she continues, "Unbelievable. I couldn't find one single flaw. He must have a little penis. I guess we could go ask Super Tits." I assume she's referring to Blonde Bombshell. There's no way those things are real. He probably paid for them himself.

I nod in agreement. "There you are. I thought you left me," Alex says, pulling my thoughts away from Nick. What the hell was he doing here anyway? I never pegged him for the social type. Although, I did kind of call the girlfriend. Figures he'd go for the not-so-friendly neighborhood supermodel. Good for him. They can spend their nights having perfect sex and making perfect babies and living perfectly happily ever after. I'm leaving with Alex.

CHAPTER NINE
Heidi

Alex leads me out of the bar to his Land Rover. He opens my door and helps me climb in. Such a gentleman.

"So, who's your friend?" I probe. Not that I'm entitled to an answer. But I want one regardless.

I watch as his dimples appear deep in his cheeks and his eyes light up. "You wouldn't know her," he replies. I feel like growling at him. I think I may have actually done it because he laughs.

"I just met her tonight so I can't say much about her. We were just getting to the good stuff when you interrupted."

I glare at him and then turn and sulk out the window like a child who just got her favorite toy taken away. "Well you're welcome to turn around and go back for her," I pout, "but don't say I didn't try to save you."

His eyes widen and he looks at me in amusement. "Save me? From?"

"An entirely wasted night of incredibly monotonous sex. Plus think of all the money you saved. You didn't even have to get me drunk," I state as if the answer bores me.

"No I didn't. Someone else did a pretty fantastic job of that. So you're saying I owe you then?"

I shrug. "Yep. You do."

"Is that the only reason you molested me among a crowd of people? To save me?" he questions. He seems amused with himself. Like there's some private joke I'm not aware of.

"Nope."

He waits for more. I reach for the volume button on the radio. Alex grabs my wrist and immediately my head darts in his direction. He wants me to elaborate. Of course he does. *Are we at my apartment yet?* How much longer can this car ride be? I let out a big huff of air. "Fine. I missed you."

He's trying to hide the fact that he wants to grin like an idiot. He clears his throat and restructures his expression. "Did you?"

Another huff. "Yes, Alex. I did. I missed your cute little dimples and your cocky smile. I missed your unruly curls and your boyish charm. I missed your sensual mouth and your big, fat dick. Happy?" I have a feeling he already knew that.

"Quite."

We pull into a parking garage I'm pretty sure doesn't belong to me. "This isn't my apartment." It's a stupid statement. He knows it isn't my apartment. Dead brain cells.

"No. It's mine," he informs me. What.The.Hell. We don't go to his apartment. Ever. I don't want to go to his apartment. My apartment is safe. I can kick him out whenever I want. Why can't we just go to my apartment? I can't be stuck here with no way home. What if he makes me spend the night? I do not want to spend the night. This is way out of my comfort zone. I'm feeling a little claustrophobic. See what happens when you drink?

"Alex," I start, but he is quick to put his index finger over my lips. "Sssshhhh," he warns. "Don't make this a big deal. Just come in. I won't make you stay if you don't want to. Trust me."

And I do. I believe him.

"You live in The Lofts at Creighton Heights?"

"You were expecting something else?"

"No," I lie, "it's very nice." The second part was not a lie. It is nice. I've done some design work in this building. I love the architecture. I have never thought about where Alex might live, but I can say I never imagined it to be somewhere like this. Who knew? I should have been a boxer. They live the life. His loft is very industrial. Brick walls, wood flooring, high ceilings showcasing exposed duct work and floor to ceiling windows along one wall. Open concept with a black metal spiral staircase in one corner. What is it with men and black leather furniture? And big screen televisions. He has red leather barstools, glass top accent tables, a white shag rug and a few art canvases with a geometric print on them. I wonder if he decorated it himself.

"I'm glad you approve," Alex says as he lifts me up and carries me to a room off the dining area. This must be his bedroom. There's a king size bed with a white upholstered headboard and a dark walnut dresser and mirror. He lays me on top of the dark gray comforter and stands over me. He pulls off my boots and drops them on the floor. "Relax and enjoy this, love. There is no thirty minute time limit tonight." *Yes!*

His hands run over the tops of my feet, along my calves, and up my thighs, sliding my dress up as he goes. His actions are slow and deliberate. He pulls me to the end of the bed and drops to his knees between my legs. I feel the soft skin of his lips on my ankles. His mouth inches its way tenderly up my leg and stops behind my knee. His wet tongue snakes out and licks me in the sensitive spot there and I feel it in my core. I'm so ready for him yet at the same time I'm savoring every pleasurable second of his little expedition. He moves to the inside of my thigh. I can feel his

49

hot breath increasing in intensity as his mouth works its way to its destination. My body is anxious for what is coming. I can't keep still. My hands fist in the covers and my hips buck up in anticipation. Alex hesitates when he reaches the top of my thigh. He places both hands on top of my legs and rubs his thumbs along the outer seam of my panties. He is driving me crazy. I urge him on with the roll of my hips. He lowers his head back between

my thighs and breathes on me. Achingly slow. His breath is so hot. "Alex, please," I beg him. My feet don't quite reach the floor so I can't push myself further into his face. I grab his head with both hands and pull him closer. I feel the hard tip of his tongue trace the crease of my mound through the thin, lacy material. He groans. The vibrations stir up an electric current in my body. I grip his hair tighter and buck my hips again. He pulls his head away long enough to grab my hips and lift me off the bed so he can remove my panties. Once those are out of the way, his skilled tongue goes back to work. He wastes no time in tasting me. The minute my panties are on the floor, his tongue is on me, in me. Licking and sucking and fucking me. His long fingers spread my lips apart as his tongue explores and teases me. I move my hips, greedy for more of him. I can feel my release coming. The tingle starts in my toes and creeps up my body. I moan and cry out his name as I come. He laps up every drop like it's his last meal, before standing between my legs, which I cannot move. He's staring down at me. His expression is dark and wanting. He unfastens his jeans and slides them off his body. I sit up and reach for his shirt, pulling it over his head. He is standing in front of me in nothing but his underwear now. I can see his erection begging to be set free. I reach forward and stroke him. He thrusts his hips forward and I slide my fingers under the waist band of his boxer briefs and tug them down. I lick my lips at the sight of his cock. I haven't tasted Alex yet. We're both treading into new territory tonight but he looks delicious and the alcohol running through my veins has taken away any reservations. Instinctively I move forward, swirling my tongue around his thick head. He makes a deep growling noise in the back of his throat, giving me the encouragement I need to keep going. I run my tongue down the full length of him and all the way back up. My mouth opens around him and my tongue sweeps over his head one more time before I take him all the way in. I can feel each of his veins bulging from the blood pumping in his body right now and he feels so thick in my mouth. I repeat the motion, increasing in speed and suction each time I slide my mouth over his fullness. The insides of my thighs are soaked with my own arousal. In one swift unexpected movement, Alex slides himself out of my mouth and brings my legs up so my ankles are resting on his shoulders. The backs of my thighs are against his abdomen and my ass is lifted off the bed.

"Not yet. Not before I get the chance to be inside of you." His cock is well lubricated from my saliva so it doesn't take more than one thrust and he's inside of me. His body leans forward onto mine as he places a hand on either side of my head to hold his weight. There is no slow and steady rhythm to his movements. He is pounding me. Hard. From this position I have no choice but to take all of him. He is going so deep. I swear I can feel it in my stomach. It's painful but at the same time my body doesn't want him to stop. Another orgasm is rapidly building. I can tell Alex is on the brink as well because his thrusts are getting more urgent and I can feel the sweat from his body beneath my thighs. He pounds in me one last, hard time before letting out a loud groan. The pulsing of his cock as he fills me sets free my own release and I thrust my hips onto him and moan his name as the intense pleasure rolls over my body.

Alex lifts me up and scoots our bodies up the bed so my head is resting on his pillow. He is still between my legs but is no longer inside of me. My inner thighs are covered in a sticky wet mixture of his DNA and my own but I'm feeling too good to care. He rolls off onto his back and lies beside me. I turn to my stomach and prop myself up on my elbows so we can see each other.

We stare at each other for what seems like hours when he finally speaks.

"I want to know you Heidi. Tell me something personal," he requests.

Well that came out of nowhere.

"Okay," I agree, "I'm an only child." There. That wasn't so bad.

Alex shakes his head and gives me a look of disapproval. "Something more."

I file through all of the complex little details that define me and try to find one of the least invasive.

"I love the water," I confess, "I have been swimming since," I pause a beat to think, "Well since the womb pretty much.

"I started young and kept up with it all through school and even now. It's a huge stress reliever for me. So it's always been a dream of mine to live by the water. Ocean. Lake. It doesn't matter. As long as I can walk out my back door and see the water. It's so soothing. Especially the ocean. It's so calm and serene.

But then there's always the knowledge that it is one of the most powerful forces on earth. It's majestic."

His eyes light up in approval. I guess I answered correctly this time. I lean forward and press my lips against his. I feel his body shift as he reaches for my face. His tongue traces the top of my bottom lip before easing inside and molding with mine. I climb on top of him and straddle his stomach. My hair forms a curtain around us as I withdraw my mouth from his. "You want personal Alex? I can give you personal." I inch my way down until I feel his hardness trying to make its way inside of me. With a slight lift of my hips and some careful maneuvering he is back inside where it's nice and warm. This is the kind of personal I don't mind sharing with him.

CHAPTER TEN
Heidi

Sunday, June 1

I roll over and grab the extra pillow on the bed, holding it with both arms and snuggling it close to my body. It's morning and I'm not ready to get out of bed yet but I have too much to do to be lazy so I let go of my pillow buddy and turn to get up. *Oh crap.* No way. This is not my bedroom. That means this is not my apartment. *I spent the night.*

I look around the room for Alex but don't see him. I listen for the shower or some hint that he's near but still, nothing. Then the smell hits me like a freight train. Bacon and coffee. The scent is heaven to my rumbling stomach. I think I overdosed on alcohol and sex last night. I really need the coffee and bacon. And is that cinnamon rolls? I summon the energy to crawl out of bed. Laid out on a chair to my right is a tee shirt with a sticky note that reads simply, *For you.*

After I slip on the shirt and help myself to some toothpaste and mouthwash, I saunter into the kitchen and find Alex busy scrambling eggs. He is wearing the sweatpants he wears when he comes to visit me after our kick boxing classes. They are soft and baggy. He's shirtless. His hair is wet. He must have just showered. He smiles when he sees me although I'm not sure my appearance is worthy of his smile.

"Good morning sleeping beauty," he greets me.

"What? No kiss to wake me up?"

"As a matter of fact, I did kiss you but since I pretty much fucked you into a coma I doubt you were aware of it. Hungry?" He walks around the island, pulls me into his arms, and places a soft kiss on my forehead.

"Starving," I respond with enthusiasm.

After breakfast I talked Alex into bringing me home, even though he tried to convince me to stay for an encore of last night's performance. He didn't give me any grief about spending the night, thank goodness, and I didn't bring it up. I did leave my phone number on his bathroom counter, however. Baby steps.

A long, hot shower soothes my aching muscles and clears my mind so I can focus on taking care of my errands before Cole brings Hudson home at five o'clock. By three, the apartment is clean. I've gotten three loads of laundry down, and managed to make it to the grocery store. I turn on the television but fall asleep on the sofa without actually ever watching anything. A knock on the door wakes me up.

I open the door and my boy jumps right into my arms almost knocking me down. "Mommyyyy," he screams.

"Hey monkey butt. I'm so glad you're home!"

Cole brings Hudson's bag inside and sets it next to the sofa. We have a decent relationship. It's been two years since we've split. There's none of the fighting or pettiness you see in other situations like ours. He moved on shortly after I left. Cole has a hard time being alone. And Michelle is a great woman so I'm happy for him. He gives me a brief run-down of the weekend, saving the details for Hudson, then they say their goodbyes until next time.

Hudson fills me in on the details of his weekend over dinner. Apparently there is a ten acre pond not far from where his dad lives and it has the biggest fish he's ever seen. Hudson caught three but chose to throw them back because they have families who will be lonely without them. We snuggle on the sofa and watch a few of his favorite shows until it's time for his bath.

"Mom, dad said I can get a mohawk," he informs me as I'm washing his hair.

"Is that so?"

"Yes ma'am. Annnnd he said I can color it blue." He's so excited about his news.

"Why blue?"

"Because mom, that's my team colors. All the other kids have mohawks. Can I? Please?"

"I'll think about it," I tell him, then I smile knowing I'll eventually cave. He gives me an aggravated sigh but ultimately gives in. "Okay," he says reluctantly.

At bedtime he sings to me and I read to him and we cuddle until he falls asleep.

Monday, June 2

Nick told me on Friday that we would be coming up with a game plan today. We have a meeting at 9:30 so I pop in my store, say my good mornings, get everyone set for the day, and then make my way to his office. I consider stopping to get him a coffee on the way but that seems a little like sucking up so I don't. The guy has a coffee maker in his office. He'll be okay. I waste way too much time coming up with ways to impress this man. It took me forty-five minutes to decide on my outfit this morning. Teetering back and forth between *I want him to notice me* and *I want him to take me seriously*. I settle on what I feel is a happy medium; dark gray dressy trousers and a loose-fitting, gold chiffon, short sleeve top that criss-crosses just between my shoulder blades but drapes open down the rest of my back. I go for a black bandeau underneath in lieu of a bra and some yellow gold accessories to finish it off. Classy but sassy. Oh goodness, now I'm naming my outfits. I told you, I am putting way too much effort into this.

I don't call to confirm our meeting. I just show up. I'm a little OCD so it makes me feel like I've forgotten something important, like underwear. I make my usual path through security and down the hall before walking up to Thing One's desk and announcing myself. She eagerly informs me that Mr. Knight is expecting me so I should go right up. What's with Perky Polly all of a sudden? People who are too nice make me nervous. No one likes anyone that much. I don't trust it. Oh well. I shake the thought and head upstairs. Thing Two greets me with the same enthusiasm. Weird. She stands and opens the doors to Nick's office, guiding me in.

"Good morning Heidi," Nick says from behind his desk. He stood when I walked in the room but didn't walk around. Today he has forgone his usual suit and tie combo and is looking delicious in khakis, a white button up, rolled up to just below his elbows, and a black vest. He left the top three buttons of his shirt undone. Just to tease me, I'm sure.

"Good morning Senator," I politely reply. "May I?" I ask, pointing toward the chair in front of his desk.

He grins and takes his seat. "Please do."

He watches as I sit and waits a moment before speaking again. "Heidi," he starts. I wait a second for him to continue. When he doesn't, I realize he is waiting for me to respond.

"Yes?"

"There's no need to be formal. Call me Nick."

I mentally whine. But I like calling him Senator. It reminds me how powerful he is. And I like that he is powerful. It's kind of hot. I haven't found much about this man that isn't hot. I don't want to make him uncomfortable so I decide to just call him Nick like he asked but inside I'm pouting like a two year old.

"Nick," I say to confirm my obedience, both to him and to myself.

I notice one corner of his mouth turn upwards. He does this often. It highlights his dimples. I love it. It's like he wants to smile but won't quite commit.

"Did you enjoy your weekend?" he inquires. Instantly I replay the events of Saturday night in my head. I remember seeing him. I remember the biceps. I remember the jeans. Oh lord, those jeans.

"It was nice." I'm not sure Alex would appreciate it being called nice. Now is not the time and this is not the place to be thinking about my Saturday night sexcapades. *Change the subject. Talk about him.* "So I didn't peg you as the going out type. Guys night out?" I ask but immediately regret it. I might as well just have straight up asked him if Blonde Bombshell was his girlfriend.

"Something like that. I prefer to call it networking. I *am* just a man, Heidi. I clock out and go home just like the rest of the world. Unless you can think of another way for me to enjoy myself?"

"Well....no," I reply, not sure if it's a statement or not. I can think of tons of ways for him to enjoy *me*. Or for me to enjoy him. Or us to enjoy each other. *Get your mind out of the gutter Heidi.*

"No?" he probes.

"I guess I just pictured you going home, throwing your tie on the bar, popping a cold one and watching CNN all night while a couple of security guards keep the riff raff away." It seems like a pretty typical senator thing to do.

Nick laughs at my response. "Import or domestic?"

"Import, of course," I say.

There he goes with that slanted grin again. "Well you're right about the tie. But I'm a scotch man. As far as the news goes, if I have to wait until I see something on tv to know it's happened, then I'm not doing my job very well. Am I?"

"I guess not." Great. Now visions of Nick Knight throwing his tie down and unbuttoning his shirt while he sips on a glass of scotch are dancing around in my head. His chest and abs are exposed and he's leaned back on a plush sofa with those long legs stretched out in front of him. Shit. It's getting really hot in here. He never brings up Blondie so I don't either. Even though I am really curious.

He's looking at me with that *look*. His eyes are narrowed and focused. His mouth is closed but his lips are toying with whether or not they should part. Does he look at everyone that way? And just like that it's like he's in my head. Watching me, watch him. And the thought amuses him. Just then, his phone rings, interrupting my daydream.

"Hold that thought," he tells me. *Believe me buddy, that thought ain't going anywhere.* I almost forget why I'm here again. I find this is becoming a regular occurrence. I briefly wonder if there's a support group out there for all the women addicted to Nick Knight. A-Nick-ted. Here I am, quietly laughing at my own joke again. Good thing he's focused on his phone call. There's no way I'd tell him what's so funny.

CHAPTER ELEVEN
Nick

There's something off about Heidi today. She's distant. Not here with me where I want her to be. I spend too much time trying to make her more comfortable and end up not even discussing the reason she's here. It's a midterm election year and I have an important meeting in about fifteen minutes so I need to think fast.

"I apologize for cutting this short but I have to go. I would like to take you to lunch this afternoon though." It's more of a statement than an invitation. I don't want to give her the chance to decline. I'm enjoying her company too much.

Her mouth parts but no words come out. *She's surprised.* She takes in a deep breath and looks at the ground before looking back up at me. She's regained her composure. It was only gone for a moment but I caught it. And I wonder if my assertiveness offended her or if she's just taken by surprise at the thought of having lunch with me.

"Sure. Lunch is good. Just let me know when and where." She pulls her tote over her shoulder and reaches inside for her keys.

I don't have to think about it. I know the perfect place. "Bistro 129. I'm not sure what time so I'll call you."

"Okay." Her answer is hesitant but compliant nevertheless. She pulls her bottom lip into her mouth like she's thinking of saying something else but decides not to. Why? Maybe she's dating someone. Fuck him. I'm taking her to lunch.

As she leaves my office I notice the back of her top is open, exposing the slight curve in her figure just above her ass. There's a thin black band of material underneath and it hits me. She isn't wearing a bra. Just when I thought she couldn't get any sexier. *Fuck me.*

Two hours later, I walk in to the small, locally owned restaurant. The atmosphere here is ideal for someone who wants their privacy. I come here often. Heidi is sitting on one of the benches near the entrance. I was expecting to beat her here. I just called her less than twenty minutes ago.

She stands when I walk in. How polite. The hostess greets me by name. My hand finds its way to the small of Heidi's back, urging her to follow the young lady. I feel the warmth of her skin beneath my fingertips and immediately recall that her shirt is open in the back. She shudders for a split second but quickly relaxes. Instinctively my fingers slip further under the thin fabric and around her waist as we wait for the hostess to finish placing our menus on the table. Her body doesn't move but I'm gauging her other reactions. Her chest rises as she inhales deeply and she swallows hard as she exhales. Her eyes are

fixed intently on the hostess. She's concentrating on staying focused. She doesn't want to break. She won't let me know I affect her. Not yet anyway. But she will. I play the gentleman card and pull out her chair. What can I say? She brings it out of me. The waiter introduces himself and takes our drink order as soon as we are seated.

"So. You come here often?" Heidi questions. Her face indicates she already knows the answer but prefers to try to make me uncomfortable.

"I bring business associates here, yes," I reply. Her eyes narrow and her lips twist to one side. It is absolutely fucking adorable. She doesn't accept that answer. She takes in a breath and gears up to challenge me but I stop her before she can start. "It's quiet and they serve alcohol. Pretty good combination for sealing the deal, don't you agree?" She doesn't answer. She still thinks I'm fucking with her. Not that I owe her an explanation but I want her to know this isn't some *'go to'* place of mine for getting laid. I'm not a wine and dine kind of guy. Most of the women I sleep with aren't interested in what's for dinner anyway.

"Look Heidi, I don't want you to get the wrong idea about me," I clarify. I'm just about to expound when I witness a palpable shift in her demeanor. Her shoulders square up, her chin lifts, and she straightens up in her seat. *Holy shit. It just got frosty in here.*

"I don't have any ideas about you, Nick," she retorts, placing heavy emphasis on the word ideas.

Whoa. What the fuck just happened? I'm getting ready to explain that I don't serial date and she flips shit on me. I must look like a deer caught in headlights. That's how I feel anyway. My eyes roam the room while I search for something to say.

"Seriously. I get it. This is where you take *business* associates. This is a *business* lunch. Why would I get the wrong idea?" She laughs to herself and takes a sip of her wine. She is looking past me, not at me. Well shit. That didn't go the way I had planned. We were at the same stop but she got on the wrong bus. I wasn't fending her off. I was trying to make myself not look like an asshole and ended up doing exactly the opposite.

"There's a conference room in the back by the bar. That's normally where I sit. This," I wave my hand around the space encompassing us, "is a first."

Her face softens a little and I breathe a sigh of relief. What the hell is happening here? So I offended her. Who cares? She'll get over it. I don't have to explain myself.

"Well then. Where do you take all your dates if it's not here?" She's smiling. Not a full on, pearly whites, my cheeks hurt, smile. Just a simple upturn of the lips. But it lights up her eyes and I know she's moved on.

"I don't date." It's an impulsive response to a question I'm sure was meant to be light-hearted. But it's the truth. And she deserves the truth. She contemplates my answer for a minute. "So the blonde. She wasn't a date?"

She's talking about Taylor. The woman she saw me with Saturday night. I am definitely not dating Taylor. Taylor Montgomery is a local news anchor I fuck occasionally. Two or three times a month for the past six months, actually. She's dating a well-known local musician but I guess his creativity ends with his guitar because she damn near grovels for my cock. Taylor knows I am not exclusive to her but that doesn't keep her from getting all possessive and shit like she did when she saw Heidi. I don't blame her. If I were a woman, seeing someone like Heidi with my man would make me nervous too. "I don't date," I affirm.

"Yea, me either," she states. Well isn't she just full of surprises? Normally when I tell a woman I don't date, she is quick to dismiss it as a joke or an excuse. Followed by the cliché *you just haven't met the right woman.* I can't say I've ever had one actually agree with me. So she isn't fucking anyone after all. *Or is she?* She said she doesn't date. She didn't say she doesn't fuck.

"No happily ever after for Heidi Lemaire?" There's no way she meant it. Every woman wants the fairy tale. It's in their DNA.

"Nope." She takes another sip of wine. I'm figuring out that's her way of avoiding further conversation. She's waiting for me to change the subject but she's not getting off that easy. I don't break eye contact with her. Finally, she gives in.

"Cinderella figured out that the ball was nothing but an overrated costume party. And she wasn't the only one wearing a mask." It's vague but I sense there's a deeper meaning behind it.

She expounds, "People aren't always what they seem. Sometimes it's easier to keep them at a distance. You don't see all the flaws that way."

"Some people are exactly what they seem." *Like me.* I am exactly what I seem. I make no promises and I make no apologies. It's as simple as that yet I feel an overwhelming need to prove something to her. This woman does things to me like no one I've ever met. I think about her when she's not around. And when she is around, I don't seem to want her to leave. I want to know what motivates her, what she cares about, and what she doesn't. I can't decide if this should excite me or piss me off.

Thankfully the waiter shows up with our food before this conversation goes any further. Over the meal we talk about how delicious everything is and our mutual fondness for local businesses. She tells me more about what she does and how she got started. Her dream is to one day go nationwide. I'm talking franchise this shit. I'm completely engrossed. This woman has so much drive and determination. She started with a laptop and a Facebook page. And now she's heading up major design projects and planning million dollar weddings. Which gives me a brilliant fucking idea. I can hire Heidi to plan an event for me. Every year for the past four years, I hold a political fundraiser party at my home. They aren't always for my own benefit but they do offer a good opportunity for me to solicit potential benefactors for the future. This year's fundraiser is for a friend of mine running for a state senate seat. It's four weeks away and I've been so wrapped up in trying to get in Heidi's pants that I forgot to hire someone to organize it. Fortunately for me, she does that. Talk about your good luck. We've finished our lunch, I've got the bill, and until now I haven't even noticed that we haven't even talked about her situation at all. I don't think she's noticed it either. And if she has, she hasn't mentioned it. Oh well. Guess we'll have to have dinner now.

I walk Heidi to her Jeep Wrangler. Now there's a contradiction. Here is a woman, elegant and graceful in every way. And then here's this rugged, four door, solid white, off road vehicle that I'm positive she has to climb a ladder to get into. I was expecting a Lexus or BMW but for the second time this afternoon, she blows my mind.

Heidi is shuffling things around in her purse and digging in her pockets. She lets out a frustrated growl and blows her hair out of her face then starts digging again.

"Something wrong?" I inquire, although the growl made it obvious.

"Can you see if my keys are in there?" She points to the driver's side window of her Jeep. I peek inside and sure enough I see them lying on the seat. I turn around and give her a sympathetic nod.

"Crap. You have got to be kidding me."

I reach in my pocket to pull out my cell phone and she eyes me curiously. "I can call a locksmith. It's not a big deal." I start googling the number but she interrupts the process.

"I can call a locksmith too. But I have a spare key at my apartment so it would be cheaper to just call Shelly to bring it to me." Her tone is sharp and determined. She is clearly used to doing things her way. I'm gonna have to show her how to let that go.

"Or you could just let me drive you to your apartment to get it yourself. I'm here. Ready and willing," I tease, hoping to make light of a potentially stressful situation. She sighs but gives in.

I plug in her address on my GPS. On the way there we finally discuss the cocktail party. She tells me she normally has an assistant by the name of Hannah head up her event coordinating. I immediately shoot that plan down. I didn't come up with a bullshit reason to see her more just to have some assistant take over. After some cunning persuasion on my part, she reluctantly agrees and I'm feeling extremely lucky today. We arrive at the gated entrance of her complex just a few minutes later. She spouts off a code for me to punch in and I pull inside. Her building is the last one before the curve. She invites me in but I decline. It's probably not a good idea to be alone. Near a bed. Near *her* bed. Not yet. Not because I'm not ready. I don't think she's ready. But then again, she has managed to surprise me more than once today.

"I have to make a phone call," I lie.

She looks…surprised? Disappointed? Hurt? Whatever it is, it doesn't last long. The wall comes back up and the mask goes back on. "Okay. I won't be long," she promises.

I watch as she walks to the door of the first apartment on the bottom floor. She lifts a potted plant from a ceramic container and pulls a key from the bottom and goes inside. She needs to come up with a new hiding spot. Anyone could guess that one. And if she's alone…There I go. Thinking shit I have no business thinking about. What the hell is wrong with me? She's a grown woman. Let her figure it out. Heidi quickly returns all bright eyed and bushy tailed with her spare keys. I bring her back to her vehicle, feeling oddly disappointed that our time together has come to an end. For today.

CHAPTER TWELVE
Heidi

Thursday, June 5

I have to meet Joel this morning to go over menu options for Nick's party. I have four weeks to pull this thing together. No problem. What with all the free time I have lately and all. I guess it could be worse. He could have waited until the week before. I really talked Hannah up, hoping he'd go that direction. Events are her thing. Design is mine. He could have brought her in and it would have been fine. I'm convinced Nick just likes seeing me stressed. He's making me crazy. And what was with the hand under my shirt thing? Is he trying to kill me? You have no idea the willpower it took not to moan right then and there. His touch was so soft and warm. *No.* More than warm. *Hot.* My body was begging for him to keep inching those fingers up my side. Can you blame me? You can practically hear the panties dropping when he walks into a room. And he plays these Jedi mind games with me every time I see him. Subtle insinuations and sexy half-smiles. The way he looks at me with those eyes. I can feel it all the way in my soul. It's intense. I wonder if he's that way with all the women he knows. He must get laid on a daily basis. He said he doesn't date. I can't say I blame him. When you have that much booty on speed dial, why waste all your time on just one? Variety is the spice of life after all.

After Joel and I come up with a preliminary menu, I call Nick to schedule a taste testing for Monday. He lets me know he'll be out of town until then but to call if I need anything. After our lunch yesterday he gave me his cell phone number. No more going through Thing One and Thing Two, which is a definite plus. I stop by a local stationary and accessories shop to order a couple of sample invitations and take the rest of the afternoon off to take Hudson on a mommy/son date. We load up on tickets and race each other on Mario Kart until he tells me he's tired. Then we call it a day and go home so he can rest before baseball practice tonight.

Hudson was born with ASD, a heart defect. Kind of like a murmur on steroids. He has a hole in the middle of the four chambers of his heart. For most people, your blood pumps through your heart then through your body. With Hudson, his blood pumps through his heart, then through his heart again before going through his body. So the organ works overtime causing him to have an accelerated heart rate all the time. It hasn't required surgery so far but it does limit what he feels up to doing most days. The past two weeks something has been off with him. Two nights ago I noticed a big purple bruise on his shoulder when he got out of the bath. He couldn't remember how he got it. Then this morning there was another one on the front of his leg. He had no clue it was even there. He's also been nauseated more than normal lately. At first I attributed it to the summer heat but the worse he feels, the more worried I get so I go ahead and make an appointment with his pediatric cardiologist for next Friday.

We spend most of the afternoon cuddling in my bed and our evening making homemade pizza for dinner. Hudson puts extra pepperoni on his side. Then we have root beer floats for dessert. He asks if we can make a picnic in the living room, which is not something we do often but it's a fun twist on our routine once in a while. After I load the dishwasher, we play Go Fish and watch cartoons until he falls asleep.

I tuck him in then try to read some before falling asleep. It's pointless. I lie here awake thinking of Nick. And his unbuttoned shirt and glass of scotch.

Friday, June 6

"Do I have to go to grandma's today?" Hudson asks as I lay out his clothes for the day.

"Do you want to go to grandma's today?"

"Ehhh, I figured we could use some time apart," he says. He sounds so grown up but there he stands in his tiny little camoflauge boxer briefs and bed hair.

I chuckle and help him with his shirt. "You're not tired of grandma already are you?"

"Mom, she farts when she cleans. And she feeds me coffee beans and tells me it's candy." He makes a face like he just ate something horrible. "It is most definitely not candy," he explains.

Why is she feeding my kid coffee beans? Seriously grandma? Coffee? But I would never undermine her decisions in front of him. "Okay, fart is a gross word. And I like coffee beans," I tell him.

He looks up at me with accusing eyes. "Really mom? Coffee beans?"

"Okay, you got me. We'll call grandma and tell her we have plans. Fro-yo date?" I offer.

He jumps up and down and hugs my legs. Of course he's happy. You see, Hudson doesn't eat frozen yogurt. I fill my cup with a sugar-free strawberry/New York cheesecake blend and goes straight for the toppings bar, filling his cup with all the candy toppings. No yogurt.

Monday, June 9

It's only been one week since we've seen each other but I am looking forward to seeing Nick this afternoon. I have two other appointments before meeting him at Joel's for our tasting because, let's face it- the bills aren't going to pay themselves.

Those end up being a breeze so here I am, fifteen minutes early at Joel's. He and I have been working together for the past two years. He knows my preferences and I know how to persuade him to work within my budgets. We've actually become pretty close friends. He's a hot mess and loads of fun to go out with. Joel is also extremely talented. He has a full service, well-known, restaurant as well as a very popular catering business. I don't know how old he is but my guess would be mid-forties and very attractive. He is rather tall with dark brown hair and brown eyes. His smile is contagious and he is a habitual flirt. Flirting to Joel is like breathing is to most people. He's never been married and swears he never will be.

I walk in and head straight to the back of the restaurant where I know he will be preparing today's menu. I find Joel standing in front of an eight foot rectangle table that is beautifully decorated with a variety of trays and platters, candles, and fresh florals. He's wearing his usual black shirt, black slacks combination. He turns when he hears me approach and immediately smiles.

"There's my beautiful girl," he croons. He meets me halfway and greets me with a hug and quick kiss on the cheek.

"You've already got the job Joel. No need for flattery," I tell him.

"I always get the job. I'm still waiting on the girl."

I playfully shove him away and shake my head. "This is gorgeous! It looks absolutely delicious," I change the subject, indicating the spread in front of us.

Joel moves in right behind me, looking over my shoulder at the food. "What would you like to try first?"

His closeness doesn't bother me. I'm used to his games by now.

"Strawberry," I reply, pointing at the tray of chocolate covered strawberries to my left.

"Mmhm hmm. You go for those every time," he says as he moves around me to grab a strawberry.

He holds the fruit in front of my mouth and I give him an agitated glare. "I can feed myself."

"Humor me," he pleads, placing his other hand on my shoulder.

I roll my eyes and open my mouth. He places the strawberry on my tongue and I bite off most of it, leaving only a small portion and the crown. "Mhmm ohmigod Joel. Amazing. As always."

The sound of footsteps coming towards us interrupts my affair with this delectable chocolate-dipped fruit. Joel's eyes move from mine to the person approaching. He grins. It's mischievous. He seems pleased with himself for some reason.

I hear Nick's voice behind me. "Excuse the interruption. Should I come back later?" His tone is inquisitive and....irritated? I can't tell. Either way, I note the sarcasm in his comment.

I turn to face him, silently wishing I could rewind time about forty-five seconds. I would have snatched that damn strawberry out of Joel's hands.

"Nick...Hello...This is Joel. Joel, this is...Nick," I stutter, struggling to introduce them.

The two men shake hands and lock gazes for a moment longer than I'm really comfortable with. Then Nick looks back at me. His eyes quickly drop to my mouth and my lips part automatically. The effect he has on my body is unreal. He brings his hand up to my face and slowly runs the pad of his thumb over the top of my bottom lip. I freeze. I'm frozen. What the hell is he doing? Joel watches in amusement at the gesture. And holy freaking crap if Nick doesn't take that same thumb and stick it in his mouth and then very, very slowly draw it back out again. Then, he licks his lips. All the while, staring at me. Or more like *into* me. Holy shit, I need new panties. Silence. Until finally, Nick speaks. "Well, that was," he pauses a beat before continuing, "delicious." Here he goes with the sideways grin. I wish I had a photographic memory so I could randomly pull up that smile when I'm having a bad day.

"Where did it come from?" he asks.

I don't answer immediately. I'm still mentally licking his gorgeous body from head to toe.

"Heidi? The chocolate?"

Shit. He's talking to me. Just as I'm about to answer him, Joel steps forward. "The strawberries. They're Heidi's favorite."

Nick's eyes never leave mine. He doesn't even acknowledge Joel. "Are they?" he asks.

"Yes." My response is soft. Breathy. Like I just got punched in the gut.

"Are all of these your favorite?" he inquires, scanning the table.

"Most of them," I reply.

Joel moves to stand beside me. I forgot he was even in the room until now. "Once you figure out what Heidi likes," he says, "she's pretty easy to please."

Alright, they might as well just lift their legs and pee a circle around me. This is ridiculous.

"I have to make a phone call. Nick, please try a little bit of everything and I'll get with you later on what you like," I tell them.

Nick smirks and nods his head. "Later," he pauses to look at me, "you'll find out *exactly* what I like." He moves his eyes to Joel. "Take her favorites and put them on the menu, Joel. It's been a pleasure." His tone is clipped and he seems suddenly eager to leave. He gives me a wink and a smile and walks out of the room, leaving me wondering what the hell just happened.

"You're kidding me! He *licked* the chocolate off your mouth?" Shelly blurts out.

After the "tasting," I came back to work and soon called Shelly in my office because let's face it, I had to tell *somebody*. So why not my best friend? Now she's announcing the event to the whole store. I shove an index finger over her lips. "Sshh. Not off my mouth," I whisper. "Well, technically off my mouth, but not literally off my mouth," I explain as I close the door to my office.

"Technically. Literally. That shit was hot. I don't care how you put it," Shelly states.

"I know, right."

"He definitely wants *the business*," she says, her eyes moving down my body and stopping at my pelvic area to emphasize her meaning.

"You think?" *Okay Heidi, don't be a moron*. You know what he wants. Apparently Shelly is thinking the same thing I am because she's giving me the *"you're an idiot"* look right now. "I think it's time we had the talk honey. You see when a woman likes a man, and a man likes a woman..." she starts, making an "o" with her index finger and thumb on one hand when she says woman and aiming her other index at the hole when she says man.

I grab her hands and pull them to her sides. "Ohmigod STOP! I don't need *the talk*. Go away," I spit out mid-laugh. She is mental. For real. But I love her. I take her by the shoulders and lead her out of my office.

I spend the next two and a half hours putting together design boards and emailing vendors. And reminding myself that Nick Knight is just a guy helping me keep my business. That's his job after all. So he hired me to organize an event. *That's my job.* No crazy story here. Just business.

CHAPTER THIRTEEN
Heidi

Tuesday, June 10

The girls and I usually change at the store before Alex's kickboxing class and tonight is no exception. Once we're ready, we head over to the gym. When I walk in I notice Alex wrapping up a new girl's hands. She's flirting with him. I don't blame her. I flirted too. We all did. He's hot. Can't blame a girl for trying right? I get through the class without saying much. I let him have his fun with new girl. Every man could use an ego boost. I'm not jealous. He manages to walk past and grope my behind a couple of times and occasionally he comes up behind me and whispers inappropriate comments in my ear. After class, new girl is making an attempt at getting to know Alex better. I grab my bag and walk past them to leave when he stops me.

"Heidi. Do you mind staying a minute? I need to go over something with you," he says.

"Sure," I reply, dropping my bag and waiting for him to say goodbye to his new friend.

She's the last one out the door. Poor thing waited around for nothing.

Alex locks the door and walks toward the back of the gym. I guess I'm supposed to follow him. So I do. He is wiping off with a towel. He looks so sexy with his satin shorts and bare, sweaty chest. He turns out the lights in the front by the windows, leaving only the ones by the showers and lockers on.

"I'm not going to make it over tonight," he informs me.

I'm a little disappointed because I look forward to our weekly one-on-ones but it's not the end of the world. I tease him, "You made other plans?" I walk a few steps closer toward him, stopping a couple of feet away. "You should probably tell her Tuesdays are mine. Wednesdays are good. Or Fridays. Sundays and Mondays even. But Tuesday is taken."

He's trying not to smile but I can see the arrogance bursting out of him right now. He throws the towel on the ground and steps forward. We're almost touching but not quite.

"Heidi. Are you jealous?"

"No." It's the truth. Kind of. I'm not *that* jealous. What Alex does when he isn't with me is his business. But on Tuesdays and sometimes Thursdays, he is with me. So. See? It is my business.

"Well, you're very sexy when you're not jealous," he flirts. He places his hands on my hips and pulls me to him.

I look up with curious eyes. "Your plans?"

"A buddy. Who is a male. Who has a penis. Is having woman problems. He needs a distraction," he explains.

"So you are blowing me off for a penis? I always knew there was something off about you." I'm joking but he's not finding it funny.

Alex walks me backwards until my back is pressed firmly against a wall. He places a hand on either side of my head and leans forward to look me in the eye.

"I never said I wasn't going to fuck you, love. I simply said I wouldn't be doing it at your place."

Two hours later I'm in bed relaxed and reading. Thanks to Alex and my weekly orgasm. He definitely fucked me. My body pinned against the wall, his shorts around his ankles, both of us breathing hard and sweating as he pounded me with an almost painful determination. I'm just about to fall asleep when I hear a knock on my door. *So he decided to come over after all.* It's strange to me because Alex knows when Hudson is home, there's pretty much a standing *Do Not Disturb* sign on my front door. But I get up to answer anyway, guessing the quickie at the gym wasn't enough to hold him over til next week.

I open the door just a crack and find none other than Nick Knight standing outside. What the f-bomb is he doing here? He's wearing a plain white t-shirt and jeans and just standing there with one hand braced against the door jamb.

"Nick." I'm sure my voice sounds shaky and confused. Most likely because I *am* shaky and confused. How the hell did he get in? Then I remember giving him the gate code last week when he brought me to get my spare key.

"Heidi," he replies. He smells like he took a bath in a barrel of whiskey. I can't believe he drove like this. In traffic. And made it in one piece.

I reach out my hand to him. "Here. Come inside." I open the door a little wider to welcome him in.

Nick moves his eyes over my body, making me suddenly self-conscious. I forgot I'm in my usual t-shirt and panty combo. Cut me some slack. I thought it was Alex at the door.

"Were you expecting someone else?" he inquires, reading my mind. The Twilight Zone theme song plays faintly in the background. *Okay, that's just weird.*
Yes.
"No," I lie.
"Do you always answer the door dressed like this?" *Yes.* But it's usually just Alex or Shelly and neither one of them care. I don't have visitors.
"No," I lie again. "But then again I don't usually have visitors at 10:00 at night." I step back behind the door.
He decides to come inside, closing the door behind him, leaving nothing for me to hide behind. So I just stand there. What else is there to do? The damage is done. Besides, I'm sure he's seen plenty of women in their underwear. Hotter women. Sexier women. It's not like I belong in a Victoria's Secret catalog or anything. It's just me. Heidi. He moves to stand directly in front of me. His eyes are dark and serious. He traces his index finger along the side of my face then tucks a strand of hair behind my ear. I'm nervous. I'm confused. I am glad to see him but have an overwhelming suspicion I should proceed with caution.
"Heidi," he says again. Like he's reminding himself that's my name. He is definitely drunk. I'm halfway there just breathing the same air.
"Are you okay?" He's kind of freaking me out. He's touching me. I'm half naked. He's been drinking and I have no idea why he's here.
"Tell me, are you fucking him?" His hand has moved from my face to my arm now. His touch is gentle yet his tone is anything but. Normally that question, in that tone, would send me running for the hills. Too many memories of accusations ending badly. But I'm not afraid of Nick. I can sense that his question comes from a different place. Not the usual *I'm asking because it hurts my inflated male pride* place. This feels like it's more from the *I'm asking because it hurts my feelings* kind of place. He's running his fingertips from my shoulder to my elbow and back up again as he speaks. It's an intimate gesture. One I could definitely get used to.
His question catches me off guard. "What? Who? What are you talking about?"
"You know who. The chef. Busy hands, wandering eyes, smart mouth" he spells out.
What the hell? And why is this any of his business? We aren't dating. We aren't sleeping together. He has no justification in asking me something like that and I definitely don't owe him an answer. But I feel like I need to tell him the truth. Why do I feel that way? I have no idea. Why is he even asking me this question? I have no idea.

71

"No. I'm not." I'm hoping this pacifies him.

His hand stills at the top of my shoulder. He cocks his head to the side and studies me for a minute. I'm thinking maybe he's trying to figure out if I'm telling him the truth. I lean forward on my tip-toes and run the tip of my nose along the outline of his jaw up to his ear. My lips are slightly parted so he can feel my breath on his skin. He stands completely still as I move back down to his chin, my nose barely skimming his bottom lip. I lift my chin just enough for my open mouth to hover over his. Nick parts his lips as well. We both remain still. Just breathing each other in. I close my eyes and move ever so slightly to one side and softly kiss the corner of his mouth. Then I lower myself back down and look up at him, allowing him the chance to make the next move. If there is a next move. *Please let there be a next move.*

"Fuck," he swears. More to himself than to me. "I'm sorry. That was none of my business. I need to go."

"Nick, you really shouldn't be driving right now."

He smiles and shakes his head. "Now, Ms. Lemaire. Are you suggesting I stay here?"

I roll my eyes and take a step back. If I keep standing that close to him, I'll be asking him to do more than just stay here. "No. I'm offering to call you a cab," I say, attempting to convince both of us that's what I really want to do.

He inches his way back close to me. "Or you could just give me a ride," he says with that sexy little half smirk I've grown to adore.

His hand inches down my arm to my hand. His fingers intertwine with mine and he pulls me even closer to him. I want this. Good god do I want it. But not this way. Hudson is sleeping in the other room. Nick has had way too much to drink. And I'm not *that girl*.

I lay my forehead against his chest and inhale his woodsy, masculine scent. "Nick," I say, the word a near whisper leaving my lips. I want to tell him he should go. I want to ask him to stay. I've never *not* known what I wanted this much in my life. I look up at him hoping to find some sort of answer to my internal contradiction.

He looks down at me and grins. "Maybe another time," he says. "I really need to get going."

We spend several seconds looking at each other. It reminds me of when I was in eighth grade and had the *you hang up, no you hang up,* conversations with my boyfriend. One of us needs to hang up, and since I'm the only one functioning with all of my brain cells at the moment, I decide it should be me. I walk to the door and turn the knob. Nick stops just in front of me and gives me a final once over before walking out. He graces me with one more beautiful, beaming white smile.

"I'll see you soon Heidi," he promises.

I respond by returning his smile with my own and watching from the doorway as he climbs into the back seat of a big, black SUV.

It's two a.m. when I finally stop thinking of him long enough to fall asleep.

Friday, June 13

Dr. Collins goes through the usual routine of running an EKG on Hudson followed by an echocardiogram. Hudson hates the EKG. He says it hurts when the nurse pulls the stickers off. I don't know of anyone who likes having things stuck to their body only to have them ripped back off just minutes later. But it's something we have done every six months since he was three months old. Even during my pregnancy, the doctor sensed something wasn't right with his heart. I recall more than once being sent directly to the ultrasound room for them to monitor Hudson's heart because something didn't sound quite right during the routine exam.

He doesn't have to take any medication or anything. It's just always been something we keep a close eye on. And Hudson knows his body well. When he starts to feel tired or out of breath, he tells me, and we rest. I make sure his appetite stays healthy and watch what he eats. His cardiologist said let him live a normal life outside of those few things. Who am I to argue? I'm not the one who went to med school.

The echocardiogram is taking longer than usual this visit and I'm starting to fidget in my seat. I have no idea what I'm looking at on that screen. Dr. Collins is clicking and typing numbers and clicking some more. I know from experience she's measuring the hole but I can't tell what else is going on.

She asks him to turn over onto his side so she can view things from another angle. *That's a first.* Now I'm really nervous. I wish she'd hurry and finish so she can tell me what the hell is wrong. And there *is* something wrong. She usually talks to Hudson about baseball or what he's been up to but today she is quiet. Concentrating. Measuring and clicking. Today is definitely different. I want to speak out. I want to point at the screen and ask, *"What is that?"* I want to ask why she turned him onto his side. I don't want to wait for her to finish. I want to know now. But I sit here. Completely silent. Because even though my brain wants to know, my heart isn't ready to find out just yet.

She moves him onto his back and wipes the goop off his chest area then turns on the lights. I brace myself.
"You know we've been monitoring him to see if the condition will self-correct. And in most cases, they do," she says. I sense a *"but"* coming.
I nod. "Yes." It's all I can manage until I know where this is going.
"Hudson's hole has grown. It's gotten bigger," she explains. *Yes, I know what* grown *means.*
"Okay?" I'm still waiting for the rest. I scoot to the edge of my seat and sit up completely straight, somehow thinking the closer I am to her, the more sense her words will make. I glance at Hudson but he is busy putting his shirt back on.
"The right side of his heart is becoming enlarged. We may need to consider corrective surgery. I have a few other concerns based on how you answered some of my questions earlier, so I'd like to run some blood work on him before we talk about surgery options."
This isn't happening. They told me it would correct itself by the time he was four. When it didn't, I told myself he was just a late bloomer and he would be fine by six. It wasn't supposed to get bigger. He doesn't need heart surgery. That is not part of the plan! Get it together Heidi. The doctor is staring at you.

I guess she realizes I have nothing to say at this point. "My nurse will give you the orders. You can take him next door to the Specialty Clinic and they'll take care of the lab work," she prompts.
I just nod and reach for my baby. I take him down from the paper covered table and hold him on my hip. Like I used to do when he was just a toddler.
Dr. Collins gives me a reassuring smile before leading us out of the room. "He will be fine, mom. This is just a precaution. I just want to check on some things."
I thank her, handle my business at the sign out window, and then go hold my little boy in my lap while the nurse next door draws two vials full of blood from his little arms.

CHAPTER FOURTEEN
Nick

I'm not sure what the hell I was thinking Tuesday night. Going over to Heidi's loaded like I was. I take that back. I know exactly what I was thinking. Nate told me I was lacking. There I was, gushing like an idiot to my best friend over a bottle of scotch how this woman has completely exasperated me yet captivated me at the same time. On the outside she's controlled, calm, and collected. But I can sense on the inside, she needs *something*. And I am the man who can give it to her. He's tired of hearing it. Says I have an extreme case of blue balls and I *"just need to fuck this girl already."* Easy for him to say. That fucker gets laid on a regular basis. Talk about being tired of hearing of it. It's all he talks about. I'd even go as far as to say he may actually even be in love. Pathetic bastard. But he doesn't know Heidi. He doesn't understand that this isn't a girl you take home from a bar one night and forget about the next day. This is the type of girl you lock in a room for a week and play out all your twisted fantasies with. I'm talking Beauty and the Beast type shit. So that my friends, is what I was thinking. I was going to fuck the shit out of Heidi Lemaire so maybe I could start thinking straight again. Boy was I wrong.

She opened the door in nothing but a t-shirt and panties. My first instinct was to shove her against the wall and take what I went there for. Then my mind started to wander. Who the fuck answers the door half naked? What if I had been a stranger? Or a burglar. There's no way she's protecting herself dressed like that. Wait. What if she wasn't surprised by the knock? What if she was expecting someone else? Whoever she left Jackson Street with that Saturday night. The chef seemed pretty cozy with her. Is she fucking him? My mind was racing but all I cared about was seeing what I was up against. I had no right to ask. I have no claim to her. She doesn't belong to me. But I wanted her to. Right then, at that moment, in her oversized t-shirt and messy hair piled on top of her head. God she looked so innocent. So vulnerable. Nothing like the *all work and no play* Heidi that comes to my office asking me if I'm okay. Worrying about me. I knew then that I have to make her mine. Then, she does this fucking thing with her mouth. This thing where it felt like she was touching me. Kissing me all over my face. But in reality it was just her breath. Soft, sweet, and hot. Everywhere. My dick was hard as a fucking rock at that point. I swear it was some sort of voodoo brainwashing bullshit because I have been walking around with a perma-rection ever since. It took all I had in me to lasso in every ounce of self-control so I didn't take her right then and there. I know that's what I went there to do, but something changed. Seeing her that way, outside of the fierce business woman. Seeing her vulnerable. That was a game changer. No. When I take her, it won't be because of an alcohol induced testosterone overload. She'll want it just as much as I do. In fact, she'll beg me for it.

Wednesday I sunk to a new low. Heidi had me running around the city like a fucking stalker. I should just have a GPS tracker activated on her phone. I have people who can do it. But there I was, stalking her. I went by her office with some bullshit guest list for the event she's planning. She wasn't
there and I wasn't satisfied with just being told she wasn't coming in. I had to see her. Like I said. Voodoo bullshit. I drove by the chef's place but didn't see her Jeep. I have to admit I let out a little sigh of relief at that observation. By then, Jimminy Cricket was standing on my shoulder telling me I probably need counseling. And that I used to recommend women get restraining orders against guys like me. I tell that aggravating mother fucker to shut up and drive by her apartment. She's not there either.
Two hours later she's texting me.

Heidi: Hey you! How's the head?
Me: Fine. Is there some reason it shouldn't be?
Heidi: Well, unless you're Irish, I'm guessing you probably had a rough morning.
Me: You've obviously never drank with a Latino.
Heidi: Latino huh?
Me: Yes, Cuban. Any more questions Ms. Lane?
Heidi: Well, Clark. Maybe just one. Where do you rip off your clothes since they did away with all the phone booths?
Me: Where ever I feel like it. Are you taking notes?
Heidi: Yes, actually. Writing a book. Want to read it?
Me: Perhaps. After dinner, tonight?
Heidi: Not a good night for dinner. But you have my address if you happen to be in the neighborhood. ;)

There she goes with the winky shit again. I didn't reply to her last message. Did she seriously just turn me down? This woman is driving me crazy. Why would she turn down dinner but invite me over? I finish up a few phone calls and emails at the office before going home. I'd normally be in Washington D.C. right now, but we're out of session until next week. Which leaves me plenty of time to think about Heidi. I didn't stop by her apartment. I'll be damned if I'm begging anyone for pussy. Doesn't matter how much I want it.

That was Wednesday. It's been two days since I've talked to her and I can't stop thinking about it.

When I get home, the smell of fresh lemon and clean cotton hits me as soon as I walk through the door. Monica is my live in housekeeper and Friday is deep cleaning day. The rest of the week is just maintenance. She lives in the guest house with her four year old daughter, Olivia. Monica and I don't have your typical employer-employee relationship. She got burned when things went down with Elise and Matthew. See, she happened to be dating the guy Elise cheated on me with. Two months later she discovered she was pregnant and I'll be damned if I let her go crawling back to that asshole just because of it. I offered her a full time job and a place to stay. I also pay her tuition for nursing school. In a fucked up way I feel like I owe her that. It was my fiancé that helped ruin her relationship. Her future. We have more of a friendship than a business relationship. She tells me like it is and most of the time I tell her to mind her business.

The house is quiet and dark. And clean. I switch on the surround sound and head upstairs to take a shower. The water spits out from six different sprays on three sides of the shower and pours over my head from the large, square rainfall showerhead up top. I close my eyes and relax. All I see is Heidi. Waiting for me in her t-shirt and panties. I lather up my hands and gently rub my swollen flesh. And it feels really fucking good. I lean back against the wall and begin to stroke my cock. The more I stroke, the harder it gets. I look down at it and see her mouth. Her big green eyes looking up at me. Just like she did the first day in my office. I stroke a little faster, pull a little harder. The water is so warm and soothing. I lean my head back and suck in deep breaths between my teeth. My hips start to move with my fist. Before I know it my balls tighten up, muscles flex, and I'm spitting baby gravy all over my hand. Fuck me, that felt good.

After my shower therapy, I throw on some black sweatpants and a tee and pour myself a drink. My balls are still tight and my dick is still hard. So much for shower therapy. I think about Heidi's invitation and decide I'm going over there. And this time I'll have her begging me to stay.

I pull out my phone as I reach her doorway and text, *"Knock, Knock."* Within seconds she opens the door and invites me in. "Well, well. What a surprise."

She's wearing baggy pajama bottoms with colorful polka dots on them and a tank top. I'm beginning to grow fond of the messy pile on top of her head. And she's wearing glasses. She's so freaking sexy like this. She's hot on a daily, but this- This is sexy as fuck.

"You didn't have to dress up for me you know," I tease.

"Sure I did. It's not every day Superman comes to visit," she says, her smile lighting up her eyes.

"Not quite. More like the Joker," I tell her.

She laughs and shakes her head. "Wrong comic, genius. That's Batman,' she states. "But you're actually better off with that one. Batman could kick Superman's ass any day. And he's way hotter." She shrugs and gives me a quick wink before turning to walk into another room.

I could get used to this adorable little playful side. Despite the fact she has me thinking words like *adorable*. I scan the space around us. It's cozy. It's clean. Feminine. Lots of grays and blues. It suits her. I notice two glasses on the counter next to two dirty plates. "So, you live alone?" I inquire, secretly hoping the extra dishes belong to a roommate and not previous company.

She looks away before answering, as if to think about it, and then looks directly back at me, "No."

I wonder if she lives with the girl I met at her store earlier today. The friend from Saturday night. I don't see anyone else here. I don't hear anyone either. "Should we be quiet? Is she sleeping?"

"*He* is asleep. So, yes, we should probably be quiet," she replies.

He? He? I remember how she answered the door last night. She's walking around here in t-shirts and panties when another man is living here?

"So he's gay then? Your roommate."

She giggles. "Not that I know of."

I don't know why but suddenly I'm jealous. I'm *really* fucking jealous. I'm not the territorial type and I'm never jealous. But this eats at me. This guy gets to see her every day. He gets to eat with her. Cook for her. She cooks for him. He watches movies with her. And god knows what else.

Right now I want to walk in there and wake the mother fucker up and...
Heidi interrupts my thoughts as if she's reading my mind.

"He's not just a roommate," she tells me. And I'm about to lose my shit. I can't stop thinking about this woman and I'm not even going to get the chance to find out what she's all about because she is living with another man.

"He's my son," she explains.

Holy shit! All that for nothing. She has a kid. So what. I'm just thanking God it's not another man. I easily picture her as a mother, a really good mother. I wonder things like; how old he is, what his name is, where his father is, but I don't ask. She'll tell me more about him when she's ready.

"And here I was about to get jealous," I admit. I'm smiling to mask the truth in the statement.

"Well he *is* better looking than you," she jokes.

"If he looks anything like his mother, I don't doubt that."

My compliment surprises Heidi. Her face changes from a playful smile to curiosity. She's scanning my face to see if I'm paying her a serious compliment or just going along with her joke. I hold her gaze when she reaches my eyes. She swallows hard but doesn't say anything. So she doesn't do well with flattery. I can't imagine she never gets compliments. She's beautiful. After a few long seconds of silent staring she clears her throat and walks toward the kitchen.

"Sorry about the mess," she says, "I didn't think you'd actually come." She gathers up the plates and glasses and loads them in the dishwasher.

"Well you do owe me a bedtime story."

She wipes her hands on a towel and joins me in the living room. Coming off of this room is another room with an arched opening and two circular columns at the entrance. The entire outside wall is a set of floor to ceiling windows. It looks like it may be a sunroom or something. On one side of the room is a set of bookshelves with a white desk in the middle. On the other side of the room is a white bed hanging from chains, a swing bed I guess you could call it. She catches me staring off into the room, imagining her working or lying in that cozy little bed.

"That used to be my office," she explains. "And I guess before long, it will be again." She stares into the room and lets out a deep sigh. Her body is standing right next to me but her mind is a million miles away. I have an overwhelming urge to wrap her in my arms and tell her I will take care of it. That she isn't going to lose her dream. I want to tell her I'm the man who will fix this for her. But those are promises I know I can't keep. She's up against something-someone bigger than me. We live in a nation where money talks and the biggest wallet wins. I let her stay lost in her daydream a few moments longer.

"What do you use it for now?" I ask, trying to bring her back to me.

"Reading, mostly," she answers.

"What's your favorite book?" I'm not asking to simply make conversation. I really want to know. No bullshit. I want to know everything she likes and even the things she doesn't. I want to know what makes her smile. What makes her sad. What turns her on.

"*Pride and Prejudice*," she replies without taking any time at all to think about her answer. "What's yours?"

I laugh. I don't read. Nothing holds my attention long enough. I can barely sit through a whole movie, much less read an entire book. But I answer her anyway, "The one you're writing."

Now she laughs. She leans back against one of the columns and crosses her arms. "I was joking about the book thing. I read books. I don't write them."

I walk over to her, stopping just inches in front of her, and look down into those bright green eyes. "Then I guess the one you're reading will have to do."

It takes a little persuasion, which I happen to be quite good at, but soon enough we are both sitting cozy on Heidi's bed. She has her Kindle on her lap and I'm happily awaiting my bedtime story.

CHAPTER FIFTEEN
Heidi

Today definitely ranks in the top five of the "crappiest days of my life" countdown. Scratch that. Let's go with top two. Hudson is sleeping. After the lab we went to Toys R Us where he spent forty-five minutes picking out one toy, then spent most of the evening dressed up as his favorite Ninja Turtle. I spent most of the evening praying for a miracle. Even if I were comfortable with my six year old undergoing open heart surgery. Even if I knew his body could handle the recovery. Even if I trusted Dr. Collins with my baby's life. There's no way I'd ever be able to afford it. So that leaves me here. Waiting. Waiting for them to tell me I can't save my son. Waiting for the bottom to fall out.

I can't change the inevitable so I decide to focus on the things that take me away from the harsh reality of what the future holds. Like watching Hudson play hero in his make-believe world until it's time for bed. Then pouring myself a glass of wine and downloading a book on my Kindle. And thinking about the senator. A couple of hours later he is in my bed convincing me to share my romantic fantasies with him.

"Nick, I'm sure you have better things to do than sit here listening to a bunch of girly fantasies," I try to convince him. Talk about asking for trouble. I'm supposed to sit here and verbalize a sex book to Nick Knight and still be able to act casual. Tuesday night was bad enough. If there were a scale for measuring sexual tension, alarms would have been going off all over my apartment building.

Nick doesn't budge. The guy is impossible. He's hell bent on embarrassing me. He settles down a little further in my bed. We're on top of the covers of course. This is so far out of my comfort zone. I don't have company when Hudson is home. But here we are…in my bed….about to read mom porn. What the hell am I thinking?
He clears his throat and looks over at me with arched eyebrows. "Ready when you are."
I hold the device in front of me and skim over the page to remind myself what part of the book I'm on. *Great.* He's about to take her virginity. Screw it. I clear my throat and begin to read. We get to the part where training is mentioned and Nick eyes me curiously.

"Training?" He obviously is out of the loop. Well I guess now is not the time to be awkward. We're both adults here right?

"Yes. He is training her to be submissive. This is a story about a dominant man who meets an innocent young woman, decides he wants her as his next submissive, but ends up falling in love with her and changing his whole way of thinking."

His face remains stoic. He's processing. He sits up and runs his fingers through his hair. "Someone actually wrote a book about that shit?" he asks. *Ohmigod, he's serious.* "And you're actually reading it?"

I nod. "And now it's a movie." Which is the reason behind my reading it again. Refresher course.

He shakes his head and sinks back down to his former position. "Now I'm curious. Keep going."

I read the rest of the chapter. Hesitantly. I can't look at him. I can feel him staring at me but there's no way I'm looking away from this screen. This is about as awkward as having the sex talk with your mom. I know I'm a grown woman but seriously, you read a sex scene to a man like Nick, who happens to be lying in your bed, who you happened to almost kiss, while he was at your house, drunk, and see how easy it is. *Awkward.* "Okay, enough for now," I tell him, shutting off the Kindle and setting it on the nightstand.

"So that's considered *'girly fantasies'*?" he asks, amused.

Yea. I asked for that one. I sigh and narrow my eyes at him. "Well, not that part. And not all girls." I hope this satisfies him.

He sits up. *Oh yay.* He's all propped up and ready for a formal discussion. "What about you?" he inquires.

Why did I know he was going to ask that? I sit up straight, turning my body to face him, and tuck my legs up under my butt. "I think it's a nice story about how love can surprise you." I try to veer away from the whole *sex* topic. "It's a pretty classic move really. Like Jane Austen with *Pride and Prejudice*. Darcy was arrogant at first, but his love for Elizabeth changed him. Authors have been doing this since the beginning of time. It's no big deal." There. Short and sweet. Conversation over. *I hope.*

"How do you think would Miss Austen feel about the whole submissive situation?" *Annnnd I'm not so lucky.*

"I don't see her being comfortable with it," I tell him.

"Maybe that's why she stayed single," he laughs. "And what about Ms. Lemaire. How does she feel about something like that?" His tone is more serious now. Like he really wants to know. *Oh god. Is he...does he...* Well I guess it would make sense. He certainly fits the part.

I think for a second about my answer. "I don't think anyone could really answer that question truthfully without ever having experienced it for themselves. I don't think it would be my thing, but to each their own." It's the truth. I like being the one who decides what I do and when I do it. I don't need anyone telling me what I want.

"Don't you think it would be nice to have a break, Heidi?"

His expression is serious. He's looking at me and it's almost as if he's pleading a case. "All day, every day, you make decisions. You decide how to run your company, you decide how to run your household, what to wear, what to cook, how to spend your time, what things take priority and what things don't. Men like this guy you read about offer a reprieve. A chance to just....not think. A chance to just feel. Just for a little while. An escape. I can't think of a single woman who doesn't need that."

Well when you put it that way. A break in the form of an orgasm does sound pretty nice. *Okay Heidi, now is not the time and this is not the place.* Nick hasn't moved his eyes from my face, even though I'm nervously looking anywhere but back at him. I'm trying to think of a good rebuttal but I got nothing. So I look him in the eye and tell him the truth. "And I can't think of a single man I trust enough to take a chance like that."

His eyes drop to my mouth and he licks his lips. "Well, I'm sorry to hear that. Maybe one day you'll change your mind."

I *want* to change my mind. I *want* to trust him. I *want* to believe he can take all of this away, even if just for a moment. But not even a man like Nick has that much power. He gets up to leave and I stand to walk him out. He stops just as I approach the door. I have my hand on the knob, preparing to open it, but he stops me. He's standing behind me with his palm flat against the door right next to my head. I feel him inch closer, his body heat seeping into me. He smells like fabric softener and vanilla shampoo. I sense his head dipping and I can feel his breath on the back of my neck. His five o'clock shadow tickles the top of my shoulder. His forearm is flat against the door now and the weight of his body is pressed against my back. His other arm wraps around my front, dangerously close to the bottom of my breast. My heart is beating faster and I find myself forgetting to breathe. "Tell me what you're thinking. Right. Now," he whispers. His mouth is just below my ear lobe, his lips leaving feather-light kisses against the most sensitive part of my neck when they move.

I lean my forehead against the door in front of me and let my body melt into his. He is just as hard as I am wet. All I can think about is how good it would feel to have him inside me. His hand moves up and his thumb skims my nipple. "Heidi," he prompts.

"I..I don't know," I answer, my words forcing their way out. The truth is, I'm not thinking. Holy shit. *I'm not thinking.* I'm just feeling. He was right. It's amazing.

He must have read my mind because he backs away and lets out a soft chuckle. "Maybe you're more ready to trust than you think," he states with a cocky grin.

I open the door and feign irritation. "Goodnight Senator," I say, purposefully mocking his distaste of the title.

"Goodnight Heidi. To be continued?"

I'm not sure if he's talking about our own tortuous version of the hunger games or the bedtime story. I'm taking the safe route and going with bedtime story. "To be continued," I confirm.

He smiles my favorite crooked smile as he walks down the sidewalk.

Sunday, June 15

Yesterday was just another typical Saturday at the baseball park. Hudson had a tournament this weekend. Two games on Saturday, play til you lose on Sunday. That's how we spend at least two weekends out of our month. His team won both games yesterday. He plays an inning and sits an inning so he doesn't get too tired. It doesn't bother him. He just likes being a part of the team. Last night, Nick came over again, all fired up about his *bedtime story* as he likes to call it. We made it through chapter nine- *the oral exam*- without any deep conversation regarding my thoughts on oral sex, thank goodness. Halfway through I decided that humility was pointless and it's better if I just think of it as words on a page. I mean, it's not like either one of us has never had sex before. Nick left without any further physical altercations. His thoughts didn't seem to be one-hundred percent with me, but before he left he promised to be back for more.

This morning Hudson and I got all packed up for a day of baseball. Sunflower seeds, bottled water, and sunblock. His team made it through the first two games but lost in the playoffs. It's always heartbreaking when they lose. My baby really wanted that championship gold ring. There's always next time. And a silver ring is not so bad.

After dinner, a movie, and baths, I find myself watching the clock. I'm counting down the minutes until Nick comes over again. I've never been this anxious to see anyone. And we aren't even dating. Hell, we aren't even having sex. But I need to see him. Just as much as I need to eat or sleep. He's become my therapy. I don't even care why he's coming over anymore. We could be reading The Cat in the Hat for all I care. As long as I see him. *Feel him.* Just knowing he's here, with me. In my mind I know it's ridiculous, but my body has decided not to listen to my mind. It just wants him near.

I don't even spend this much time with the guy I *am* actually sleeping with. Speaking of that, I'm cutting it off this week. It just doesn't seem like a good idea anymore. It seems like weeks since I've seen Alex, even though it's only actually been a few days. The quickie in the back of the gym seems like a lifetime ago. Hudson interrupts my thoughts by telling me he's tired so we go to his room and get him all tucked in to bed. The song of the night is *Take Me out to the Ball Game* and our story is about a little boy who lives with penguins. I lie beside him rubbing his eyebrows until he stops talking and falls asleep.

An hour and a half later I'm coming to the conclusion Nick has decided not to come. Little sparks of disappointment flutter around in my heart. I get aggravated with myself for even caring. I can't believe I've let him affect me this way. I decide my feelings have nothing to do with…feelings, and everything to do with hormones. Purely physical. The man oozes sexuality. Any woman in her right mind would react this way to him. So would a few men I know. See, I'm perfectly normal.

I shut off the lamp in the living room, leaving the stove light on in case Hudson gets up for some water, and head to bed. Just as I'm climbing under the covers, my phone buzzes. My stomach flutters. I look at the screen: *Knock Knock.* His usual text.

Nick is in his typical late night visit attire, sweats and a tee shirt. He could wear denim overalls and a straw hat and look sexy. I wait until we're in the bedroom before I speak. "I didn't think you were coming. I was getting ready to start without you," I flirt.

He glances over at the down-turned comforter and then back at me. There's something different about him tonight. His gaze is intense, dark, almost….primal. He dons the crooked smirk I love to see and inclines his head toward the bed. "Don't let me stop you. I have a feeling I'd enjoy the show."

Uh. Uhm. Holy shit. "I was talking about the book, pervert."

"*Pleasure Seeker* is a much better term, wouldn't you agree?" he states. He's not smiling with his mouth but his eyes have a slight twinkle. I can't tell if he's serious or being sarcastic as well, so I keep the conversation light.

"Creative. You should put that on a tee shirt."

"If I did would you wear it? Only it? To answer the door when I text. Like you did the first night I came over?"

The twinkle is gone. It's been replaced by the intensity from earlier. His gold-green eyes are dark brown and burning into me. They move from my eyes to my lips, down to my bare neck, then my breasts- stopping there for a split second before moving further down my body. Slowly. So agonizingly slowly.

Every inch of my body heats up as his eyes roam over it. I let him ogle me. It makes me feel sexy. Like knowing he wants me, gives me some sort of power over him. Even though I know the complete opposite is true. Deep down I know it's him who has the power. He knows it too. So I go with it.

"If that's what you want," I comply.

His eyes quickly shoot back up to mine and he tilts his head slightly. As if he's trying to decipher what I just said. "You want to know what I want, Heidi?"

He moves closer to me. With every step he takes toward me, I take one backward until the backs of my knees hit the edge of the mattress. He nudges one of his feet in between my feet and maneuvers them apart until my legs are spread, sandwiching the one he used to manipulate his way in. I have to reach up and grab his bicep to keep from losing my balance and falling on the bed. As soon as I touch him, the atmosphere changes. It's like we're suddenly surrounded by some invisible force field of sexual electricity. The air all around us is charged and I feel like we're ready to spontaneously combust at any given moment. I've never felt this attracted to another person in my entire life. As cheesy as it sounds, it's magnetic. I'm drawn to him. I can't pull myself away. Especially when he's looking at me this way. Talking to me this way. I look up at him and gasp when I see his face, my lips parting slightly. I will never get used to his beauty. Yes, he's beautiful. Like a waterfall, a garden full of tulips, or an amazing piece of architecture.

He watches me carefully. His hands cup my face, holding my head in place. He licks his bottom lip and dips his head, stopping just centimeters from my mouth. He's going to kiss me. I want him to kiss me. Good god do I want him to kiss me. I want him to do a lot more than just kiss me. I have to put on the brakes. This can't happen right now. I can't move. I'm hypnotized. "Nick..this...I," I plead, not quite able to form a coherent thought.

He moves his hands from my cheeks back into my hair, his fingertips gently massaging my scalp. I'm still holding onto his arm. Still breathing him in. His eyes narrow and he moves his mouth to my ear, understanding my unspoken words. "Don't worry. I'm not going to fuck you Heidi. Not yet."

Oh.my.god. I should be offended. That was vulgar. Such a stark contrast to the gentle way he's touching me. I swear the guy has more willpower than Edward Cullen. Which is probably a good thing because my body is screaming for him to throw me on the bed and go balls deep inside me. This is becoming a pretty regular feeling around him. And this is most likely why I'm not offended by his choice of words. Instead I'm completely turned on by the promise that he, indeed, will be fucking me one day. I'm pretty sure I'm dripping on his leg right now. If he would just move it up....just a few inches. Apply a little pressure right where I need it. Give my body the relief it seeks. The message goes un-intercepted from my mind to my body and I find myself lowering my hips in search of his thigh. He pulls his head back and smiles at me. Not a happy smile, or a cocky smile. A knowing smile. No teeth. Just a slight upturn of the lips. "Soon enough baby. Tonight, we just read. Okay?"

CHAPTER SIXTEEN
Nick

I wasn't planning on coming here tonight. Not because I don't want to see Heidi, but because when I do see her, I don't ever want to leave. I need a break from this game we're playing. I need a break from *her*. I wanted to ask her what she did all day yesterday. It was Saturday so I know she didn't work. Then I realize it's none of my fucking business. I don't have the right to demand to know what she's doing. I imagine her with her son. Then, suddenly I want to meet him too. I wonder if he looks like her, acts like her. Does she think of me when she's doing her normal, daily things? Does she spend time with another man the way she spends time with me? Does she touch herself at night when I leave? All these questions are driving me fucking nuts. Meet a woman. Take her home. Fuck her crazy. Say good bye. That's the routine. That's the way it works. No lunch dates. No texts. No nightly visits. No sitting around wondering what the hell she's doing. Why does this one have to be any different?

I know Heidi wants me. The physical attraction between us is stronger than anything I've ever felt. The timing totally sucks ass, however. I'm not a serial masterbator but the past couple of weeks have me practically rubbing blisters on my dick. And this book. This fucking book. The woman should be a marriage counselor. I'm fairly certain housewives all over the world have stripped their husbands down and fucked the shit out of them because of this book.
So there I am, watching tv, but not *really* watching it, drinking Johnnie Walker, and wishing I were there. With her. *Not* touching her. *Not* kissing her. *Not* fucking her. And that's when I decided it all changes tonight. I know she has her standards about freaky shit with her son in the house. And it's probably a good rule to have because all the screaming might send the little boy to therapy for life. But I'm going over there tonight. And I'm making damn sure she knows playtime is over. When I leave tonight, it will be with the knowledge that soon, very soon, Heidi Lemaire will be diligently and thoroughly fucked.

I don't waste time beating around the bush. We've barely made it to the bedroom and I'm making my intentions crystal clear. I don't force anything on her, but I'm not leaving any doubt as to what I want. I need her to know I respect her boundaries but I'm done playing games. Her body responds to me exactly the way I knew it would. She doesn't want me to stop any more than I want to stop. But the first time I have her won't be centered around peeking over my shoulder and trying to be quiet. No. I can wait. I'll just have to make damn sure it's worth waiting for.

I pull my body away from hers, stroking her jaw line with the front of my index finger. Her eyes close as she savors my touch. "Come on Heidi. Read to me."

She opens her eyes when I move away and follows me around the side of the bed. We settle in and she begins to read. I love watching her. Especially with the naughty parts. Her cheeks flush but she keeps going, never missing a beat, as if it doesn't affect her. Half the nights I lie here with a hard on the size of

the Washington Monument, listening to those words come out of her mouth. Her mouth. I have so many plans for that mouth. This particular chapter captures my curiosity. I listen to her read and watch intently for any sort of reaction to the words she's speaking. Every once in a while she'll pause, as if to think briefly about what just happened, but quickly regains composure and starts right back up again. I find this to be a pattern with Heidi. Any hint of emotion is quickly shoved aside and replaced with new words or thoughts. She finishes up the chapter and sets the device to the side. She's quiet. I wonder if she's thinking about the book or about what happened before we started reading.

I'm thinking about the book. I avoided discussing last night's chapter due to the fact that I didn't think I could endure it without ripping her panties off and burying my face between her thighs. So I just left. Tonight is different though. Tonight I want to talk.

"How do you feel about sexual dominance Heidi?" I ask.

The question catches her off guard and she shifts on the bed. She takes her glasses off and sets them on top of her Kindle. When her eyes meet mine, they're curious. "I don't know much about it. Just this. What I read," she tells me. "Why? How do you feel about it?" she continues.

I'm far from experienced in that sort of thing. I know people who are into it. It's not that I have anything against it, hey everybody has their thing. I've just never dabbled in dominance. But I hear things. I know what I'm about to say is going to pop her whole romantic little bubble, but I need to say it.

"I'm indifferent, honestly. You could say I like things the way I like them. I wouldn't consider myself *dominant*, but I do enjoy being in control. At all times. I enjoy giving pleasure and I like to take my time doing it. I also know there can be great pleasure in pain, if done correctly."

I don't need to give her a play by play of my sexual inhibitions. She'll find out soon enough. But I need to make this point, "But telling someone when to eat and what they may or may not discuss with their friends is not sexual dominance. It's being an asshole. Tell me you see nothing sexy about that."

She considers my words for a moment. "Who says he's not just showing concern?"

Her response startles me. I figured an independent woman like Heidi would completely agree with me. Go off on the asshole for thinking he can boss this woman around. But here she is challenging me. It's like she's defending him. Why the fuck would she defend that? What's going on in that pretty little head of hers? Suddenly I feel very protective. A woman like Heidi should never feel a guy like that is boyfriend material. *Concern?* Concern is what I feel for her right now. Getting upset because she talks to her friends or prefers diet Pepsi over white wine isn't concern. It's mental. I have to go. I'm getting all worked up over some bullshit work of fiction that has my imagination in overdrive. Heidi follows me out of the room, grabbing my arm right as I reach the doorway. "Nick?"

Great. Now I'm being the asshole. I turn to face her, giving her my best attempt at a comforting smile. I don't want to give my thoughts away. She looks up at me with sad eyes. "Are you okay? I'm sorry if I said something wrong," she starts.

I reach out and place a finger over her lips. "Heidi, stop. You didn't say anything wrong. I just need to go. It's late and I have an important meeting in the morning," I lie. She parts her lips beneath my finger as if preparing to draw it into her mouth. If she's trying to convince me not to leave, it's working. The tip of her tongue snakes out and softly licks the back of my finger. Her mouth opens a little more, allowing my fingertip to fall inside. She gently sucks it further in, swirling her tongue around it once before I pull it back out. *Fucking-a.* I grab her hips and pull her closer to me. I lower my head so our foreheads are touching and look her dead in the eye. I'm positive she can feel my erection pressing against her stomach but I don't give a shit. I just move my hands to her ass and pull her even closer. She gasps. "I'm going to ask your permission to kiss you soon. But you should know that once you say yes, you're mine."

"Yes," she whispers.

"I haven't asked yet." With each word, my mouth moves closer to hers. Now our lips are touching, slowly parting, compelling the inevitable. "Kiss me Nick. Please."

Please. Good god. That was it. Willpower shattered. Strength crushed. Resilience snapped. I close the remaining gap between us. Her lips are so soft, so full. I relish the feel of them against mine before pressing harder, slipping my tongue through her parted lips. Our tongues collide and I move my hands up her back, to her head, weaving my fingers into her hair. I swear a current is running through our bodies. I tug gently on the roots of her hair as the kiss intensifies. She groans softly in my mouth, turning me on even more, if that's possible. Her hands move up my chest and twist in the fabric of my shirt. I could kiss her forever. Her mouth is so warm. So sensual. I move my hips forward, pressing my dick into her. Hard. She groans again. Fuck. I force myself to end this before I get carried away. Because I am quickly getting carried away. I take a step back. Her eyes find mine and here we are staring at each other from inches away. Both of us breathing heavy. My heart is racing and even though we're no longer touching, I still feel the current between us. I say the only thing I can think of at this moment, looking at her swollen lips, knowing I'm the cause. I reach forward and cup her cheek. Her head leans into my touch. "Mine."

CHAPTER SEVENTEEN
Heidi

Monday, June 16

I don't think I slept a full hour last night. Nick left right after he kissed me. *"Mine,"* he said. I keep hearing his voice, speaking that word. All night, all I could think about was what that meant for me. Mine as in: mine to visit every night? Mine as in: mine to kiss? Mine as in: mine to touch? Mine for how long? Just one night? A million different mines bouncing around my head. No matter which one he meant, I know today I live in a completely different world than the one I was in yesterday.

I have to try to concentrate on work this morning. Nick's fundraiser is a little over two weeks away and I have to finalize plans with the florist, the band, and the photographer. He's having it at his home so I'm sure I'll end up there at some point to discuss decorations. Oh god. I have to go to his house. That's so...personal. Will it be all like *hey girl, come see my bedroom?* Or will it be all business-like and formal? Thinking about it makes me nervous. Focus Heidi.

Shelly barges her way into my office about five minutes after I get comfy at my desk.
"You slept with him," she declares.
I place my hand over the end of my cell phone, thanking goodness no one has picked up on the other end yet. "Sshh," I tell her, pointing to the device in my hand. As if she couldn't already see that I'm on the phone. She purses her lips and arches her eyebrows at me, silently telling me she isn't going anywhere any time soon. I roll my eyes and end the call. I'll call back later. I was on hold anyway. I huff at her. "Fine," I say. "I did not sleep with him. Happy?"
"You saw him naked?"
"No."
"He saw you naked?"
"No."
She narrows her eyes and contemplates her next move. She walks over to my desk, plops her butt down on top of it, and crosses her arms. She knows me too well for me to get away with telling her nothing happened. "He kissed me. Like....kissed the shit out of me, kissed me," I confess. She seems satisfied with this answer. Good. I don't feel like getting into the

whole *mine* thing. Or the bedtime stories either for that matter. Somewhere inside of me is secretly afraid if I talk about it too much I'll jinx it or something. This way if things go bad, it never was really a big deal anyway.

Shelly hops off my desk and bumps my shoulder with her booty. "Kissed the shit out of you huh?"

I lay my head back, open my mouth, and roll my eyes back, imitating a feeling of pure pleasure. "Yessss," I moan. She laughs as she walks out of the room. "All that just from a kiss? I can't wait to hear what the sex is like!" she yells down the hall. I shake my head and retry my phone call.

Twenty minutes later I have appointments scheduled with all three vendors for tomorrow morning. I take advantage of my few moments of silence and reminisce about the past three nights. I'm lost in my daydream when a number I don't recognize pops up on my screen. "Hello, this is Heidi," I answer.

"Hello Heidi, my name is Rhonda LaSant. I work for Dr. Collins," the voice on the other end announces.

Good. They must have Hudson's test results. "Hello Rhonda. How may I help you?" I hold my breath and wait for her response. *Please let it be good. Please let it be good.*

"We got Hudson's lab results and there are a couple of areas of concern. Dr. Collins would like you to come in this afternoon."

Come in? Why can't she just tell me over the phone? *Because it's bad you idiot.* They never tell you bad news over the phone. No. This isn't happening. I can't do this. Breathe Heidi. You *can* do this. "I'd like to come this morning if that's possible," I tell her. Now or never, right? I mean, who wants to sit around all morning waiting to hear bad news. Not this girl.

She places me on hold for a few seconds and comes back to inform me that coming in this morning is fine. I grab my purse, let Shelly know where I'll be, and take off.

The drive to Dr. Collins' office is painfully long. It feels like I'll never get there. Just as I'm pulling in the parking garage, Nick texts me. Great timing, Romeo. "Meet me at my office at 2?"

I don't reply. I can't. At this moment I have no idea if my heart will still be beating at 2:00. All I can think about is my precious baby boy and how there's no way he's sick. *He's not sick.* I repeat the chant over and over in my head all the way up to her office.

I'm fidgeting in my seat. Crossing and uncrossing my legs. Sitting up straight all the way back in the chair and sitting up straight all the way at the edge of my seat. I have every word on every poster in this room memorized by the time she walks in. I can even tell you where she went to school and what color her kids' eyes are.

She takes a seat in front of me. "Ms. Lemaire, thank you for coming." I nod and fidget some more.

"Hudson's white blood cell count is abnormally low and his platelet count is high so I'm referring you to a hematologist oncologist." Well she sure gets right to the point. Oncologist? *Cancer.*

She must note the look of sheer terror on my face because she continues. "Don't let the word scare you. I'm only sending you to him because he has a more thorough testing procedure and can get to the root of the problem better than I can," she explains.

That's supposed to make me feel better?

"Okay," I manage to say. What choice do I have, really? I mean, I can sit at home and pretend none of this really happened. Or we can fix it and move on. The more doctors involved, the better our chances are at nipping this thing, whatever it is, in the bud. Right? So this is good. At least that's what I tell myself. We exchange a few more bits of information and she gives me the oncologist's number, informing me that his office should be calling me to set up an appointment soon. I thank her and say goodbye. It takes me the entire walk back to my Jeep to process the conversation we just had. My child, who has a heart defect, now may have cancer as well. He's six. *Six!* How is he supposed to fight cancer? He can't even fight a cold. How am I supposed to tell him what's about to happen to him? How do I explain that the needles and the medicine are all *good* for him? That he will have to endure all the pain in order to feel better. *Normal.* Will he ever be a normal kid? Will he be able to keep playing baseball? Will he lose his contagious energy?

As soon as I get in my car I break down. I sit there, in the parking garage, crying and screaming at God. It's not fair! Hudson is the most loving, kind, and charismatic child I have ever seen. He's all I've got. We're a team. This isn't supposed to happen.

Here I sit, snot dripping, mascara running, close to hyperventilating, and my phone rings. It's Nick. I can't talk to him. I don't even really want to. He can't fix this. He can't fix the situation with my business. He's just a big fat distraction. And that's the last thing I need right now. I calm down enough to drive home where I draw myself a hot bath and sulk until the water gets cold and I have the hands and feet of a ninety year old woman. I call Shelly and let her know I'm not coming back in to the store today. "Senator Super Kisser called. He said it's important. I think he misses you," she tells me.

"Thanks, but I can't deal with him right now."

"You can't hide from life Heidi."

I hate when she says something that actually makes sense. Sometimes I wish she'd just stick to sarcasm and twisted humor. "Blah," I reply and then hang up on her.

A few seconds later my phone dings. "Get out of the tub and put on your big girl panties."

How did she know I was...because she's Shelly, that's how. I take her advice and text Nick back once I'm out and dry.

"Sorry to keep you waiting. Rough morning. If 2:00 is still open, I'll be there."

It's not as flirty as I would have normally been, but today sucks and flirty isn't a priority. He texts back almost immediately. *"No apology needed. You're worth waiting for. See you at 2."*

Why is he so awesome? Doesn't he know I'm trying to forget that I like him? I take my time doing my hair and make-up so I don't look like I've been crying all morning. I consider going in yoga pants and a t-shirt but some persistent crazy part of me still actually cares what he thinks. So I carefully choose an outfit I'm sure he'll like. I go for a tan shirt dress with gold buttons, leaving the top two undone so he gets a nice little cleavage shot. The dress hits me just above the knee and has a small slit on each side. I throw on some nude, strappy heels and I'm ready to go.

I shoot Shelly a quick text before I walk out the door. "Left the panties at home. On my way to kiss a senator ;)"

95

CHAPTER EIGHTEEN
Heidi

Thing One and Thing Two get more pleasant every time I come to Nick's office. This time around Thing Two even complimented my dress. She may not have good manners but apparently she's got good taste. She lets me know Nick has been waiting for me so I should just go ahead and go in his office.

He's leaning back in his chair watching me like I'm an antelope in a field full of lions. "Come here Heidi," he commands. His tone is firm and serious, making me wonder if he's upset that I ignored him all morning. Too bad I can't give him a good explanation for that. I don't want him to think I was blowing him off, but I'm not dumping my personal crap on him either. So I just cross my fingers and figure out a way to make him happy again, deciding a good way to start would be by doing as he asks. I'm standing next to his chair, facing him, when he cocks his head forward, indicating the space directly in front of him. "Here."
I move to stand in front of him, leaning my butt against his desk. He has one leg on either side of me, holding me in place. He sits up straight and places his hands on the outside of my thighs just above my knees, right where the slits in my dress are. My heart could win an Olympic gold medal right now, it's racing so fast. His office door is open. Thing Two is right outside. He's said all of four words to me since I arrived and already my panties are soaked. I'm looking down at him, watching him concentrate on where his hands are placed. His eyes roam up my body but never make it all the way up to mine. They stop at my breasts and I have no doubt he notices the cleavage. He gives a sexy little smirk before moving his gaze back down to my thighs. I give myself a mental high five for my choice of outfit. I stand still and wait for his next move. I'm barely breathing. My lips are parted. My mouth is dry so I slip my tongue out and wet my bottom lip. His long fingers inch further around the back of my thighs so that they are now just barely underneath the hem of my dress. His thumbs stroke softly up and down the front of my leg. I can hear my pulse in my eardrums. He's so focused, so centered on the lower region of my body. I wish I could read his thoughts. "What's all this about leaving panties at home," he says, finally.
What? I snap out of my sexual hypnosis and focus on what he's saying. What panties? What in the world is he...Oh god. *No.* Please tell me I did not send Nick the text I meant to send to Shelly. Well, this is

embarrassing. He thinks I'm not wearing panties. He thinks I came here to seduce him. Okay so I kind of did, but I didn't mean to tell him that in a text message. And even worse, I *am* wearing panties. Boy is he going to be disappointed here in about two minutes. *Shit.* "You read the text," My tone is a cross between a question and a very vague answer. Technically, it could be taken either way.

Nick stands and looks over my shoulder. "Enjoying the show?" he inquires. *Thing Two.* I knew I should have closed the door. Nick runs a hand over my back in a comforting gesture.
"Oh, don't stop on my account."
My hair stands on end and my ears perk up. That voice. That accent. Alex. There's no way. What the fuck is going on? Is this why Nick asked me here? To confront me about personal stuff? Stuff that started before I even met him. I need to turn around to validate what I already know, but I'm frozen in shock. I can feel the color drain from my face while my heart stops beating altogether. I'm staring straight ahead but not really looking at anything. My mind is processing in slow motion the many different scenarios that could be about to take place. The voice continues, "Unless I've been invited here to join you?"
Nick looks away from our visitor and back at me. He offers an encouraging smile before looking back over my shoulder. Did he do this on purpose? How does he know? I guess I need to turn around. I can't stand here with my back to him forever. That would just be rude. For a brief moment, I forget Nick is in the room. I still haven't figured out why Alex is here and I am feeling increasingly guilty by the second for what he witnessed when he walked in the office. I'm urgently searching my mind for something to say to him. Luck jumps in and I don't have to because Nick chooses that moment to break the silence. "Forgive his manners," he says as he glares at the man behind me. "He doesn't see many beautiful women." Nick smirks at Alex before continuing. "Heidi, meet Nate. My best friend, slash, attorney for the client proposing to acquire your property."
Nate? Not Alex? *Thank goodness.* I can breathe again. It's just some guy who sounds like Alex. *Exactly* like Alex. I force a smile as I turn to face him. "So you're the man who doesn't return phone calls?" I joke.
My words stop short as soon as I see him. Sure as shit, there he stands. Alex. Yes, *the* Alex. Hot Alex. My Alex. The moment he sees my face, his eyes widen and his mouth falls open. Just a bit and only for a split second. "*You're* Heidi Lemaire?" His voice is full of curiosity laced with a tiny hint of accusation.

I swallow hard before answering, "It would appear so."

"And you're *Nate*? Is that right?" I make sure to place heavy emphasis on the name. This dickwad has been lying to me. And he wonders why I wanted to keep it casual.

He catches the sarcasm in my tone and takes a few steps forward so that he's standing right at the edge of Nick's desk, directly opposite me. It's a bit intimidating. He looks over my shoulder at Nick. "Actually, this asshole is the only one who calls me that." He then transfers his gaze to me. "I prefer to be called Alex. You see, my father is called Nate and this world isn't quite big enough for two Nathan Alexanders."

Oh. I see.

Nick chuckles behind me. "Old habits die hard. And it's not my fault your dad's a cocksucker," he says.

If awkward were a color this room would be painted in it. Nick has to know something is up. He's a smart guy. Do I let on that I know Alex? Or do I pretend I'm clueless? Shit if I know. This is all new to me. I just follow Alex's lead. "Why don't you have a seat so we can talk?" he asks. Nick backs up so I can move from my current compromising position and sit. Alex looks me in the eye almost apologetically. "Before we begin Heidi, I need you to know I'm not the bad guy here. I'm just an attorney hired by a client to do a job. That's it. I never meant to hurt you."

I can't have this conversation with him right now. Not here. Not like this. "But you had to know. You had to know it would hurt *someone*." I want to tell him how incredibly fucked up this whole thing is. I want to yell and scream and throw things at him. But I don't do any of those things. I sweep those emotions under the rug and pull the mask over my face. "You know what? It's fine. I get it. Business is business." I need to get through this as quickly as possible. If Alex wants to apologize, he can do it later. I can't do this right now.

"We have options. As soon as Nick told me how important this is to him...how important *you* are to him...I called my client and worked out a deal."

"So, what? What's the deal?" I ask, avoiding his reference to my relationship with Nick.

"My client is willing to pay all relocation expenses. Whatever it costs to get you set up at another location." I sense a "but" coming. He doesn't say anything else so I say it for him. "But?"

"But?" he repeats.

98

"Yea, there has to be a catch. For example, do I pick the new location or do they?"

"They suggested the new location be their choice," he answers. *Thought so.* Pricks.

I shake my head and huff my disapproval. *"Doesn't matter if we stick her in the ghetto. Just give her something to shut her up. We did our part. Anybody want another beer?"* I mimic the way I hear their asshole voices in my head. "Right? Is that about how the meeting went?"

I'm too irritated to remain seated. I get up and pace the small area beside my chair, stopping a moment to face Alex. "I pick the new location. I pick everything. Not them."

"Heidi, I can't negotiate your terms."

"What? Why not? You're a lawyer, Alex. That's what you do."

He lets out an exasperated sigh and runs his hands through his hair. The way he always does when he's aggravated with me for whatever reason. Like my kickboxing wardrobe, for example. Nick is watching our interaction intently. He hasn't spoken a word since Alex and I started our little back-and-forth. "He's their attorney, baby. It's a conflict of interest for him to negotiate for you," Nick says, finally.

Alex and I both give Nick our devout attention as if he's just spoken some long lost prophecy. We were too caught up in our argument with each other to remember he was still in the room. The mere sound of his voice soothes me. My heart rate begins to slow, my breathing regulates, and the tension that was creeping up the back of my neck into my head fades away. I calmly sit back down. "So, what? Now I need my own attorney?" I question.

"Don't worry. I'll take care of it," Nick tells me.

"Nick, I'm not letting you hire me an attorney. You've helped enough already."

The side of his mouth turns up in an irresistible crooked grin. "I'm not going to *hire* your attorney. I'm going to *be* your attorney."

"Nick, you know you can't do that," Alex states.

Nick ignores him. The look on his face is one of a man who shouldn't be messed with. "I'll handle Graham. We want relocation expenses as well as compensation for time lost."

I don't understand what he's saying. Who is Graham? And why would Nick have to handle him? I'm still trying to wrap my head around this whole situation. Alex is an attorney. The attorney who sent me the letter. And he

99

is also Nick's best friend. It's like a tornado of thoughts swirling around in my head. I can't sort this out right now.

"Nick," Alex starts to argue but Nick interrupts, "I'll have the paperwork sent to your office tomorrow."

"Heidi, talk to him. Tell him I can fix this. Give me the chance. I *will* fix this," Alex promises, and I'm not sure anymore if he's talking about my business or this seriously screwed up threesome we've just become a part of.

Just then my phone rings. "I'm sorry. I have to take this," I explain. It could be Hudson's doctor. I excuse myself, taking the call in the foyer. And as luck would have it, it was. Hudson has an appointment with a Dr. Amir Morad on Wednesday. This morning's visit with Dr. Collins is now fresh in my mind again. I'm suddenly very overwhelmed. This is too much at once. I step back in Nick's office long enough to excuse myself for good this time. "I have to go," I tell them. They both stand at the declaration. *Awkward.* Alex remains in place, watching carefully as Nick walks toward me. "Is everything okay?" he asks.

"Yea, everything is fine. I just have a...thing...it's kind of...I'll call you okay?" *That was smooth Heidi.*

Nick tilts his head and narrows his eyes to study me. I give him a reassuring smile. "I'm fine." I look to Alex, who also looks concerned. Can't say I blame them. It is a pretty weird way to end this meeting. "It was a pleasure Alex. Thank you for all your help." He simply nods his head in response.

"I'll walk you out," Nick offers.

"No, really. I'm fine. I'll see you later. Okay?"

I hurry out of there as fast as I can without attracting any attention to myself. The minute I'm in my Jeep, I have mental breakdown: episode two.

CHAPTER NINETEEN
Heidi

The hot water from the shower is therapeutic. I'm standing here letting it rain over me like people in California aren't suffering a drought right now. I've been in here at least thirty minutes. I'm surprised it's still warm. I'm not sure where it came from, but water has always had the ability to relax me. Whether it's a taking bath, a shower, a dip in the pool, or standing with my feet in the ocean, I love water. One day I'll have a house on the water. One day when my life is simple and drama free. Hudson and I will spend our mornings watching the waves and our afternoons having picnics on the dock. We'll admire the reflection of the moon on the water and take spontaneous outings on our boat. *One day.* When he is well and I am not worrying about things like relocation and attorneys.

What a seriously twisted joke fate decided to play on me. Not only is Alex the attorney for the big corporate bullies, he is the best friend of the one man who makes me *feel* something. I was so mad at him in that office! Even though in my head I knew he had no idea it was me he sent those letters to or me he never called back. I still felt betrayed. It's my own fault though. If I hadn't played stupid games with him, he would've known who I was and what was happening. I would've known he was friends with Nick. And I wouldn't be in this ridiculous situation.

I can't see Nick anymore. Not like I have been. I can't resist him. I'll be naked in no time. And I can't get naked with Nick. Not knowing I've already been there with his best friend. Talk about messed up. I can't see Alex anymore either. Not that I was going to keep riding that bus anyway. I had already decided to take a different route before any of this even happened. But today's revelation pretty much sealed the deal on that one. So here I am, washing my worries away under scalding hot water. No more Alex, no more Nick, lots more doctors, and starting from scratch with a business it took me years to open to begin with. Yea, I'm going to go ahead and ask for a do over for today.

I don't bother with make-up or curling irons. I throw on some yoga pants and a tee-shirt, put my hair in a messy pony tail, and go get my boy. Cole's mother keeps Hudson during the day while I work. Or in today's case, while I have a mental breakdown. When I get there to pick him up, she drills me on what's happening with his health. I explain that I don't really know much right now but when I do, I'll make sure she's not left out of the loop. My ex mother-in-law and I get along pretty well. During my marriage to Cole, she basically took the place of my mother. She taught me how to cook and make nifty little household remedies for stuff. My mom lives in Texas and we don't talk much. Let's just say, I'm a better mother because she never really was one. I learned at a young age how not to make your kids feel and made a promise to myself that if I never accomplished anything else, my children would know beyond a shadow of a doubt that they are loved. It's really your one real job as a mother. *Love your children.* Seriously. You have one job. Do it. The rest will fall into place.

Hudson and I spend much of the rest of the afternoon playing Monopoly. He wins. As always. He shows me how he learned to dance like Michael Jackson, which leads us to a youtube marathon of dance videos. Over dinner, I let him know he'll be going back to the doctor in a couple of days but it's no big deal. They just want to check some things.
"Are they going to poke me with needles again?" he asks.
I've never been the mom that lies and sugar coats things. I'm not brutally honest either. He is just six years old after all. But I want him to trust me so I always try to keep as close to the truth as I can. "Probably, but it will be quick, and I'll be there to hold you. Just like last time," I assure him.
He doesn't get upset like I thought he might. He just takes a bite of his grilled cheese while he thinks. "Can dad come with us?" he asks once he finishes chewing.
"Dad? Why?"
"Because he's big. And he can put the doctor in a headlock if he hurts me," he explains. As if it makes perfect sense to him.
I try to look offended. "Oh, so you don't think I can put him in a headlock?"
He laughs and shakes his head. "Mom. Seriously? You're a girl."
I scrunch my nose up and mouth his words back to him. He laughs again. "Fine. Dad can come. If you want him to."
He smiles and nods in approval. We finish our simple meal of grilled cheese and homemade soup, followed by our nightly routine of songs and stories. I lie with him even after he's fallen asleep and hum to him. I catch myself dozing off and determine it's probably my bedtime too. It's been a long day and I'm ready to get it over with.

I take my phone out of my purse, where I've purposefully left it all day, and check my messages. Two missed calls from Shelly, one from Nick, and three from a number I don't recognize. I text Cole about the appointment Wednesday, text Shelly, and stare at the screen which now displays my messages to Nick. I laugh to myself when I see that I *did* send him the panty message. I remember the way it felt when he touched me. I wonder what was going through his mind. If Alex hadn't shown up when he did, what would have happened? I shake the thought and lay my phone on the nightstand. Next to my Kindle. I don't even feel like reading. It reminds me of him. And I don't want to think about him right now. I just want to sleep. As soon as I switch off the lamp, my phone rings. It's the same number from earlier that I didn't recognize. I answer it because I assume if they've called three times it must be important.

"Heidi." *Alex.* Maybe I shouldn't have answered after all.

"Oh so now you decide to return my calls," I say, half joking, half serious.

"We need to talk," he states, not reciprocating my attitude. Serious Alex doesn't come out to play much. Thank goodness.

"We do. But not now. I'll call you tomorrow, okay?" I hope this appeases him so I don't have to do this now. I was actually starting to believe this horrible day was coming to an end. Dream on sista.

"You always do this. You are the queen of avoidance. Look, just give me ten minutes. Please?" He sounds serious. I hate when he sounds serious. And I can't seduce my way out of this one. So I guess I'll have to suck it up and deal with it the grown up way.

"Ten minutes Alex," I agree, almost instantly regretting it but what the hell. I have to face it sooner or later. He's not going away. I put some pants on and wait for him to show up. It's only 9:00 but it feels like midnight. Days like today are why they invented wine. I pour myself a glass while I wait. Twenty minutes and two glasses later I hear a soft knock and know it's him.

He's still in his dress slacks and button up. The sleeves are rolled up to his elbows now and he's lost the tie. I'm so used to seeing him in athletic shorts and tee-shirts, but I could get used to Business Alex. *Stop it Heidi.* That's not an option. He looks like a lawyer now that I think about it. A very young lawyer, but a lawyer nonetheless. It definitely explains the loft. He's standing in the doorway with his hands in his pockets, looking like someone just shot his dog. Why can't I have sex with ugly men? It would make dumping them so much easier. He is so freaking attractive. And I am so, so stupid. *Okay, really Heidi.* Even if they weren't best friends, did I really think I was going to be able to keep both of them anyway? "Hey," I say, not really knowing what is appropriate.

"Hey," he replies. We stand there staring at each other for a moment until he speaks again. "May I come in?"

Right. That is why you're here. "Sure," I say, stepping back to allow him to walk past.

He walks toward the sofa but I grab his arm to stop him. He turns quickly, his eyes falling to my hand then lifting back up to meet mine. "Not here. Hudson is asleep. Let's go on the patio." I don't say the bedroom because that would probably end up being a bad idea. I sit across from him on the outdoor furniture. It's a pretty night. My patio overlooks the courtyard of the apartment complex. There are fountains, flower beds, and trees of different sizes and varieties. At night, spotlights highlight certain areas. It's really pretty and actually one of the main reasons I chose this unit.

I try to keep my tone light even though I know the conversation is about to get heavy. "Okay, you have ten minutes. Go." I fire an imaginary gun like they do at the beginning of a race.

"For chrissakes Heidi, just once, can we have a serious conversation?" he pleads.

I sigh. "I've had enough serious for one day Alex. But I promise you have my full and complete attention. What do you want to talk about?"

He leans forward and runs a hand through his hair. His elbows are propped on his knees and he's looking at me like a dying man would look at the doctor. Welp, I can't change the diagnosis here buddy. We're pretty much screwed. "I'm sorry. I know you feel like I hurt you intentionally, but you need to know I did. not. know." He speaks the last three words slowly and deliberately. "I will do everything in my power to make sure you're taken care of. You have my word."

I believe him. "Thank you," I say. And I mean it.

Alex swallows hard and looks away for a minute. Collecting his thoughts, I assume. "Nick is a good man."

Oh god. Not this. I don't want to talk about this. "Alex..."

"Let me finish," he urges. "I should've known it was you all along. The way he described you. The way you affect him." He stares right through me. "The same way you affect me."

"Alex..."

He keeps going. "In the seven years I've known him, Nick has never spoken of a woman the way he speaks of you." He snickers. "Hell, he's never spoken of a woman. Not in depth anyway."

He pauses and I try again. "Alex..."

"Heidi, please. Let me say this. If I don't do it now, I won't be able to at all," he implores. I understand that so I shut up and listen.

"I guess what I mean to say is, if I have to lose you to someone, I'd prefer it to be him." He pauses again but this time I let him gather his thoughts. Breaking up with a booty call isn't supposed to feel this bad. Is it? "I hear the way he talks about you. I see the look in his eyes when he's thinking of you. I felt the energy between the two of you the moment I stepped into that office. Nick has had that stolen from him once by a man he called "friend." I'm not going to be the one to do it to him a second time. I'm not that man. I'm not that friend," he explains.

I wait for a minute to see if he's going to continue. When he doesn't, I finally say what I need to say. "Alex, you aren't losing me to anyone. No, we can't do….what we do…anymore. But that doesn't mean I'm going to go running straight to Nick. In what universe would that even be fair? To anyone. Even if I were selfish enough to do that, which I'm not, there's no way once he finds out about us that he would be okay with it."

"You can't tell him Heidi. He can't know. It would kill him. To have to look at you that way."

"I'm not dating him, Alex. I barely know him. You and I….our…*relationship*. It started long before I ever knew Nick Knight. He has to understand that. It's not like we planned this. Or did it on purpose. He can't get upset over it."

Alex stands and looks out into the courtyard. I have an overwhelming desire to comfort him. To touch him. But I don't. I can't. Instead I stand next to him, looking out at the same view. He keeps his eyes forward while he speaks. "I'm okay with losing you for the sake of a friend's happiness. At least then I know it was a worthy cause." He turns and looks down at me, his expression solemn. "But to lose you, then have you turn around and break his heart in return. Well then I've lost you for nothing. We all
lose."

Is he for real? What is he? Superhuman? Most guys would be pissing circles around me right now, claiming some *'You're mine, not his'* caveman bullshit. Not Alex. He's worried about not only my happiness, but Nick's as well. Completely selfless.

"I can't lie to him," I affirm.

"You'd rather hurt him?"

I chuckle. "Hurt him? Alex, you're talking like we have some epic romance. We haven't even had…" I catch myself before I say something I shouldn't. The intuitive lawyer skills kick in and Alex finishes my thought.

"I know," he says. "But you will. And believe me, the thought kills me."
This is the first time tonight he really sounds agitated.
"You're talking about things that haven't happened yet. Things that may never even happen." I'm getting upset. I am exhausted. His ten minutes is up.
He must sense that I'm tired because he moves toward the patio door.
"All I'm asking is for you to give it some thought. We don't all have to lose here. And truth is you and I weren't long term material anyway."
Ouch!
He grins and cups my cheeks. "Not by any fault of mine, love."
He's right, though. He did try. I was the ice queen with all the "rules." And now I see how truly amazing he is and I feel like a complete ass. But if I'm honest with myself, even now, seeing him for the astonishing man that he is, I don't feel with him the way I feel when I'm with Nick. I return his smile and assure him I won't make any rash decisions. He states his approval and gives me a kiss on the forehead before leaving. I go back to bed, checking my phone one last time before calling it a night. A text.
"Knock, knock"
That was fifteen minutes ago. Crap.

CHAPTER TWENTY
Heidi

Tuesday, June 17

I didn't return Nick's text last night. I figured if I plan on faking a headache then I probably should just keep quiet. Thank goodness for the three meetings I have this morning. The wine helped me sleep. Even after freaking out that Nick was outside my apartment at the exact time Alex was on my patio. See? This is why I don't sneak around. It stresses me out.

The whole time I was getting ready for work, the whole drive to my meetings, and every second in between, I have thought about the next time I see Nick and about what Alex said last night. I've had a dozen different conversations with him in my mind. Some of them end well, some of them not so much. I'm leaving my last meeting of the morning when Shelly calls.

"Did you lose a hot senator? Because one's been hanging around your office all morning," she informs me.

"Well piss," I say. So much for avoidance.

"Yep," she says, "I told you not to feed him. They never go away after that."

"Can he hear you?" God, I hope not.

"Nope," she quips. "He's snooping around in your office."

"Shelly!"

"Kidding," she says flatly. "But he is in your office. Want me to go get him?"

"No!"

"Oh.*Kay*?" I know she's wondering *'what the hell'* right now.

"Okay. Here's the deal. I may or may not have recently found out that he and Hot Alex may or may not be best friends," I confess.

"Holy shit."

"Yea, my thoughts exactly," I tell her. "So Alex, who Nick calls Nate but everyone else calls Alex- long story- comes over to my apartment last night being all noble and junk. Telling me I should give Nick a chance because *he's a good guy* and that I can't tell him about how we did the nasty because of something with some other guy -who used to be a friend- that really messed him up...and I don't know what to do. I can't lie to Nick. But I don't want to screw this up. Help me!" I think I got all that out in a record ten seconds. It would be a miracle if she understood me.

"So this Nick guy, you haven't done the dirty with him?" she asks.

"No."

"But he comes to your house almost every night?"

"Yea, I guess." What's with the 20 questions? I need advice, not an interrogation.

"So, you're dating?"

"No!" Is she crazy? I don't date.

"Yes, Heidi. That's dating." She gives me a minute to process what she's saying then continues. "He's been in your office for almost two hours. I don't know much about politicians and what they do, but I am guessing he probably has more important things on his schedule. And since you aren't giving up the good-good there has to be something else going on here. For both of you."

She waits for me to argue and when I don't she continues. "This is the first time since you first met Cole that I've seen you interested in a man. Like, *legit* interested. This kind of stuff doesn't happen every day my girl."

"But Alex..." I try to argue. She's not having it.

"Yea, he's a great guy, blah, blah, blah. Alex was a Tuesday night distraction. Now he's gone and you have his absolute permission to get it on with his best friend."

Well when she says it that way it just sounds trashy. She laughs at herself. "Seriously Heidi. Come see this man. If things get serious then you can tell him whatever you want. But for now, enjoy the fact that this exquisite piece of masculinity wants you, and go make him happy dammit."

See? This is why I love Shelly. This is why she's my best friend. Nobody said I have to marry the dude. I'm jumping way ahead of myself. If the time comes and I feel like Nick needs to know all the gory details of what I did before I knew him, I'll deal with it then. For now, I'm taking Shelly's advice. I'm going to enjoy him. And I'm going to make sure he enjoys me.

Nick is on the phone when I walk in. I don't interrupt him. It sounds heated. Something about him not giving a fuck where so-and-so thinks the money should go. "If we don't start holding these agencies accountable, we'll have bigger problems than a few overpaid CEO's," he declares. "I'll be there tomorrow with my vote. This shit better pass. Gotta go." And he ends the call, smiling at me like he wasn't just ripping someone a new one.

"Well hello, Cinderella. I came to return your shoe," he teases.

I shoot him a steely look. "Come on, I didn't leave in that big of a hurry," I say as I walk towards the chair he's made himself comfortable in. Which happens to be the one behind my desk.

"No?" He crosses his arms and leans back.

"I'm sorry. I had…"

"I know. A thing," he interrupts. "Is everything okay?" He stands as he asks the question. Good lord is he freaking handsome. Today he is wearing dark gray slacks with a navy blue oxford and blue and gray tie. He looks so good in blue. He looks good in black too. And gray. And white. And I'm pretty sure he probably looks good in everything. Or in nothing at all.

"Great," I tell him. "Florist, Photographer, and the band are all set for the function."

"Well, that's good to know, but I was talking about you. Are you okay?" he clarifies.

I knew what he meant. I was just hoping to skip over that part. "Nothing a little wine and a good night's sleep couldn't fix." I feel like I owe him an explanation for not calling him or answering his text. "I fell asleep tucking Hudson in. I wouldn't have been much company."

Nick runs a hand up and down my arm. "I wasn't looking for an explanation, Heidi. Simply concerned about you. That's all." Well that's a first. I'm so used to defending everything I say and everything I do. And everything I *don't* say or do. "But now that you mention it, we do need to discuss the fundraiser." He must sense that I'm ready to change the topic. "I think it's time you see the venue. Wouldn't you agree?"

Oh crap. I can't go to his house. Alone. With him. Not today. I'm not wearing the right underwear. What if he wants to…*Ohmigod* I don't even think I shaved. He can't just spring this on me like this. A girl needs a little notice ya know? We can't just whip things out like guys can. These things take preparation. I'm having a mini panic attack. "Now?" I ask. *Please say no.*

"Do you have plans?"

Great. If I say yes, I feel guilty for lying. If I say no, I have panty shame. *Eeeny meeny miny mo…..*

"No." *Are you crazy?!*

He grins from ear to ear and gives me a swift kiss on the cheek. "Then yes, now. I'll drive."

The whole way there I feel like a virgin on prom night. Nick makes me nervous. I've never been with anyone like him. What if he doesn't like what I like? What if he doesn't think I look good naked? What if he's into crazy shit like dressing up as animals or something? We spend most of the drive making small talk about where I grew up and how I met Shelly. He gets on Interstate 12 and heads towards Northshore. Before I know it we're pulling up to a gated subdivision. He slips his ID in the keypad and the big iron gate opens up, inviting us in. Nick lives all the way in the back of the subdivision. If you can call it a subdivision. Each home is sitting on approximately five to ten acres. We pull around to the side of his home into the garage. His house is the size of my entire apartment complex. All of a sudden I feel very inadequate. It's a massive Mediterranean/Italian villa combination mansion. There is a huge two-tier stone fountain in the front, ornate iron balconies off each set of upstairs windows, large stone columns framing the entrance, which displays a set of large dark walnut and glass doors, and an arched breezeway in front of an area of the home I would assume to be an office or library because I can see floor to ceiling bookcases through the two sets of glass double doors. Damn. Where was I when he was decorating this place? This is a designer's dream.

Nick shuts off the ignition and looks over at me, a nervous expression on his face. "I have a confession. I am slightly intimidated right now," he admits.
Oh thank goodness! I thought it was just me.
"I did my own decorating. Promise you won't scream and run out."
Are you kidding me? I'm stressing about whether or not I've trimmed the hedges and he's worried about his furniture?
He looks kind of serious. He can't be serious. I shake my head in disbelief and give him a reassuring smile. "Don't worry, you don't lose points for bad decorating." By now, he's opened my door and is leading me inside. We enter through a mudroom and end up in the kitchen where he starts to type in a code on a keypad but notices something and changes his mind. Maybe he forgot to set it.
"If that were the case, I never would have made it past the first time you saw my office," he says playfully. He sets his keys down on the island and moves toward me, causing me to step backwards until my butt hits something hard. "But I suppose you were right. It could use a makeover."
"You remember me saying that?" I'm impressed.
He moves closer to me, pinning me against the counter. "You're pretty unforgettable, Heidi."

We haven't even been inside two minutes and I already don't care what panties I'm wearing or whether or not I shaved. Just his presence has me wet. Soaked. He smells so freaking good. He reaches out and traces a fingertip along my collarbone. I look up and see him staring back at me with hooded eyes. His lips twitch, making me want to lick mine in anticipation of what is coming. "I bet you get laid a lot with lines like that, Senator."

The corner of his mouth moves, just a little, as his eyes fall to my newly moistened lips. "You certainly have an interesting mouth."

I instinctively pull my lips into my mouth but he shakes his head. "No. Don't hide them from me."

I obey, releasing my lips back to their natural position, pressing them together to relieve the numbness caused by my teeth. His voice sends a delightful sensation down my body, penetrating deep into my core. His hand moves up and his thumb runs along my bottom lip. I can feel his erection pressing into me, right below my belly button. My body craves him. I move my hips forward searching for more. Every inch of me wants to feel every inch of him. His eyes never move from my lips as he dips his head and kisses me. No delicate urging my lips to part. No subtle invitation of the tongue. This is pure, uninhibited lust.

Nick pulls away long enough to prop me up on the countertop. I lick my swollen lips as I watch him undo his tie. He holds it up to my eyes and gives me a knowing smile. I sit still and wait. *He remembers the book.*

"Just kidding," he says.

Damn.

"Maybe next time. This time, I want you to watch me please you." *Even better.*

He takes my hands and moves them to the top button of his shirt, our eyes locked on each other. I inch to the edge of the counter and begin to unbutton his shirt. Every button I unfasten reveals another bit of his smooth, tan skin. Once his shirt is completely open, I run my hands up his perfectly sculpted abdomen to his chest, then over the tops of his shoulders and down the upper part of his back. I can't stop touching him. Even though I'm not looking him in the eyes, I know he's watching me. My hands are wandering back over his shoulders and down his chest. I am just about to slide his shirt off when I hear a voice. A woman. A very loud, very rude, woman.

"Nickolas, are you kidding me? I just cleaned those countertops!" She slams her hand down on the kitchen island and glares at me. "And since when did you start bringing your extra-curricular activities home during the week?"

CHAPTER TWENTY-ONE

Nick

The fuck? *Monica.* I reach up and grab Heidi's hands, holding them still on my chest, and turn to Monica. "That's enough." My tone is not angry but it's still firm. She can give me all the shit she wants later but Heidi has done nothing to earn her disrespect and I'm not having it.

"Mi hija está en la sala de estar. Lleve a su piso de arriba de basura." *My daughter is in the living room. Take your trash upstairs.* She waves her fingers above her head, indicating the space above her.

Shit. "Lo siento." *I'm sorry.*

Heidi is watching our interaction cautiously. I'm sure she's embarrassed. And probably offended. Maybe a little intimidated. I let go of Heidi's hands and begin buttoning my shirt from the bottom. I get halfway up and quit. Fuck it. That's good enough. "Heidi, this is Monica, my live-in. Monica, Heidi Lemaire."

She politely smiles at my rude housekeeper. I grab her hips and slide her off the counter, slipping a protective arm around her waist once she's standing. I lean down and speak softly in her ear. "Her daughter is in the other room. That's why she's upset," I explain. The last thing I need is for Heidi to think that there's anything more to this situation.

She gasps and her hands fly up to cover her mouth, her eyes open wide as she looks around desperately for the child. "Ohmigosh Nick. I'm so sorry." I can tell she genuinely means it. This is a woman who doesn't even allow men around her son. I know this is a big deal to her. I mean, I was about sixty seconds away from fucking her senseless just then.

I smile reassuringly and gently kiss her forehead. "It's okay baby. You couldn't have known."

I walk past Monica into the living room where Olivia sits in front of the television. Heidi remains in the open archway between the two rooms while Monica follows me into the living room, arms crossed, with a scowl on her face.

"Hey pretty girl," I say to her daughter. "How was camp today?"

Olivia gets nothing from her father. I don't think he's ever even come to visit her. I say she's better off without the bastard but I'm biased. Every kid needs a normal childhood. So, I send her to camp every summer. She goes until noon every day, Monday through Friday. It's the least I can do. It's not her fault her father is a world class douchebag.

The little girl beams at me. "It was awesome! They brought animals from the zoo to our class! I got to hold a baby kangaroo!"

"Wow!" I exclaim. "Maybe I should start going to camp."

She giggles and shakes her head. "You can't, silly. You're too big."

"Time to go Olivia," Monica tells her. I pick her up and wrap her in a big hug before she takes off out the glass doors leading to the guest house where they stay.

"Hablaremos más adelante sobre este problema de actitud." *We'll talk later about this attitude problem.* I tell her mother as she walks past me like she's pissed off at the world.

"Yo no soy el que tiene el problema Nick." *I'm not the one with the problem Nick.*

I don't know what the shit she's talking about. It's not like this happens on a daily. I can count on one hand the times I've brought a woman into my home. And not one of them has ever been a daytime occurrence. So I wouldn't exactly call this a problem.

I look over at Heidi, standing there, leaning her head and one shoulder against the wall. She's so fucking beautiful. She catches me staring and smiles at me. "Did I just witness the soft side of Nick Knight?"

"That depends. Do I lose points for that?" I grab the remote and turn the television off.

"Oh no, Senator. I believe you just doubled your points," she flirts.

I'm getting used to her calling me *Senator*. The way she does it, in her flirty little voice, actually turns me on. Hell, who am I kidding? Everything she does turns me on. I start toward the kitchen, stopping in the opening where she stands. "I'm sorry for what just happened."

"No, I'm sorry. I got carried away," she says. She's apologizing for something that wasn't her fault. Something she's obviously so used to doing, I don't think she even realizes she does it anymore. I will find the mother fucker that made her this way and beat the shit out of him one day. I lean in to kiss her. Softly. Sweetly. A world apart from the kiss we shared just a few minutes ago. Even without all the lust, there's still so much passion behind it. I place my hands on her hips and pull her close. She wraps her arms around my neck, twisting her fingers up in my hair. I put everything into this kiss. My apologies, my desire to take care of her; to make her trust again, my hunger for her touch. It's all right here. In this kiss. It's an unspoken promise that I can feel all the way in my soul. I know in this moment, as our bodies seek each other out, as our hands explore, and our tongues collide, that I can't let her go. I am hers every bit as much as she is mine.

I would kiss her like this every minute of every day just to see the look that's on her face right now. She's completely relaxed, carefree, and...happy. Whatever shit she usually has running through her head is gone for now. There's just me and her and this feeling.

"I believe we were supposed to discuss an upcoming party," she says. Well, so much for that. She's still got her arms wrapped around my neck so I know the feeling isn't entirely gone. She's just causing a distraction so it doesn't go any further. I reach up to take her hand and lead her through the living room to the space outside.

There is a large set of glass sliding doors in my living room, kitchen, and dining room. As a matter of fact, the entire back side of my home is mostly glass doors and windows. Running the full length of the rear of my home is a covered patio. The west side of the patio ends with a breezeway that opens up into a covered pavilion. This is where I entertain. Even though you can see into my house through the glass, it's locked down during parties. I don't necessarily like strange people roaming around my home.

Heidi is admiring the view. Every few seconds she tilts her head and twists her mouth to the side, mentally visualizing and planning I assume. I watch and wonder how she sees things. Her mind obviously sees things in a completely different light than mine. I see things for what they are. She sees things for what they could be.

Her eyes wander the property, moving to the infinity pool right off the patio nearest the living room, and then down the hill to the walkway that leads to the pier on the river that lies about 100 yards from my house. She begins walking the path so I follow her. We stop at the bottom just before the entrance to the pier. "Yours?" She asks, noticing the 50-foot Horizon in the boat dock.

"The love of my life," I answer. True story. I spent more on that piece of workmanship than I did on my home. Well, not really, but close. Some of my best weekends are spent taking *Tranquility* out on Lake Pontchartrain. Just me, her, a bottle of Johnnie, and ESPN. Her name suits her perfectly. Peacefulness is exactly what I experience. Every time I set foot on her.

"Should I leave you two alone?"

"I guess I can share. Just this once." I pull the corner of my lips up in a genuine smile and reach for her hand. "Come. I'll introduce you," I say, pulling her toward the gangway leading onto the boarding platform. I've never brought a woman on my boat. This is my sanctuary. It was never meant to be shared. But here I am bringing Heidi on deck like I bought it just for her.

"You know how to drive this thing?" she inquires, looking over the many screens and buttons. "It's huge," she exclaims.

I feel an overwhelming sense of pride in this moment. She's impressed. The one thing that means the most to me has her mesmerized. Forget the fact that I serve in the United States Senate, or live in a million dollar home. She's never appeared affected by those things. Not one bit. But here on my yacht, on my pride and joy, Heidi is in awe. "This is beautiful Nick."

"I'll take you out one day. You'll fall in love. There's nothing like it. No disruptions. No distractions. Just us and the water." She's watching me intently as I speak, her attention to the boat completely forgone.

"I look forward to it," she tells me, never moving her eyes from mine. I move to where she's standing and tangle my hands in her hair behind her neck. She tilts her head back, inviting me to do as I please. I lean down and place soft kisses from her temple to her jaw line, trailing further down to her neck, stopping just above her collarbone. Her breathing is getting heavy and she's licking her lips. She is wearing a loose, thin, black top that falls off one shoulder, revealing the strap of a black silk camisole. I hook a finger under the strap and pull it off her shoulder, placing kisses along that path. Her breaths are short and heavy now. I'm hard as a fucking rock, knowing she's as turned on as I am. Our legs are intertwined with the top of my thigh flexing against the heat between her thighs. I move my hips forward, my erection jutting into her hipbone, letting her know how badly I want her. She rolls her body slowly against mine as I move my mouth back up into the dip in her neck. I bare my teeth and bite her very, very gently. She moves her hips forward and moans, making me mentally smile. *So she likes that.* "Let go baby. Let me make you feel good," I tell her as I lift my leg just enough to create more pressure between her thighs. Right where she needs it. She bears down on the flexed muscle, steering her body in the direction it craves. I can feel her heat through her thin linen pants.

She reaches underneath my arms and grabs a hold of the back of my shirt, balling the material in her fists as she pulls my body closer to hers and grinds against my thigh. At that moment, I lick the spot on her neck, now marked by my teeth, with the tip of my tongue and kiss my way up to the sensitive spot just below her ear. I nip and kiss, nip and kiss, at that spot as I reach down and pull her leg up and prop it on my hip, opening her wider so she can get what she needs. "Now, Heidi. I want to hear you." One more roll of her hips and she throws her head forward, screaming and biting my shoulder through my shirt, then throws her head back again as she rocks slowly against me. Her eyes are closed and her mouth is open but she's holding her breath. When she finally lets it out she moans, "Holy shit Nick."

Fuck me. That was the sexiest thing I've ever witnessed. "Oh baby, I am going to thoroughly enjoy pleasing you."

She is still licking her lips and catching her breath while she brings her leg down from my hip and pulls her bottom lip between her teeth. Her hand sneaks between our bodies and she rubs my crotch through my pants. She lifts up on her tip toes and places a soft kiss on my lips, still stroking my cock. "Your turn," she says behind a sly smile.

No fucking way. I almost made a mess in my pants just from watching her just now. I'm not being pegged as a three-minute man the first time I fuck her. I've had swollen balls since we met. A few more days won't kill me. Especially now that she's had a taste of what I can give her. She's not going anywhere. But damn, her hands on my dick feel so good. I let her stroke me for a minute longer before I pretend I just remembered something. "I have a meeting in an hour. We need to go."

It's not a total lie. I do have a meeting in an hour. But if I really wanted to, I could reschedule. She keeps rubbing my dick this way and I may rethink that possibility. Her sneaky little fingers move to unbuckle my belt and then unfasten my jeans. I want to stop her but I can't. She reaches inside, her touch now only separated from me by my underwear.

"I want to touch you Nick," she pleads. Her hand moves down to cup my aching balls, then back up the length of my erection. "Please. Let me touch you."

There's that fucking word again. It's like witchcraft rolling off her tongue. She says it and I'm dumbfounded. I have no choice but to let her do whatever the fuck she wants. With that one little word. I don't answer her but she isn't really waiting for me to. She's just waiting to see if I'm going to stop her. I don't. Her soft hand moves inside my boxer briefs and my cock jumps at the feel of her skin against my flesh. Her thumb spreads the liquid already gathered at the tip, then her hand wraps around me and she begins to stroke, slowly yet firmly, from tip to base and back again.

She looks up at me, open-mouthed and wanting. Her other hand slips into my underwear from behind. She cups my ass cheek and pulls me against her. My personal opinion on hand jobs is that they're for middle school boys, but Heidi is working my dick like she's doing it for money and I'm starting to think I could get used to it. I don't think I even make it the full three minutes when I feel the pressure building. I reach to replace her hands with my own so she doesn't get messy, but she shakes her head and tells me, "No. Let me." Then she pumps me dry. The electric sensation lasts a full minute it seems before the first spurt of semen ever comes. That's a first. Afterwards, I show her to the galley so she can wash her hands. I sidle up right behind her, wrapping my arms around her waist, dipping my head to speak softly in her ear.

"Heidi, what the hell am I going to do with you?"

CHAPTER TWENTY-TWO
Heidi

After what will now be referred to as the *Tranquility Experience*, Nick drops me off back at my store. After he changed clothes of course. Dark clothes and bodily fluids don't work well together. You can be as careful as you want, there's always going to be a little evidence in the end. He walks me in and Shelly gives me an *'I know what you've been up to'* look. "Anything happen while I was gone?" I ask, avoiding her curious eyes. "I don't know. Did it?" she says slyly. "Oh. Wait. Mrs. Landry called. She wants you to email her paint selections today."

I smile and nod. "Got it," I reply as I continue walking down the hall to my office with my man right behind me. *My man.* Oh he is definitely all man. As far as being mine, I don't really know. Don't really care. As long as he keeps giving me supernatural orgasms like that, I don't care who he belongs to. Okay. That's a lie. I do care.

We get to my office and I'm suddenly feeling like it's naked karaoke night at the Cat's Meow and I'm on stage. Yea. I'm nervous and there aren't any words on a screen for me to cheat with. "Your meeting?" I inquire. It's more of a suggestion that he go than a question, but I phrase it as though I'm asking. He stalks toward me, stopping just inches away. "Yes?"

He's going to make me tell him to leave. Dirty little shit. His hand reaches up to cup my cheek, the pad of his thumb stroking my cheekbone. "You're going to be late." The words don't want to come out. I don't really want to speak. I just want him to keep touching me.

"I'm just saying goodbye," he says as his other hand wraps around my waist and slips underneath the back of my shirt. Oh god. Not again. My heart rate has doubled and the thrumming sensation has begun between my thighs. I squeeze my legs together to relieve some of the tension slowly building there. He hasn't even touched me yet. I'm going to be a sloppy wet mess if he ever gets inside of me.

"Nick," I say, offering a distraction.

"Yes, baby?" His head is inching into the curve of my neck. I can feel his breath on my skin when he speaks. The tip of his nose grazes the side of my throat. Every single cell in my body is alert and aware of his presence. Even though my eyes are closed, I know exactly where every part of him is. I think I moan. Actually, I'm pretty sure I do, because he chuckles. Not out loud. More like a breathy huff. I'm sure he's proud of himself.

I open my eyes and come back down to earth. "You should go. Neither one of us is going to get any work done like this."

Nick sighs heavily but complies, backing up a step. He leans down and kisses me sweetly on the lips. Then he smiles the crooked smile that I've grown to love, before walking to the door. "I'll see you later," I say.

He continues smiling and winks. "Later." Oh man, I hope that's a promise. He isn't gone a full minute before Shelly is bursting through the door. Took her longer than I thought. "Details," she demands. "You weren't gone long enough for seconds so it must not have been good."

"Shelly." I glare at her for being so crass. I should have known though. It is Shelly after all.

"So, does he have a little penis?"

"Shelly!"

"Come on! The man can't be perfect. It wouldn't be fair."

"Oh. Mygod." I take a seat behind my desk and roll my eyes at her. "Well, considering there wasn't even a first, then no. We didn't go for seconds. And he does *not* have a little penis. It's big and beautiful. Just like him. Now go away. We are not talking about this now." I declare.

A familiar voice chimes in from the doorway. "Am I interrupting?" *Oh. Shit.* Why is he back?

Nick is standing in the door of my office looking like the cat that ate the canary. That grin. So smug.

Shelly looks nervously from me to Nick. Then back to me. "No, not at all. She was just leaving," I tell him. Shelly turns up the corner of her lip at me and goes back to her desk. "Forget something?" I ask him.

He doesn't answer right away. He's holding a manila folder in one hand and staring at me with an amused expression plastered all over his face. *Yes. I said you have a big dick.* Get over yourself. I mentally roll my eyes at him. *Men.*

"Actually, yes. I did. I came here earlier to show you this. But we….got distracted. So I forgot," he says, placing the folder on my desk and opening it.

"I need you to sign these. They're your terms of the agreement. I'm giving them to Nate. The relocation requirements. And a couple of other simple requests. I can go over them if you like."

I look at the documents then back up at him. I'm guessing I look confused because he walks around and tucks a piece a stray hair behind my ear. It's a comforting gesture. "I'm on your side Heidi. You have to trust me."

"Okay," I reply, simply.

He points to different sections of the paper that are highlighted by little neon post-its that look like little arrows. "Initial here. Sign here. Initial here."

I do as he says and when I'm done he closes the folder and gives me a reassuring smile. "It's going to be okay baby. I'm taking care of you."

He gives me one last kiss on the forehead before he leaves. For real this time. I really like when he calls me baby. The word sounds so sexy coming from his lips. I need to stop this. I'm starting to fall for Nick Knight. And I have a feeling it's going to be fast and far and there will be more than just a few scrapes and bruises when it's all over with.

The rest of my afternoon consisted of emailing Mrs. Landry her paint selections and creating a reception layout for an upcoming wedding. Tonight is Tuesday night. Any other Tuesday I would be gearing up for kickboxing with Hot Alex followed by a one-on-one with Hot Alex. But that's not happening tonight. Or ever again for that matter. So I skip kickboxing and go to baseball practice with Hudson and his dad. Halfway through practice Cole comes to sit next to me on the bleachers. "How have you been?" he asks.

"Good. I've been good." I smile courteously but quickly avert my attention back to the field.

"You look great," he continues. *Is he serious?*

"Thanks. You too." The compliment is disingenuous but I don't think he cares.

"How's business?" I guess he's looking for small talk. He wasn't this interested in my life when we were married. I could have stood in front of the television naked and he would have asked me what the score was. Sports and work. If he wasn't on the phone, he was watching whatever game was on. Most of the time flipping between two or three of them depending on what team he bet on that week. You know those couples you see out and the guy is on his phone the whole time, leaving his date to stare at the menu for the hundredth time? All the while, they're having dinner together without actually having dinner *together*. That was Cole and I. Only it was the same way at home. Maybe worse.

"Business is good." I don't really see why I need to go into detail with him. I keep watching Hudson field ball after ball at first base. He's really good. I'm a proud momma.

"Glad to hear that. So you must stay pretty busy?" he presses.

"Yes, pretty busy. I'm actually getting ready to change locations soon. So it's hectic." Hopefully that's enough to shut him up. It's not.

"Wow. You haven't been in this location long. Everything okay?"

"Everything's fine. Just thinking ahead. Long term. Change of scenery. Stuff like that," I explain. My business is no longer his business. Literally. No need to give him the low down on my personal stuff.

"You deserve it. You really are an amazing woman. I'm sorry I never noticed it before now." An apology. That's a first. In ten years of marriage he may have apologized for something twice. And that may be exaggerating a little. I look around for signs of snow.

"That means a lot. I know it was hard to say. So thank you."

He tells me he means it. It doesn't matter if he does or doesn't. I have forgiven him and moved on. What's done is done. But it's nice to hear I suppose. Practice is over and Hudson and I are on our way to the car when Cole stops us and invites us to dinner. I tell him we're fine but he insists. A little over an hour later our stomachs are full of pizza and coke, and it's time to call it a night. Dinner wasn't so bad. We spent most of the time listening to Hudson talk but had decent conversation in between. He's doing well with Michelle and work and I tell him I'm enjoying my time with Hudson and my friends. I'm heading out the door when a familiar face greets me. "Hey! Heidi, right?" she says.

Hey! Thing Two? Right? "Guilty," I say lightheartedly. I feel a little ashamed I don't know her name. I knew I should have asked before now. She's walking in with a decent looking younger guy. They're holding hands so I assume it's a date.

"I'm Candace. I don't think we've ever officially met." She giggles and scoots closer to her date. "Hey I need to apologize for being a bitch the first time you came to the office. It's just that you never really know, you know? You wouldn't believe the crazy stuff these women come up with just to see him." She shakes her head in disbelief.

"It's okay. I can imagine," I assure her all is forgiven with a smile. I turn to continue walking out but she keeps talking.

"You have no idea," she exaggerates the sentence and rolls her eyes. "Like Taylor Montgomery with her fake smile and faker boobs. She's forever showing up for interviews," she makes air quotes around the word "interviews" then groans.

Faker? Is that even a word?

"At least once a week. Ugh! She was there today for over an hour! God, that woman drives me nuts. I wish he'd tell her where to go already. I mean, she does have a boyfriend. Hello." Well she sure is talkative all of a sudden. I'm just staring at her, waiting for whatever she decides to blurt out next. "Sorry. I know you don't care about all that. I don't know why he

122

can't just find a decent woman…You know..like you…and actually date her. Anyway. It was good to see you!" She waves as her date pulls her to a table.

I wave back. "You too!" I feign enthusiasm.

The whole drive home my heart is in the pit of my stomach. The way Candace was talking, Nick had another woman in his office this afternoon. For over an hour. I guess that was the meeting he had to get to. The meeting I encouraged him hurry to so he wouldn't miss. A meeting with a woman he meets with once a week in his office. *A weekly.* Oh my gosh. He has a weekly. Like Alex was my weekly. But he still met with his weekly. Just hours after the Tranquility Experience. Dickhead. I mentally growl at him. Hudson wants me to sing along with him and the radio but I just don't feel like it. This feeling right here. This is yet another reason I don't date. It's so much easier when you don't know. It's easier not to care. This is why I don't ask for names. Or numbers. Or dates. Give me what I need and go home. Maybe take the trash out on your way. Simple. I like simple.

Once we're home and Hudson is in bed, I pour some wine and take a long hot bath. All I know about Taylor Montgomery is that she is one of two anchors on a local news show that is set in a bar type atmosphere and focuses on the more cultural part of the news rather than the hardcore stuff. She is supposedly dating a musician she met on set. But I guess he's not hitting the right notes. So far nothing from Nick since he left my office, but Alex calls while I'm in the tub.

"Just because we aren't banging isn't a reason to let yourself go, love," he says as soon as I answer. I can hear the grin in his voice.

"It's bound to happen sooner or later." I sigh and sink further into the bubbly water.

"True. Before you know it you'll be wearing moo-moos and feeding your cats in between soap operas and game shows."

"Oh yeah. Living the dream." I sigh again and growl a little. I know he's trying to make light conversation but I haven't had enough wine to be in the mood yet.

"Heidi, are you alright?" The grin voice is gone. I sit up straight in the tub. Like somehow if by doing that I'll convince him I'm fine. He can't see you dumbass. Right.

"Nothing a hot bath and a bottle of wine can't cure."

"So you're in the bath? Now? Alone?" That's a lot of questions all at once. I try to remember the order in which he asked them.

"Yes, yes, and of course I'm alone." I smile proudly.

Silence. Then he says, "Well that's a pity considering it *is* Tuesday."

He clears his throat and quickly changes his tone. "A runner brought your documents by this afternoon. I should have a response by week's end. I'll call you and we can meet up. Okay?"

Well that was a quick transition from playful to business. "Okay," I reply simply.

"Goodnight Heidi."

"Goodnight Alex."

And once again I'm left alone with my wine and my thoughts.

CHAPTER TWENTY-THREE
Heidi

Nick does finally text me. Just as I am climbing into bed. It's a picture of his boat followed by: *Thank you for an unforgettable day.*

Players gonna play. This guy is definitely at the top of his game. He knows how to make a woman feel good. In more ways than one. Of course the smart ass inside of me is telling me to ask him if he's sure he's thanking the right person. The Riesling is telling me I should be impressed by his stamina. I went back and forth with this all evening. Part of me is hurt. The part of me that was starting to like Nick. Like, really like Nick. Then the part of me that swore to never fall into that trap again is saying: *Suck it up buttercup. He's not doing anything you haven't done.*

It's not like we made any sort of commitment or anything. Good grief Heidi act your age. Just because you jacked him off doesn't mean he has to put a ring on it.

The Riesling wins out and I text him back a picture of me. In bed, my head on my pillow, hair splayed around me, blowing a kiss, and captioned: *Sweet dreams.* Sixty seconds later my phone is ringing.

"Let me guess, you wanted to hear my voice." I decide to go ahead and humor him.

"Something like that." His voice is so smooth. So sexy. It infiltrates through the phone line and seeps into my veins. Suddenly my whole body is hot just from the sound of it. He continues, "Do you have any idea what you do to me?" It can't be near as crazy as what he does to me.

"Why don't you tell me?" My voice is low and sultry. I forget I'm mad at him.

"Touch yourself," he commands.

"Do what?" I'm a little shocked at his bluntness. Not completely shocked, just startled I guess.

"If you need me to elaborate, I can. Slide that pretty little hand under those Egyptian cotton sheets and touch yourself. Do it slow. First stroke your collarbone. With your fingertips. Just like I would do. Now run a hand over your plump beautiful breast. God I can't wait to get my hands on your breasts."

Holy hell. He's talking to me like he's giving me a grocery list. But my head is spinning, my mouth is dry and fuck me, I am wet. My hips roll as the words roll off his tongue. My hands respond accordingly, moving just as he told them to.

"Are you doing what I asked, Heidi?"

"Yes." The word is barely a whisper. I envision him smiling a twisted sexy smile.

"Good. Don't stop." His tone is assertive, commanding my full attention. "Glide your hands over your stomach. Slowly. Go lower. Lower. Stop at the tops of your thighs. Anticipate your touch. It's all about anticipation, baby." He pauses for a moment then continues, "Now run your hands over your panties. Are they wet? Are you wet?"

Oh god yes. I'm arching my back and rolling my hips with every word he speaks. I am too busy rubbing myself to answer his question.

"Heidi? Answer me."

"Yes."

I hear him make a noise like he's sucking air in through clenched teeth then he groans. "Slide your hand inside your panties. Spread yourself open and tell me how wet you are baby. How swollen and slick it is."

I'm surprised he can't hear for himself. My finger slips right in. I'm soaking wet. And hot. I lick my lips and spread my arousal over my clit, rubbing small slow circles around it.

"Heidi," he warns. I can't speak. I can only feel. It feels so good. Just keep talking. His voice is a trigger. It sends electric sensations all through my body, intensifying the feel of my own touch. I defer my attention from my stimulation long enough to answer him. "It's so wet Nick. It feels so good."

"Tell me what you want." I want him to keep talking like this. Just one..more..minute. I want him to touch me this way. I want to feel him. I have one hand holding my panties down while my other one is busy rubbing my throbbing clit. My eyes are closed so I can see his face. I'm bucking my hips as I imagine how good it would feel to have him inside of me. "I want to come," I blurt out. It's not what I meant to say but it's the truth nonetheless. I feel the sensation getting more and more intense. I'm almost there. I rub faster. Harder. I can hear myself moan.

"Come with me baby. Right now." He makes a low, guttural sound and I shatter. I dip one finger deep inside and press on my g-spot, feeling myself contract and pulse as I come to pieces with him. I hold it there while I come down, moving my hips slightly to draw the feeling out as long as I can. I'm panting. He's panting. The line is silent aside from our breathing for a minute. "Fucking amazing," he says, finally.

"Sweet dreams Nick," I tell him. No need for small talk at this point.

"Sweet dreams Heidi."

Wednesday, June 18

Today is the day. Today is the day fate decides whether she's going to kiss me gently or bite me in the ass. I make Hudson his favorite breakfast of cinnamon butter toast and chocolate milk. Then I get ready for the day. I try to look as put-together yet approachable as possible. I pair up my trouser jeans with a dressy turquoise tank and leave my hair down and curly. I put extra concealer under my eyes to hide the puffiness there from last night's wine overdose. Brief flashbacks of an x-rated phone call pop into my head. I shove them aside to evaluate later. Right now I have other priorities.

Cole meets us at Ochsner's. Dr. Morad has found his calling. The man is wonderful with Hudson, making him feel totally at ease. He speaks English, rather than Doctor, to Cole and I, making sure we completely understand why we're here and what happens next. Hudson had some abnormal blood work. The kind that throws up red flags. It is Dr. Morad's job to find out where those flags come from and whether or not they pose a serious threat. He does this through a more extensive testing procedure. Unfortunately, this means more discomfort for my baby boy, but in the end we all have the same goal in mind. To find out what's wrong and fix it. After a few questions and some physical examination, we are directed into what is called a 'Consultation Room' to speak with a woman named Sheila. She talks to us about our financial obligations, has us fill out a privacy form denoting who may or may not have access to Hudson's medical information, and goes over the standard procedure should we not get the test results
we're hoping for. She's going over this like it's a recipe she found on Pinterest. I'm reading and re-reading the form, not certain I'm ready to sign off on this just yet. There is a very real possibility that they may need a bone marrow biopsy or even a spinal tap. Are you kidding me? I personally have never experienced either one of these procedures but from what I have heard they are both extremely painful. I start to argue that there have to be other ways to test. How does she know Hudson will even need all this stuff? Why do we have to agree to something that isn't even going to happen? I rub my temples and close my eyes tightly. Maybe when I open them I'll be back at home and realize this is some sick nightmare. I'm getting very overwhelmed and I'm sure if someone checked my blood pressure right now it would be through the roof.

This is one of those moments. You know those moments in your life when you feel as if you're not really you? The moments when it feels like you're watching someone else's life from far away. Those times when you know this can't possibly be your life. Because things like this don't happen to you. They happen to other people. People you read about. Sometimes even people you know. And those people are strong and they have support systems and seem to always come up with all the answers. I am not strong. I am alone. And I damn sure don't have any answers.

Cole takes my hand and assures me that Sheila here is just doing her job and that this is protocol. Everyone that comes through these doors signs the same papers. And that Hudson will be fine. I take a deep breath and sign on the dotted line. This isn't a moment anymore. This is real. This is very real. While most moms are fighting off runny noses and doctoring mosquito bites, I'm signing forms about bone marrow biopsies and discussing different forms of cancer treatments. It's not fair. It's just not fucking fair.

Four vials of blood and half a cup of urine later, we're done and Hudson is ready for ice cream and a toy. He has no idea what he may be facing. And I intend to keep it that way. No need to burden him with the worry of what might be. He's a kid and I'm going to let him act like a kid. He keeps finding reasons for Cole to stay with us throughout the day. I know what he's up to and it's not going to work. I think Cole hangs around for the mere fact that he's worried I may actually have a nervous breakdown before the day is over. The nurse was great when she took Hudson's blood. She kept us both calm and very comfortable. He sat on my lap and we counted like we always do until she was all finished. Today we made it all the way to sixty. He got a ninja turtle band-aid and a couple of stickers.

One of our favorite places to eat as a family was PF Changs so naturally that's where Hudson decided he wants to have lunch. Hudson is showing his dad and me how he can use chop sticks to eat his lo mein when I hear a familiar voice. My heart speeds up before I'm even able to look up to confirm who is standing there.

"Well this is a pleasant surprise." Nick's voice is calm and poised, even though the look in his eyes is anything but. He regards me first, then Cole. I see a slight twitch in Nick's jaw as they make eye contact.

"Nick. How are you?" I sound like we're meeting for the first time in years. Like he's an old family friend. Instead of the man who made me quiver with pleasure...twice...less than twenty-four hours ago.

Nick smiles at me and his eyes twinkle. Like he knows I'm uncomfortable and he's not planning on making this easy for me. He opens his mouth to speak but Hudson interrupts him. "Wanna see me eat with chop sticks?" he asks.

Nick looks down at him and continues smiling. "There's no way you can eat with chop sticks! I can't even eat with chop sticks," he goads.

Hudson accepts the challenge and digs in to his noodles and chicken. A few of them hang off his chin, but he sucks them in his mouth and smiles proudly as he chews.

"Well I am impressed," Nick tells him.

I take the opportunity to divert his attention from Cole. "Nick, this is my son Hudson. Hudson, I'd like you to meet my friend Mr. Knight." So not how I planned on this going down. I had never really planned on Nick meeting Hudson. But on the off chance that I thought it should ever happen, it definitely wasn't supposed to be while I was at lunch with my ex-husband.

Hudson extends his hand to Nick. Such the little gentleman. "Nice to meet you Mr. Knight," he says with the confidence of a grown man.

Nick arches his eyebrows and shoots me an amused glance as he reaches to shake Hudson's hand. I respond with an amused smile of my own. "It's nice to meet you too young man," Nick says as his eyes note the band-aid. "Who's your favorite ninja turtle?" he asks, nodding towards Hudson's arm.

"Donatello," Hudson replies. "He's the blue one. Blue is my mom's favorite color," he explains as if he's known Nick for months. He looks at the band-aid and sighs heavily. "We just went to the hospital. They had to take blood. Again. I hate when they do that. I don't get why my mom is so worried. I don't even feel sick," he declares, palming his forehead the way I do when checking him for a fever.

I'd say Hudson has done a great job channeling Nick's attention from his dad now. Way to over share son. Leave it to kids.

Nick leans in close to my son and speaks lowly, directing his words specifically to Hudson. "You know, sometimes there's a battle going on inside our bodies. And we don't even know it. But we have to go to the doctor because they can see inside of us and make sure the good guys win the battle and our bodies feel better again. Your mom just worries because she loves you." He ruffles the hair on the top of Hudson's head and winks at him. Hudson gives an exaggerated wink back, along with a thumbs up. And there go my ovaries.

Nick stands up straight and looks at me with a knowing expression. I give him a feeble smile then focus on taking a sip of my drink. He cuts his eyes at Cole for a split second then back to me. There's the jaw twitch again. "It seems we have a few things to," he pauses to collect his composure, "discuss. When you have time," he continues. He leaves his purpose vague. On purpose I'm guessing. He's making sure Cole questions me once he leaves. But I have nothing to hide so his little game doesn't bother me. He's the one having nooners with other women in his office. I'm not doing anything wrong. Just remembering Blonde Bombshell and her conjugal visit yesterday gets my blood boiling. He can't just come over here, interrupt my lunch, buddy up to my child, then make little jealous accusations like this. Who does he think he is? So what if I'm on a date? Which I'm *so* not. But if I were, why should he care? And what is there to discuss? And I'm mad at him all over again. This man drives me crazy.

"Today is pretty much a no-go, but I can make an appointment to come by your office tomorrow," I offer. There. If he thought he was going to make Cole think I saw him on a personal level, I just squashed that. Score one for Heidi.

His mouth slowly turns up in a crooked smile. He's on to me. Shit. "Or you could just meet me on the boat. You remember my boat, don't you Heidi?" *Oh, that was dirty.* I glare at him. He keeps smiling and I swear I hear him chuckle.

"I'll call you," I say, my tone clipped, hoping it dismisses him.

He narrows his gaze and I feel his eyes burning into me. It's suddenly very hot in here. I have to adjust myself in my seat. If I keep sitting here, I'm positive I'll slide right off.

"Mom, he has a boat! That's so cool!" Hudson exclaims, distracting me from Nick's intense stare. Nick laughs and looks over at my son.

"It is pretty cool. Maybe your mom will bring you sometime." He winks at Hudson again then turns his attention back to me. "I'll see you later, Heidi." And with that, he turns and walks back to his table of men. I see Alex there and wonder if he has been watching our interaction. Nick says something to the gentlemen and they all turn to look at me. Uncomfortable much?

"Who was that guy, mom?" Hudson questions.

I look at Cole, who has been respectfully silent this whole time, then back at Hudson. "He's just a man who is helping mom do some new things with her business, baby." The look on Cole's face tells me he's not buying that explanation. At all. But he says nothing as we finish our meal. I feel Nick's eyes on me all the way out the door and I'm positive I haven't heard the end of this.

CHAPTER TWENTY-FOUR
Heidi

Friday, June 20

Nick didn't bother me the rest of the afternoon after seeing me at the restaurant Wednesday. As a matter of fact, I didn't hear from him all day yesterday either. I guess seeing me with Cole wasn't as bad as I liked to believe.

Hudson and I played HORSE on the basketball court at the apartment complex when we got home. He won. He always wins. Afterwards we spent the evening having coloring wars and playing card games. About three games in, he decided he was a magician and spent the next thirty minutes showing me magic tricks. Then we cuddled in my bed until we both fell asleep.

This afternoon I have to set up for a rehearsal dinner taking place this evening so I figure I'll stop by Nick's office this morning. Get the double standard speech out of the way bright and early. Getting through security and past Thing One has become pretty easy lately. The main security guy named Brian even knows me by name. I know he has a wife and two kids, and he's been working here three years. Friendly guy. The minute I step off the elevator, Thing Two, who I now know as Candace, makes a disgusted face and nods her head towards the doors to Nick's office. Her lipstick is bright purple today. It must be nice to be young. I could never pull that off.

"You might as well get comfortable. Betty Boobs just went in. He didn't close the doors this time though, so maybe today's visit isn't conjugal," Candace informs me then giggles at her own private joke.

I don't find it funny. I'm glad she feels like we're friends and she can share her stupid comments with me though. "Twice in one week. It must be getting serious," I quip.

Candace rolls her eyes and shakes her head. "Gross. I say you walk in there and interrupt them. Shake things up a bit." She smiles and wiggles her eyebrows. "In that dress," she says as she runs her eyes up and down my outfit, "You'd give him a taste of what he's missing."

If she only knew. And what's wrong with my dress? It's feminine. I mentally *hmmph* at her. It's a simple, knee length, peach chiffon slip dress with spaghetti straps and a thick black lace hem around the bottom.

"I'm kind of in a hurry and he's not really expecting me, so if you don't mind would you just tell him I came by?"

I really want to go in there and drag blondie out by her hair then shove a really sharp pencil up Nick's ass, but I go with the more civil option. I make the mistake of glancing in the office as I walk back to the elevators. Nick is in his chair and Taylor is bent over the opposite side of his desk, shoving her cleavage in his face and poking her ass in the air. He's looking at a paper lying in front of him and paying no attention to her silicone valleys. I guess when you've seen them once, the thrill is gone. Lucky for him.

Fifteen minutes later my phone is ringing. I haven't even made it back to the store to pick up Hannah yet. I guess Candace relayed the message. My momma taught me if you don't have anything nice to say, then don't say anything at all. So I don't answer the phone just yet.

After Hannah and I get everything set up for the evening I drop her off at the store and grab Shelly for an afternoon of shopping. There are three things that boost my self-esteem when it's been bulldozed by…a tall blonde with fake boobs…for example. Shopping, random sex, and rum. The second one most likely inspired by the third.

"If you're going to keep bringing me along on your impromptu shopping sprees, I'm going to need a raise," Shelly tells me on the way to Canal Street. She is such a ray of sunshine on my cloudy days.

"I'm giving you the day off. With pay. There's your raise," I say.

We park and walk to the shops. I love to walk in the city. I wish I could walk everywhere. I don't like to drive. It makes me nervous. I am directionally challenged. I get lost easily and if you've ever been lost, you know that feeling really sucks. I don't know how I ever drove before the invention of GPS. The roads in this part of the city are mostly one way streets and the parking is crap. And I like parking even less than I like driving. So that brings us back to walking. We spend a couple of hours in the shops then grab an afternoon coffee, and go back to work.

Just as we're getting ready to head to the cathedral that evening, Nick texts me. He called twice while I was shopping, thus inspiring me to buy the sheer pink underwear I'm wearing right now. I wasn't sure when I bought them if I was buying them to show Nick I can keep up with blonde bombshell, cleavage or not, or if I was buying them to make myself feel pretty, or if I was buying them because I planned on playing a game of tit for tat and finding my own blonde bombshell.

Keeping Candace's observation of my dress in mind, I decided to keep it on. I add a black, silk kimono cardigan to make the look a little less hooker, a little more professional. *Oh yeah.* I'm feeling sexy. Too bad I'm only going to a church with a bunch of married and soon-to-be-married people.

Nick: *Either you're very busy or you're trying to ignore me.*
I'm hoping you're very busy baby, because I plan on
being hard to ignore.

Tell me about it. I've been trying to ignore him all day but he keeps popping up in my every thought. It's extremely frustrating. I came up with a hundred reasons I shouldn't talk to him today. Followed by a hundred more excuses why I should. And so I text him back. Game over. He wins.

Me: *I don't doubt that. Busy day. Getting ready for a*
wedding this weekend. It's kind of a big deal.

Nick: *It would appear so. Are you home?*

Me: *Still working.*

Nick: *Where?*

Me: *I'll be home in about an hour.*

I'm working the mysterious angle here.

Nick: *That's not what I asked.*

And apparently he's working the alpha angle.

Me: *I know what you asked.*

Nick: *Why won't you tell me where you are?*
Are you alone? Or with a chef perhaps?

Oh hellllll no! He did not just go there.

Me: *Are you alone? Or with a reporter perhaps?*

I hope he noted the bite in that text.

Nick: *Fair enough. Now, tell me where you are.*

Me: *St. Louis Cathedral. Fucking the chef in a church.*
Right between the altar and the crème brulee.

I should probably say some Hail Mary's for that or whatever you're supposed to do. But seriously? He crossed a line. Accusing me. The nerve. Asshole.

Nick: *I'll see you soon Heidi.*

Surely he's kidding. He didn't sound like he was kidding. In fact, he sounded pretty serious.

Me: *You're not serious.*

No reply. Five minutes later still no reply.

Me: *Nick?*

Crickets chirping. *Shit.*

I venture back inside the church to get everyone in place so we can go over the order of events for the ceremony. I'm going over the presentation of the gifts when I notice Nick leaning against the wall near the entrance. He's watching me. He looks his usual sexy yet tailored self in navy blue slacks and a stark white button up. Even though his sleeves are rolled up to the elbow and the first two or three buttons are unfastened, his appearance commands attention. He's leaned back, hands in his pockets, legs crossed at the ankle, watching me intently. Even before I saw him standing there, I knew he was here. I can feel him. I'm drawn to him by some unseen force.

I ask the priest to go over the Eucharist with the bride and groom while I excuse myself for a moment. Nick's gaze never falters as I walk down the aisle to meet him. His eyes bore in to mine, searing into me all the way to my core. He removes his hands from his pockets and stands up straight as I approach him. When I stop just a foot or so away, he sweeps his eyes down my body and slowly back up. The hair on my arms stands up in anticipation. Of what, I have no idea. This is just the way my body reacts to him. It wants. It craves. Every time he's near. He runs his tongue over his bottom lip and looks me in the eye.

"Why are you here?" I finally work up the steadiness to ask.

He twitches his lips and then gives in to a full smile. "What? I told you I was coming," he replies, all cocky.

I narrow my eyes at him, daring him to keep it up. The smile grows wider. He shakes his head at me and pulls his bottom lip between his teeth. "You're sexy when you're mad."

He's playing with me. I should stomp on his toe. Instead I roll my eyes and cross my arms. "I went by your office today," I tell him, continuing my angry façade. Well, I actually am a little aggravated but honestly I know I have no reason to be. We never made any indications to be exclusive.

"I know. Why did you leave?" he asks.

Seriously? I'll take because you had your plaything bent over your desk for $100.

"You were busy," I answer quickly and simply.

"If I wasn't with you, I wasn't busy."

Wow. That was a smooth response. "I apologize for making you think any different. I came to tell you I'm going out of town," he continues. His hand reaches out to uncross my arms and pull me closer to him.

Apology accepted. I peek to see if anyone is watching. Only a couple of bridesmaids and the mother of the groom. And I seriously doubt they're watching *me.* This is so unprofessional. I could kick his butt for coming here like this. Embarrassing me. Not to mention making these women think who knows what. In a church. He should really be ashamed of himself.

Nick pulls me until we're chest to chest. Well, sort of. I'm eye level with his unbuttoned shirt. His dark, toned flesh peeking out at me, begging me to run my fingers over it. He runs a fingertip over my cheek and down my jaw as he leans in and whispers, "And I want to taste you before I leave." For the love of all things holy. Good lord. The man is good. His words have my bodily fluids on speed dial. As soon as he speaks, they come alive. I'm almost positive it's a sin to soak your panties in church. We should go outside. Definitely.

I latch on to his wrist to stop him from moving his hand any further down. "Nick, we can't do this here."

He passes a glance over the auditorium and then back to me. "Then let's go outside," he says. "I won't be long. Give me two minutes. Please." He sounds so sincere. Almost desperate, although I know Nick Knight is not a desperate man.

I excuse myself from our newly acquired audience. Guess they've finished going over Communion. Nick leads me outside to where his solid black Toyota FJ Cruiser is parked and I'm wondering *'How many vehicles does this guy own?'*

He leans against the driver's side door and pulls me forward. I wrap my arms around his waist and breathe him in. All vanilla, musk, and pure man. I can feel his hot breath on the top of my head as I rest it against his chest. "You're out of town a lot. Where do you go?" I ask. *"Take me with you,"* I think.

"Washington D.C." He inhales a long breath of air through his nose. "You smell incredible."

Way to change the subject Cassanova. He absent-mindedly runs a finger back and forth under the strap of my dress.

I pull my head away from his chest and look up at him. "When will you be back?"

Nick stops playing with my strap and places his hands on my ass, lifting me up so that I'm straddling his hips with my legs wrapped around his waist. He then turns us around so that my back is now against the door of the SUV. My dress hiked up around my waist the second he lifted me up and these little sheer panties aren't much of a barrier between his rock hard dick and my aching vagina. With the door and his hips now supporting my weight, he places a hand on either side of my head and leans forward so that his mouth is just centimeters from mine. We are sharing the same breath. And he's looking at me...no, it's more than that. We are looking at one another. *Into* one another. If the eyes were sex organs, I'd definitely be getting pregnant right now. He has the most intense gaze. It's hypnotic. I can feel what he's thinking when he looks at me this way. Like I am the only thing that matters to him. Stuff could be blowing up around us and he'd never move his eyes from mine. It excites me. It makes me nervous. It makes me hot. I feel my breath become more frequent and heavy. I feel my pulse quicken.

"Not soon enough," he says.

Wait. What was the question? Oh right. When will he be back?

He closes the last few centimeters between us and joins his lips to mine, softly at first. Then his tongue sneaks out and traces my bottom lip, urging its way in. My lips part obediently and he begins to kiss me with a fervent yearning. He grinds his erection into me as he's kissing me. Once. Twice. A third time. I moan in his mouth and tangle my fingers in his hair and move against him, creating the most amazing friction against my throbbing nub. Oh god. Not again. You've got to be kidding me.

I press harder against him, my body begging for more. I can feel his thick flesh protruding through the thin fabric of his trousers. Every time he thrusts forward it prods its way through my panties right where I need it to be. All he has to do is unzip his pants. Slide my panties to the side and I would be one helluva happy girl. I pull his hair tighter between my fingers and push myself harder on his hips. The waves start to roll over my body. I feel the pulsing in my core. It's getting more and more intense. I have to release him from the kiss to cry out. Suddenly the movement stops. He looks at me. His breaths are short and heavy just like mine. He licks his lips and tilts his head back.

"I promise this is not what I came here to do," he tells me.

"Don't stop Nick. Please. It feels so good," I plead, urging him to keep kissing me, to let me finish. I sound desperate but I don't care.

He graces me with the tilted grin and a sparkle in his eyes. He takes a step back and holds my hips steady as my legs slide down his body until my feet touch the ground. I loosen my grip in his hair and twirl my fingers in the pieces at the nape of his neck.

"I'm guessing that's a no, then?" I know he hears the disappointment in my voice. Or at least sees it in my eyes when I look up at him. Or both maybe.

The smile widens. He's so freaking cute. One minute he's got me on the edge of orgasm and the very next he's smiling like a kid on Christmas. "Soon, Heidi."

I huff. He chuckles. "I'll be back in two weeks. Try to behave until then."

Two weeks?!? And he couldn't give me one lousy orgasm before he left. I'm convinced he's trying to drive me bat shit crazy.

I run my fingertips across the skin peeking out from under his unbuttoned shirt. "That's a long time to behave." I'm teasing him. My tone is playful and I'm batting my eyelashes in an exaggerated attempt at flirting.

"You can do it. I assure you it will be worth the wait," he promises. Then he gives me a quick kiss and a wink before reaching around me to open his door. I step out of the way and let him get in. "I'll see you soon."

I blow him a kiss as he drives off and think to myself that I have no doubt what-so-ever that it will definitely be worth the wait. Now I have to go back in this church smelling like greedy vagina. This is going to be a quick rehearsal.

CHAPTER TWENTY-FIVE

Nick

Tuesday afternoon on my boat was... unexpected. I never expected to take Heidi on board. I never expected to make her come basically without even touching her. And I damn sure never expected to have her jack me off like a horny teenager. But fuck me if it didn't feel good.

And then sitting in my office as soon as I got back, was Taylor Montgomery. In my chair. Her legs propped up on my desk like she owns the mother fucker. Naturally, I closed the door behind me. I have enough respect for myself and for Candace not to have her hear the ass chewing I was about to give Ms. Montgomery. Taylor had called me earlier to tell me she had come across some juicy gossip about me and one of my campaign sponsors. I told her to go fuck herself. She said she'd rather let me do it. I go to great lengths to keep my shit private. As much as can be expected for a man in my position. I don't need her snooping around and making mountains out of molehills. So there she was. Cocky grin and notepad. Sitting at my desk. Like the Queen B that she is.

"What are you doing here Taylor?"
She pouts. An obviously over exaggerated pout.
"What? Not happy to see me? That's a first."
Actually, it's not, but I'm usually too drunk to care.
"I've already been taken care of."
That got her attention. She sits up straight, bringing her legs down from the desk.
"Well I bet she doesn't do it like me."
You can say that again. For starters, she's not sloppy. Or annoying.
Taylor is a good lay because she's game for whatever. Outside of that, she's a cookie-cutter, blonde, gold digger. That type of woman never bothered me because I never wanted anything outside of the bedroom anyway. From anyone. Now, I'm not sure anymore.
"How she does it is no more your business than how your other boy toys do it is mine. Now, Why.are.you.here?" I made sure to articulate each word slowly and carefully.
"You don't have to be rude Nick," she says as she stands. "I told you. Rumor has it you're going head-to-head with BKG, your biggest campaign sponsor, all because of some small time business no one's ever heard of. My guess is there's a woman involved."

Damn right there is. But the last thing I need is fucking rumors about my campaign.

"BKG is good. I'm happy. They're happy. No story. The rumors are shit. And of course there's a woman. There's always a woman." Taylor stares blankly at me. "Surely you didn't think you were the only one?" She glares at me and starts walking toward the door. "Give me details Taylor." I walk up behind her and take hold of her arm to stop her from going further. "Who told you this bullshit?" She backs up into me.

"Now you're interested?" she asks coyly. I run my hand down her bare arm.

Now is about the time you're thinking I'm an asshole. I have two things to say about that. One: I never promised anything to Heidi. I may be all mind-fucked about what's going on between us but I do know one thing. We aren't a couple. This isn't some epic romance. And two: I need to do whatever I can to keep Taylor quiet and happy. So I made her come. I used my fingers, not my dick. So I get credit for that right? And she never touched me. In fact, she never even turned around. And I never even got hard. So no harm, no foul, right? I got my information and she got what she came for. Win-win. Turns out some prick from BKG was running his mouth at the gym where Taylor's boyfriend works out. Looks like I'll have to shut him up.

The afternoon didn't get much better after I got home. I confronted Monica about her behavior earlier that day. Of course her first defense was that Olivia was in the other room.

"I apologize for that. I didn't know. Which brings me to the thought of why? Why was she in my living room in the middle of the day on a Tuesday?" Naturally Monica gets defensive.

"It's laundry day Nick. Sheets, towels, and sometimes I even dust. It's too much shit to get done in one day. We don't go roaming around your house all day if that's what you think." Her tone is agitated.

"Noted. I'll keep that in mind. I understand you were upset with me, but you had no reason to talk about Heidi that way."

Monica tries to lighten the conversation. "Well at least she didn't know what I was saying."

I'm not entertained. She continues in a more serious tone, "So this one has a name?"

"They all have names. But if you're asking if this one is different, then I don't know. Maybe."

"Fine. I'm sorry for insulting her. Just be careful. I would hate to see history repeat itself."

She's genuine. I know she cares. I know she's concerned. I haven't exactly been conservative in my personal life and unfortunately, because she lives here, Monica has had a front row seat through it all.

Mission accomplished. Apology accepted. Mood lightened.

"And since I don't intend on introducing her to Matthew, history should remain just that. History." I shoot her a playful wink to let her know I'm kidding. I would never intentionally say anything to bring up painful memories for her. It's common knowledge her ex is an asshole. It used to be a sore spot but we can joke about it now. She gives me a hug and everything is hunky dory again.

Walking back from the guest house where Monica stays to the main house, I caught sight of the boat and immediately flashed back to being there that morning with Heidi. I snapped a quick picture and sent her a text. I didn't expect a response but was very glad to receive one. There she was, lying in her bed, sexy as fuck with her hair spread all around her, blowing me a kiss. I needed to touch her. Right then. And since we live almost an hour apart, that wasn't happening. So I settled for the next best thing. I told her I wanted to touch her and I listened intently as she touched herself. I could see her so clearly. Eyes closed, head tilted, back arched, and mouth open while her fingers slid under some sexy ass panties. I could hear her moan. I heard her lick her lips after she came. I remembered the look on her face earlier and envisioned her making that same face. I will see that face again soon. I see it in my sleep. I dream about it and wake up hard.

The following day I had my meeting with Nate and a couple of guys from BKG. BKG is the company buying Heidi's property. They already own half the city and a good chunk of a few other surrounding areas. They are also a primary sponsor for my campaign. I knew when I saw the name, Heidi didn't have a prayer against these guys. But I know them. They fund my campaign and in return I let things slide. Welcome to politics baby. If anyone can get them to budge an inch, it's me. The first order of business at lunch was to call out the asshole that has loose lips at the gym. Of course there were denials. Quickly followed by apologies when I told them to find another official to put in their pocket because I was done. I don't play games and I don't need their money. Sponsors come a dime a dozen. Especially in this state. Everyone needs favors. Unfortunately, the only other United States Senator in Louisiana spends her time voting on piece of shit bills and doing keg stands at football games, so she isn't highly sought out by big spenders. I keep my personal shit personal and do my best to stay out of the spotlight. And I'm a damn good official. I create jobs and make sure the people who aren't able to buy their way out of things don't get screwed by the people who can. So I'm the best of two. Which gives me a pretty sturdy bargaining chip. By the end of lunch Heidi's relocation expenses were being covered, the time frame was lifted, and she'll be getting a fifty thousand dollar compensation check, which I have decided to match, for a total of one hundred thousand dollars. Trust me, they can afford it. And my name is nowhere on the documentation. All in all, I'd say it was a productive meeting.

We were wrapping up with small talk and a drink when I spotted Heidi at the restaurant. She was with a little boy and some blonde guy. He better either be gay or just a friend. I said it before, I'm not the jealous type. I don't give two shits what you do when you aren't with me. In fact, I'd rather you have a man to go home to because I'm not the snuggling kind. I'm not sending you flowers on your birthday. And I'm not taking you out to dinner and a movie. So get what you want from him and come see me for what you need. That's my role and I don't have a problem playing it. But Heidi makes me feel....very territorial. I never even felt this way with Elise. Not even when I saw her flirting with my best friend. I knew it was coming. I was just too stupid to believe it. I know better now. I couldn't sit there and watch Heidi laugh and converse with some other man. Not fucking happening. So I walked right up to her table and made my presence known.

I knew who the little boy was before Heidi ever introduced him. He looks just like her. And he spoke in such a pleasant and approachable manner, I knew he had to be hers. We hit it off right away. He actually managed to take my mind off the other man for a minute. *Hudson*. The name suits him. Hudson and Heidi. He mentioned something about going to a hospital. I want to ask Heidi if he's okay but that's another personal topic. So far she hasn't felt too inclined on getting personal with me. Although I have a feeling she's more open with me than she's been with other men. I'm sure she'll tell me when she feels like it so I leave it alone. For now. The asshat she's with never made the first attempt at introducing himself nor trying to find out who I am. I can guarantee if I were in his seat and some man walked up and started looking at my girl the way I was looking at Heidi, he would know one way or another that this seat is taken. And so is she. So that

tells me that he's either not a boyfriend, or that he's a total pussy and doesn't deserve her anyway. She tried to play it off like we were mere business acquaintances but I wasn't letting that slide.

When I got back to the table, Graham Batiste, president and owner of BKG Vantage, made a comment about me picking up women during business hours.

"No need to pick up what's already mine."

Nate shakes his head disapprovingly. He treats women worse than I do so I don't know what he's so worked up about. At least I take them home. Although, I do keep my business sequestered to a guest room. No nasty shit in my bed. I have to sleep there afterward and I'm not sleeping in your wet spot. Nate gets them a room at the W and calls them a cab before he's even showered and dressed. Well, I'm assuming this new girl is an exception. I make a mental note to ask him how that's going later. He hasn't said much about her lately. Then again, we haven't really talked much lately. "That's Heidi Lemaire. The business owner we've spent the past hour talking about," *Nate interjects.*

Graham raises an eyebrow and turns to take another look at Heidi, as does everyone else at the table. "I can certainly see why you have expressed a sudden interest," *Graham observes. He watches Heidi a tad longer than I'm comfortable with. I keep my eyes on Heidi as she leaves. She never looks at me but I know she knows I'm watching. I can see it in the way she's breathing. I can tell she's consciously avoiding looking in my direction by the way she has her chin lifted and her eyes focusing on every other part of the room.*

Apparently Graham was watching her leave as well because he comments, "Damn, Nick. If I'd have known that's what we were dealing with, I would have had you send her to my office to could discuss her needs on a more....personal level."

Graham is a womanizer to the core. He's in a relationship with Callie Morrow, daughter of Nate's legal partner, and has been for the past three years. But he spends more time on out of town visits with women who think they're the only one than he does with his actual girlfriend. Ladies, if a man has to take you to a completely different area code to take you on a date, he's shady. No ifs, ands, or buts. I actually feel sorry for the women he's with. I'm no Mr. Darcy but at least my women know what they're getting from the start. I don't make false promises and I don't give false hope.

"Her needs have been met. Business and personal. Save your energy for Callie."

Graham laughs as if I he thinks I said something funny. "Easy there, Killer. Take your time with this one. I can be patient. It wouldn't be the first time I got your leftovers."

Nate pipes in, agitated, "Cripes! This isn't a game of pass the pussy. You're talking about a woman for fuck's sake." Graham continues laughing and drinking. He changes the subject to the latest baseball game. Maybe I won't have to kick his ass today.

That night I debated going to Heidi's but due to my overwhelming desire to finally claim what's mine, resolved to stay home with Johnnie. I respect her request to keep things rated PG while Hudson is home and have no intention of breaking her trust. Half a bottle later, I called it an early night. I booked a Friday morning flight to DC and I didn't want to miss seeing Heidi before I left. I wasn't sure what time she was coming but I was sure she would stick to tradition and call to confirm. The thought made me smile. She's so predictable.

Or not. She didn't call to confirm. As a matter of fact, she never even came by. I kept myself busy with bullshit to keep from acting like a pussy and calling to ask why she didn't show, but that didn't keep me from thinking about her.

I was just about to cave and call her then I found out she had been by my office this morning. And more than likely seen Taylor there. Shit.

My flight leaves in two hours and I'm chasing a woman all over the city. How can a mother fucker be pussy whipped when he hasn't even had a taste of the pussy? I'm embarrassed for myself. But here I am nonetheless, hunting her down. Needless to say, I missed the first flight time. Thank goodness for personal jets. Otherwise I'd be pissing off airline personnel all afternoon. I'm still pissing off someone, but those guys are on my payroll so I don't care. I finally get Heidi to text me back. She definitely saw Taylor in my office and she's not happy about it. It looks like I'm not the only one who's jealous. I smirk to myself.

Once I get her to tell me where she is, I hurry my ass to see her. I won't be back for two weeks and I can't leave knowing the last time she saw me, I was with another woman. I still kind of feel like shit for what happened with Taylor on Tuesday. Technically it wasn't cheating, but I know how I would feel if I found out Heidi's hands had been all over another man's dick just hours after being on mine. I'd probably kill a mother fucker. So I feel guilty. Which is also new for me.

I walk in the cathedral and watch as Heidi directs and instructs. They must be asking her fifty questions, yet she answers each and every one with a calm certainty. She smiles and reassures the woman whom I would assume is the bride that she will be here to make sure everything goes just as planned. That all the kinks will be worked out before they leave tonight and she, the bride, will have a perfect day. Heidi is so refined and confident in this setting. She goes through the motions as if she does this in her sleep. I am mesmerized by her.

She notices me and begins walking toward where I stand. As she approaches, I become acutely aware of what she's wearing. Instinct tells me I want to taste her. She wants it too. Even though she pretends to be mad at me, I can smell her arousal and it fucking turns me on. We go outside because she's worried about having an audience but I could care less. If she keeps going the way she's going, she's going to have to get used to it because patience is not one of my virtues. I want what I want, when I want it. And right now I want to taste her. She smells so fucking good. Her skin is so soft. I want to feel every inch of it. I want to feel her skin against mine. Flesh against flesh. Dripping with sweat. I lose all self-control when I'm with Heidi. And then she moans. It sounds like angels singing. I could listen to that sound every day. I should just unzip my pants, pull her panties to the side and fuck her crazy. I am practically fucking her right now. I can feel the head of my cock pressing through the fabric of my trousers into her. If she's wearing panties, there's not much to them. I have to take a step back before shit gets out of hand. She begs me not to stop. God knows I don't want to but I really have to go.

I've already missed one meeting. I make myself a promise right then and there that the minute I get back to New Orleans I'm making her mine. Completely.

CHAPTER TWENTY-SIX
Heidi

Saturday, June 21

Nick surprised me last night by showing up like that at the church. I knew he would try to back-step out of having Taylor in his office but I never expected him to miss flights and apologize in person. The gesture did impress me though. And oh my god the kiss. That was the best goodbye kiss I've ever had. He can leave anytime he wants as long as he kisses me like that before he goes.

Hannah was originally assigned to this afternoon's wedding, but she is out of town for the weekend so I took over. I am always blown away by the end result of all of our hard work. The tent is white with white fabric draped on the ceiling. There are crystal chandeliers hung every ten feet, tall Eiffel tower vase centerpieces with white wisteria bushes and dogwood branches, a light up bar with a subtle purple glow in the back, and cabaret tables with clear votive holders surrounding the dance floor. I'm standing in the center of it all, admiring the beauty of it. The look on the bride's face when she sees it is worth all the effort it took to create. Every event, every room, is my very own form of art. Taking a client's thoughts and creating something beautiful out of nothing is my passion. Knowing they appreciate it in the end and seeing how proud they are is what motivates me. I can't think of the forced eviction as the end of my dream. I refuse. I have to think of it as a new, new beginning. Maybe this will work out better anyway. It has to.

Once the food has been served and the cake has been cut and plated, it's time for the dance set where the guests are invited onto the dance floor. Joel finds me in the back of the tent near the refreshment station. "One of these times you're going to have to dance with me. You can't put me off forever you know," he flirts.
I bat my eyes at him in an overplayed gesture. "You know I would love nothing more than to dance with you, but I'm afraid it would be extremely unprofessional."
Joel snickers at my attempt at justification. "And here I thought it was because you know if you get that close to me, you won't be able to fight the temptation."
"Am I that transparent?"

146

He winks at me and then shakes his head. "No, I'm just that irresistible."
I give him a lighthearted shove to the chest and roll my eyes at him. My phone buzzes letting me know it's time for the bouquet toss and garter throw. "To be continued," I tell him as I walk toward the DJ set.

"You can run but you can't hide," Joel yells after me. He's trying to sound creepy but his smile is far from intimidating.

Remember what I said about basking in the glow of wedding bliss and beauty. Well, by the end of the reception the glow has fizzled to a flicker and I'm in serious need of a glass of wine. Or two. Joel helps me clean up and then invites me for a drink. I think nothing of it. We've had plenty of post-event wind down drink sessions in the past. So I accept and we meet up at Jackson Street Pub about an hour later. On the way there I try to call Nick but he doesn't answer.

Joel and I catch up on life and work over the first two drinks and by the third he starts getting personal.

"So this guy. The chocolate taster. You fucking him?" Did I mention Joel has no filter?

"He's a client, Joel." I try to be serious and professional but I'm two French martinis in and it's not as easy as it sounds. But Joel knows I don't play with my clients. I don't mess around with any vendors or contractors either. As a single woman running a business I can't afford to have that kind of stigma attached to my name. I keep my professional life strictly professional. But Nick didn't technically start out as a client so I can make an exception right?

"Not as of the Fourth, he's not." He takes a swig of his vodka and cranberry.

"Then I'll fuck him on the fifth," I say with a giggle.

"It didn't look like he wants to wait that long to me." He finishes off his drink and orders us each another round.

I take a good long sip from the skinny little bar straw. I'm not quite ready to discuss this yet. Maybe after one more drink....

It doesn't take me long to knock that one back. "I doubt he's got a case of blue balls if that's what you're saying."

"Heidi, *I* have a case of blue balls right now. And I got laid last night. You can't keep blowing him off like that. Or *not* blowing him off. Semantics."
I shake my head and wave my hand around as I take another drink. "No, no, no. I meeeean, don't feel bad for him. He's not lonely. Trust me."

"He's married?! You're fucking a married man?!" The louder his voice goes, the wider his eyes get.

"No! God no!" I give him a disgusted look. "But he has plenty of...let's see...what did his housekeeper call them? Extracurricular activities. Probably doing one right now. Mother fucker won't answer the phone." I'm drunk angry. The kind of angry that makes absolutely no sense unless you're drunk. You know, like getting mad because you go to the bathroom and come back to find your drink gone so you cuss the waitress under your breath. Until you realize you're at the wrong fucking table. Then you keep on cussing because you went to the wrong table in the first place. Joel is giving me the look. The look that tells me he's about to get philosophical drunk on me. We should probably stop drinking.

"I'm not saying he does have other extracurricular activities. But if he does. You can't be mad." He finishes up his fourth glass. "See, men are not monogamous by nature like women are. Something has to happen to make us that way."

I narrow my eyes and tilt my head to one side, giving him a classic *"what the fuck"* expression.

"Hear me out," he implores. "It's like opening the fridge and finding it empty. You don't get rid of the fridge. You just order take out." I straighten my head but still eye him curiously. "A man's gotta eat Heidi."

"But my fridge is full! I have lots and lots of goodies in my fridge. He just always opens it at the wrong time. Doesn't he know too much take out makes you fat?" I sigh and lay my head down on the table.

"Look I have never been there personally, but it does happen. When a man is satisfied with just one woman, it's for one of two reasons. He's afraid of losing something. Maybe her. Maybe half his shit. Who knows? Or he's in love. I've never been in love so I can't say."

I lift my head and look up at him. Who said anything about love? I'm just mad that he's out there giving it up to half the female population and just teasing the shit out of me. It's really not fair. I gave up my one booty call for him. Granted, it happened to be his best friend. *Psssh. Details.* I'm still a woman and I have needs dammit.

"Now. We dance," he demands, standing in front of me with his hand outstretched.

I don't think either one of us even knows the song that's playing but we are dancing like nobody's watching. And I am having fun. I don't even care that Blonde Bombshell and the man I assume to be her boyfriend are dancing right next to us. She keeps staring at me like I have three heads and all I really want to do is trip her. Now *that* would be some funny shit. The song ends and I'm ready to go. Joel takes care of the tab and calls Uber to bring us home. I go to bed thinking about Nick. And love. And

148

wondering if he's ever been in love. And what it would be like if he ever fell in love with me.

First thing this morning, I get a call from the nurse at Dr. Morad's office. She explains to me that although Hudson's count was abnormally high, there is no indication he has leukemia. We will, however, need to continue to monitor him because there is a defect with his liver. It doesn't seem to be flushing the toxins out of his body the way it's supposed to. This is what causes him to stay sick so much. There's pretty much a stagnant infection in his body and it's been there a while. This could lead to problems down the road and we have to watch for signs of serious infections. I pay attention to all that she's saying but keep repeating over and over in my head, *"HE DOESN'T HAVE LEUKEMIA!"* I can hardly wait to get off the phone to pick him up and squeeze him tight. I look up to the heavens and say a great big Thank You. It feels like I have stepped out from under a big black rain cloud and into the sun. I am practically jumping out of my skin. I think I actually may have even squealed.

I spent most of yesterday sleeping off Saturday. The rest of the day I spent cleaning, doing laundry, and debating if I should nurse my current hangover by starting on my next one. Once you hit thirty, alcohol doesn't agree with your body the way it did when you were twenty. Unless you drink for sport, which I don't. I drink for comfort. My life lately has pretty much made me a borderline wine addict.
Nick did return my call Saturday night. Late Saturday night. But I wasn't much for talking until later yesterday afternoon and by then he had called twice more so I lied and told him I was sick. Would *vodka flu* be considered a technical illness? We had our usual bedtime story conversation but this time it was followed by an unusual 'how was your day' conversation. The only people I truly care to talk about my day with are Shelly and Hudson. With everyone else it's more like going through the motions. You know, friendly talk but not a genuine conversation. I told him I stayed in bed most of the day, cleaned a little, and watched classic romance movies the rest of the afternoon. That led to a conversation about my love for classic romance. *Pride & Prejudice, Wuthering Heights, Romeo & Juliet, Tristan & Isolde*...just to name a few. Nick said he always

knew I was a romantic at heart. I told him not to read too much into it and then quickly changed the subject. I found out that a typical session day for him entails voting on the senate floor, which can be called at basically any given moment, and various committee and subcommittee hearings followed by being briefed on the following days' meetings and responding to emails. Sounds like serious business. He is a *very* busy man. The fact that he is even able to make time for me is flattering. The conversation flowed so easily, before I knew it we had been talking for almost two hours. He had to be up for an early session this morning so we said goodnight and I fell asleep once again thinking about Nick Knight.

The rest of my day flies by after my good news phone call. I have three houses to stage for a magazine shoot next week so it's pretty hectic. I don't even notice that Nick has called until midway through the second house.

It's dark when I finally pick Hudson up from his grandmother's, but that doesn't matter. We have to celebrate.

Hudson passes out in the back seat on the way home from our night out so I carry him to his room and take a long relaxing bath. I climb into bed, say one more Thank You, and turn off my lamp so I can try to get some rest. Just as I am dozing off, my phone rings. I see Nick's name and realize I never returned his call.

"If you're trying to give me a complex, it's working," he says when I answer the phone.

"I'm sorry. I promise I meant to call you. It's been…"

He interrupts, "Let me guess. Really busy."

I sigh. I know it sounds like a load of crap, but it's the truth. "It's okay. Just tell me you have time for me now." He sounds like I feel. Exhausted. I am so relieved about Hudson's results but I think the past four days of worrying have finally caught up with me. Now that I know he will be okay, my mind has stepped out of its defensive, block everything out, mode and returned to feeling normal again. And I realize I'm tired. Mentally and physically. It would feel so nice to have Nick here to hold me. Nothing sexual. Just a warm strong body here to hold on to. It's been so long since I've had that. Even in the last two years of my marriage to Cole, I never felt comforted or secure. We could lie in the same bed and never touch one another. We could spend hours in the same room, sitting right across from each other, and never speak a word. We were together, but I was alone. When I told him it was over, he didn't even seem surprised. We both knew it was coming. It was more a matter of which one would have the guts to say it first.

So here I am, fantasizing about Nick holding me. Wanting to need him. And it scares the piss out of me.

"I have all night. What would you like to talk about, Senator?"

He laughs at my use of his title. It used to irritate him when I said it, but I feel like he's gotten used to it by now. "No more senator talk. I've had enough of that word for one day. Tonight it's Nick. Just Nick."

"Long day at the office?" I ask, a hint of playfulness in my voice.

Since his office is at the White House, the conversation is kind of surreal. Here I am, on the phone with a man who just spent the day in the same vicinity as the President of the United States. I try to imagine him in one of those rooms you see on CNN or Fox news. The ones where everyone sits in a half-circle behind a microphone. I wonder what he does all day in Washington DC. One day I'll ask. But not today. Today he doesn't want to talk about it.

"You could say that," he answers vaguely. "I'm ready for the rest of my bedtime story."

Oh right. That. I almost forgot about that. Actually, I figured we had moved on from there and into creating our own bedtime stories. But if he wants a story, I'll give him his story.

The next chapter is apparently not as interesting to him as the ones before it. Nick snorts at some of the language. I assume he is critiquing as I go. His responses are typical guy responses to a book that makes them feel *less than*. When in reality, he is so much more than any fantasy I could dream up in the pages of a book.

"Hey, I didn't write the book. I'm just reading it. As per your request, mind you."

I envision the crooked smirk in response. "Very true. Please continue."

So I do until I'm burnt. One chapter is all he's getting tonight. "The end. For now," I say as I conclude the chapter. Thank goodness that's over.

"Well?" I know he has something to say about it. He always does.

"I like my stories better in person. Listening to it like this, when we're so far away, makes this bed seem pretty fucking lonely."

Well there's a surprise. He doesn't comment on anything I read. Good. Moving on. I want to tell him my good news about Hudson but being that he never knew the bad news, that would seem a little misplaced don't you think? But I *want* to share it with him. It's so weird. Normally I don't even share my last name with a guy and here I am wanting to share this incredibly personal moment.

"No bar at your hotel?" I'm picturing him watching the game and sipping his scotch after a long day. And then later lying under the sheets in some luxury hotel room.

"No hotel. I spend a lot of time here so I have an apartment."

Oh. That was a surprise. I didn't realize he was there *that* much. I guess it does make sense. I just never thought about it. A hint of disappointment comes over me at the thought of him being away often enough to need an apartment. Okay this is ridiculous.

He must sense he caught me off guard by the awkward silence. Or I wonder if he's caught on to what I must be thinking. "I have an early session and it's late here so I should go. Thank you for another insightful chapter." I can tell by his voice that he's smiling. And that makes me smile.

"Any time," I stop myself from calling him Senator, "Nick. Sweet dreams."

"Always, baby. Goodnight Heidi."

"Goodnight." I hang up and stare at my phone like I'm expecting him to jump out of it and into my bed. I go to sleep smiling like a kid who just found a bag of candy.

CHAPTER TWENTY-SEVEN
Heidi

Thursday, June 26

Today I have to finish up a residential design project I've been working on and check in on a commercial remodel. I also need to send out final reminder emails to all the vendors for next Friday. I made arrangements with Nick to do all the decorations next Thursday so Friday isn't so hectic. It's not only a political fundraiser, it also happens to be the fourth of July so I line up some last minute fireworks for the evening. I can't wait to see how they look on the lake behind his house. He sent me a good morning text this morning. Just a simple *"Good morning beautiful. Hoping you have an equally beautiful day."* But it was a nice surprise. Until I wonder if he sends anyone else *'good morning beautiful'* texts. Then the *happy me* tells the *party pooper me* to STFU and enjoy the compliment and have a beautiful day.

I'm wrapping up my walk through with the contractor for the remodel when my phone rings. It's Dr. Collins' office. *Odd.* She asks if I'm available to come in tomorrow morning. Of course I am. With all that's been going on with Hudson lately, even if I were in South America today, I'd make it to her office in the morning. There comes a point in your life when you try and try and try to see the positive in everything. The whole fall down seven times, get up eight scenario. You try to see the parade from the helicopter instead of from the road. The big picture. Like, every man you've ever cared about has been a total douchebag, but it's okay because all it takes is one to be worth it. And you'll find him. Be patient. Or spend your life building your dream so some asshole who feels entitled can snatch it away. But it's okay because at least you have a chance to try again. Or how about finding out your child doesn't have a terminal illness only to be told a few days later that... what? He has to have open heart surgery? But it's okay because... Because why? I'm having a really hard time with the *why* right now.

I finish up at the store and call it a day. Not even the fresh baked cookies helped my mood. And they usually do. They're fresh baked cookies. That's like 'happy' in an oven. At home I have a bowl of cereal for dinner, cuddle with my boy for my daily Hudson fix, and run a hot bubble bath. Nick calls right as I barely get all my clothes off and am about to step into heaven. I grab the Kindle from the nightstand before I get in because I know we'll be reading. Somehow just hearing his voice makes me feel better. My stomach flutters and my heart smiles. He doesn't say anything reassuring. He doesn't even know about Hudson's health concerns. But just the sound of his voice, so smooth and confident, is soothing. Better than cookies.

I tell him about my day, leaving out the call from Dr. Collins of course. He tells me how much he enjoys watching me work. How sexy I am when I take charge. And it makes me wish I could see him at work. Telling people his stance and going over his proposals. We finish up another chapter. I finish up two glasses of wine. I can sense a class discussion coming and I really want to avoid one so I think of a diversion. I snap a picture of me in the tub surrounded by nothing but bubbles and send it to him.

"Check your texts," I tell him. It's been a week since we've seen each other. A week since he's touched me and my body is aching for a piece of him.

A minute of silence. I'm guessing he's looking to see what I'm talking about. "Fuck. Heidi. What the hell? You're in the bathtub?"

I grin. Score. "Mmm hmm," I mewl.

"Does reading about Mr. Twitchy Palms make you hot baby?" he asks.

I close my eyes and lean my head against the back of the tub. "No Nick. You make me hot." It's true.

I hear him suck in a deep breath. "God that mouth."

My eyes pop open in offense. "You don't like it?"

"On the contrary, I love it," he assures me.

Good to know. I close my eyes again and continue my flirting. I smile to myself and mindlessly run my fingertips over my bare collarbone. "No. Not yet you don't. But you will." I lick my lips at the thought of the way he tastes. I can't wait to have my mouth on every last inch of him. I remember the day on his boat, how long and thick he was, and my mouth waters.

"Are you teasing me Heidi?" His tone bears a hint of warning. I'm not sure why but that excites me. Normally if I felt like a man might be angry or upset with me, my defenses kick into overdrive and I have a mini panic attack. But I don't get that with Nick. My senses react to him in a completely opposite way. A way I've never felt before. I like it. It's like my body knows he would never hurt me. Not with the intention of being mean or spiteful anyway. It trusts him.

"Hmm...Teasing would imply I have no intention of following through. And I fully intend on following through." My voice is deep and confident. Maybe it's the wine. Maybe it's the fact that this man drives my hormones insane.

I hear a low growl reverberate through the line. "Don't make plans for next Thursday."

"I'm already yours on Thursday. I have a party to get ready for, remember?" I remind him.

"You're mine every day, but next Thursday I'm going to show you exactly what that means," he vows.

Holy shit I can't wait until Thursday. "Promises, promises," I tease.

"No plans Heidi," he reiterates.

Okay I got it. No plans.

"Okay," I comply.

"And when you touch yourself later, make sure you're thinking of me. Not that asshole you read about." Wait. How did he know I was going to touch myself? Of course he knows. He knows how he affects me. Or maybe he's just being cocky. Either way it's still sexy.

"Haven't you figured out by now? It's always you." Pay attention ladies: The male ego can never have too much encouragement.

He chuckles. Softly, under his breath. But I still hear it. "Good night Heidi."

"Good night Senator." I smirk to myself at my use of his pet name. I know he feels like it's a formal address. But to me it's a reminder of who he is. The power he has. The title is like a uniform. It adds instant sex appeal. Not that he needs it. He doesn't correct me. He just laughs and ends the call. And he was right. I do touch myself. Thinking and wishing it was him the whole time.

Friday, June 27

I have three cups of coffee this morning. It's a nerve thing. I'm mentally preparing myself for whatever Dr. Collins has to say. I told Cole I was coming but didn't need him to meet me. I'll let him know the deal once I leave. We meet in her office. Between you and me, I'm ready for the day when I don't have to step foot in this room again. She sits down with his chart and opens it up before she begins her assault on my emotions. I strap on my imaginary bulletproof vest and get ready for her to fire.

"First of all, congratulations on the blood results," she says. Like I won a freaking coloring contest or something. Congratulations? *Seriously?* Yea, there we were, all the little sick kids, lined up in a row. And Hudson won. He made it through without getting leukemia. *Yay us!* I know she means well, but those four days were hell. Plain and simple. No parent should ever have to endure that.

I snap myself out of bitch mode and thank her. She smiles and continues, "As we spoke about on your last visit, it would be in Hudson's best interest to have corrective surgery for his ASD."

Yes. We did speak of that. I'm not thrilled about it. I nod silently and let her continue. "We have a highly qualified staff here at Oschner's. He's in the best hands possible. I'd like you to at least consider it."

I look away and then down at my hands where I've unknowingly been fidgeting with my fingernails. She closes his chart and gives me a comforting look. "Technology has come a long way. We can perform the surgery with very minimal invasion."

But you're still cutting him open. He'll still be put to sleep and they will still have to cut his heart open. She senses my apprehension and brings out the big guns.

"Heidi, the right side of the heart is becoming enlarged. There's too much blood being pumped into that side. If we don't repair the defect, he will have heart damage."

Well when you put it that way...

I sigh and give in. Reluctantly. "What exactly will you be doing? How soon do you need to do it? And how much is it going to cost?"

She explains the procedure to me and lets me know I have a little time to think about it. He will spend about four days in the hospital afterwards and there is a recovery period. The cost is the kicker. On average between forty and fifty thousand dollars. I almost need open heart surgery myself after that. There's no way I can come up with that kind of money. *Come on Heidi.* Stop feeling sorry for yourself. Right. A switch flips and I'm over being the victim. I remind myself that I've been kicked down before and got back up just fine. It's time to stand up and take control of this shit stain that is my life. Again.

I organize fundraisers for a living. Surely I can throw one together for this. Yes. I can. And that's exactly what I'll do. Then my baby boy can be on the road to living the life of a normal, healthy six-year old. I nod my head in agreement with myself. I've got this. I have to. Outside of a miracle, I'm his only hope.

I get busy sending emails and making phone calls all afternoon. I locate a venue and talk to Joel about catering. He offers to donate all the food. Yea. He's pretty awesome like that.

Tuesday, July 1

Hudson and I spent the weekend doing anything and everything he felt like doing. He's spending the next three weeks with his dad and I want to soak up all the time I can before he goes. We talk about the surgery and how it's the best thing for him. He doesn't seem too scared, and that helps me cope.

Nick and I continue our nightly ritual of two-hour phone calls, always ending with his bedtime story, making me more ready than ever to see him again. He sends me sexy pictures of himself lying in bed or just stepping out of the shower with nothing but a towel around his waist, and I return the favor with some flirty shots of my own.

He's quickly becoming someone I can't seem to get off my mind and I'm not sure if that's a good thing or something to be afraid of.

I'm tying up loose ends for Nick's fundraiser this Friday and don't even realize it's six o'clock until the girls are yelling at me to get dressed because we're going to kickboxing class.

Oh no. I can't go. Alex. Awkward. Shelly rolls her eyes and tells me to get over myself. That he's probably moved on and isn't even worried about me anymore. *Okay fine.* I get changed and go with them.

It's not as awkward as I thought it might be. Alex spends most of the class teasing my technique and saying that this is what happens when you skip classes. I vow to get him back when he least expects it. I almost forgot how good looking he really is. So different from Nick. Alex is your everyday good guy. Beautiful smile, curly hair, big brown eyes, and body to die for. While Nick is sex personified. Perfect in every physical way. The way he dresses, the way he walks, the way he talks. Even the tone of his voice says *"fuck me."*

After class, Alex corners me as I'm grabbing my bag and bottle of water. "Well this is a nice surprise." He's shirtless and sweaty and he's got the Cheshire grin plastered on his face.

I hand him my towel and return his smile. "I didn't want to let myself go, you know," I say, mocking what he told me the last time we spoke.

He moves his eyes over the length of my body. I had to go with the clothes I had at the store, which consisted of what he likes to call a sports bra (it's actually a fitted tank top that stops just above my belly button) and calf-length spandex pants.

"I say you've got a ways to go," he says as he wipes the sweat from his neck and face then throws the towel back at me.

Maybe I should have borrowed a t-shirt from someone. I suddenly feel anxious. Not in a bad way. More like in an *"I've been naked with this guy and we really shouldn't be this close with this little clothes on"* way. This was a bad idea. I shouldn't have come. I really do like Alex and I genuinely want to be friends. But he can't look at me *that* way. And he has seriously got to put some clothes on. And put that smile away. *What the hell is wrong with me?* You're effing horny that's what wrong with you. Nick has had me hanging by a thread for weeks and I am in serious need of a good hard fuck. But this is not the guy to do it. Get a grip on it and go home. Sleep it off. Two more days. That's all I have to wait.

My phone rings just as I'm grabbing it and my keys from my bag. Alex glances at the screen and sees that it's Nick.

"You should probably catch that. Don't want to keep him waiting," he says.

What in the world is that supposed to mean? The smile is replaced with an earnest expression as he waits to see whether or not I answer. Of course, I do. Alex shakes his head and laughs to himself as he walks away. I shouldn't care. I don't care.

I wave and mouth "Bye" to the other girls while Nick is telling me he only has a minute to talk. Alex is watching me from the behind the sign-in counter as I walk toward the door. He still hasn't put a shirt on. I'm betting that's not by accident. I arch an eyebrow and tilt one side of my mouth up and give a quick single wave before I go. He simply replies with a curt nod and proceeds to take a drink from his water bottle. *Men.* I can't worry about Alex now. Nick only has a minute and I need to hear his voice.

CHAPTER TWENTY-EIGHT
Heidi

Thursday, July 3

I made sure to get all my loose ends tied up for the party earlier in the week so I wouldn't have to deal with any more last minute details than I have to today. I'm hoping to start the set up early so I have most of the evening alone with Nick. I spent over thirty minutes in the shower last night paying extra attention to any areas that might need a little sprucing up. I am thoroughly shaved, waxed, exfoliated, moisturized, and whatever else you need to make sure the goods are ready for inspection. I even went as far as to get some color sprayed on yesterday afternoon. Because we all know, naked looks better tan. Talk about modesty. That lady had me lifting things and bending over and spreading things. Spray tans are not for the shy at heart. I wonder if men put this much effort into how we see them nude. Probably not. Come to think of it, I've never really seen a *"well-manicured"* man. If you know what I mean. It wouldn't kill them to get the trimmers down there once in a while. It's a two-way street boys. I'm not saying Nair it bare. I have seen that. One night on an unforgettable elevator ride during Mardi Gras. Not pretty. But a good trim occasionally would be nice. Sorry. I got sidetracked.

So here I am, sporting pretty, black, lace underwear underneath a fitted navy blue tank dress with a lace overlay. The dress stops just above my knee and I'm wearing black strappy heels to make my legs look longer. Nick doesn't get in until after noon so he arranged for me to meet one of his staff at his home so we could get started with the decorating. I have two other guys I hired for set up follow me there.

We get all the tables and chairs in place and begin working on hanging lights. I walk out to one of the two docks Nick has on the lake. The one to my left houses his yacht but the one to my right seems more for entertaining. There's a long pier leading up to a large square covered pavilion. It just sits there, out in the water. There are four rattan sofas with bright blue cushions arranged in a square with a fire pit in the center of them. A ceiling fan hangs in the middle and rope lights frame the beams on the roof of entire structure. I find myself thinking if this were my home, *this* would be my home. It seems so incredibly peaceful. I also find myself thinking I love everything about Nick's home. The location. The water. The boat. The floor to ceiling windows along the entire wall of the back, making it possible to see the lake no matter where you are inside. Then I glance at *Tranquility* and remember how it felt to finally touch him. It's like someone turned a boiler on inside of me and the heat is slowly starting to simmer until I feel it deep in my core. No man has ever affected me this way. Everything about him has me hypnotized. The more I know, the more I want to know.

I'm walking back up to the main house when I see Nick standing in the window in the kitchen. He's wearing a black suit with a charcoal gray shirt and blood red tie. His legs are spread even with his shoulders and his hands are in his pockets. He's just watching me with that crooked grin on his face. God that grin. I bypass my guys, stopping just long enough to show them where to hang the next string of round bulb lights, and walk into the kitchen where he is.

His grin widens as I approach him slowly, though his hands never leave his pockets. I stop directly in front of him and look up into his golden eyes. It feels like months since I've seen him and now that he's here, standing in front of me, every single fiber of my being is on alert. I hold it together on the outside even though the on the inside I feel like a thousand little electric currents are running through my veins. I'm excited, intimidated, and a little nervous all at the same time. *This is it.* I know it. He knows it. Today is the day. No more waiting. No more wanting. It's going to happen. *Finally.*

I reach out and run my fingers over his tie. "So were you planning on coming to help or would you rather just stand here and watch?" I use the lighthearted remark in hopes to calm my own nerves as well as to assess his mood.

His mouth twitches on one side, highlighting the adorable dimple there. He moves forward a step, bringing us chest to chest, his head right beside mine. I can feel the short hairs on his jaw against my temple. He's looking straight ahead, out the window instead of at me. My breath hitches but his voice remains calm and smooth. Like he's not affected one bit by our closeness. But I can feel the proof against my belly that he is.

"Sometimes I feel like getting dirty. Other times I just prefer to watch." I don't know if he's talking about actual work or something else but all my brain hears is *"Sex, sex, and more sex."*

I lick my lips and focus on the man in front of me. "And how are you feeling today?"

Nick moves his head so we are now face to face. He then looks down at me, finally pulling his hands from his pockets. His long fingers trace small circles on the tops of my shoulders then run down the sides of my arms.

"Today I plan on getting very dirty. Unless you've changed your mind, that is."

I'm feeling bold and I can't take another minute of him not touching me. I take his hand and slide it under my dress and up the inside of my thigh, stopping when we reach the trim of my panties. His fingers barely brush through the material yet the sensation it sends through my body is as intense as if he had ripped them off and screwed me right then.

"Does it feel like I've changed my mind?"

He traces his finger back and forth along the edge of my panties, sliding it further inside each time. God his touch feels so good. He dips a finger deep inside causing me to suck in a sharp breath. This is the first time he's touched me, *really* touched me, and I am already addicted to it.

"Goddammit Heidi," he swears as he takes his finger out and grabs my hand, pulling me out of my stupor and into the mudroom.

"You make me want to fuck you right here and now," he growls as his body presses mine against the wall. He places his hands on the wall on either side of my head, locking me in place. I reach out to unzip his trousers, sticking my hand inside to pull out the stiff flesh that has been digging into my stomach.

I pull my bottom lip between my teeth and look into his eyes. "Then fuck me," I demand.

He takes my hands in one of his and holds them against the wall above my head. With his other hand he reaches under my dress and yanks on my panties. The material digs into the flesh on my hip before finally tearing. He pulls the ripped lace from my body and bunches it up in the palm of his hand before sticking it in his pocket. My heart is beating like I just ran a marathon. I am so freaking wet I feel like we may need to watch our step when we leave this spot. He just *ripped* my panties off. And put them in his pocket. Holy shit. He's watching my reaction intently.

After a moment his eyes fall to my mouth. He licks his bottom lip then looks back into my eyes. "Such a beautiful mouth. Lips so full. So pink. So perfect. Hard to imagine words like that would come out of it." My expression is apologetic. I hope I didn't offend him.

"It drives me fucking nuts. It's like I'm looking at an angel but listening to sin," he confesses.

I don't say anything. I don't need to. My body speaks for me. My hips push forward to find his as my lips part, inviting him to kiss me. He picks up the signals and leans forward, pressing his soft lips against mine. His pants are still unzipped and my dress is slowly creeping up my thighs. As the kiss deepens, our bodies seek each other out, grinding and thrusting.

Nick pulls himself away. He nods his head toward the direction of the back patio and whispers in my ear. "Do you want me to send them home?" He looks me in the eye, breathless, "Because I will. Right now. I'll cancel the whole damn party. Shut this mother fucker down, take you upstairs, and keep you there until we don't even know what day it is."

Shit. The party. The guys. I lean my head back against the wall and take in a deep breath. I close my eyes for a second to regain my composure then look at him and smile. "Sorry. I guess I got carried away."

He releases my hands so I can straighten my dress and run my fingers through my hair for a quick fix.

Nick matches my smile and brings my hand to his lips for a soft kiss. "You think you're the only one, baby? I've been going crazy for days. All I could think about was getting home. To you."

So he was excited too. My stomach does flips and my heart dances. This amazing, perfect man wanted to rush home. To see me. "I should probably get back out there before one of them comes in here." Honestly, I could care less who comes in here or what they do out there. Personally, I like the *take me upstairs idea*, but this party is a big deal so I need to focus on that for now.

Again Nick places a hand on each side of my head and leans forward just enough to run the tip of his nose along the side of mine. He speaks softly, "Probably," and I can feel his breath on my face. He smells like cinnamon and whiskey. I resist the overwhelming urge to lift my chin a couple of inches and take his mouth again. Instead I situate him back into his pants and zip him up. I feel a quick puff of air on my cheek as he silently chuckles at the move. He takes a step back and shows me the lopsided grin. "Later, then," he says affirmatively. Then he moves his hands from the wall, allowing me to step around him and make my way back outside. Nick is right behind me, unbuttoning his suit jacket as he walks outside. He takes it off and throws it over the back of a nearby chair, followed shortly by the red tie, leaving just the black pants, gray shirt, and a black vest. He looks like absolute sin. And sin never looked so good. He unbuttons his cuffs and rolls his sleeves up to his elbows. His eyes never leave mine as I watch him get more comfortable.

"I'm all yours. Tell me what you want me to do." He smirks at the obvious double meaning.

I get him to help hang a few lights and rearrange a couple of tables while the other guys set up an outdoor tent for the band and dance floor. About forty-five minutes later, we're all done for the day. Nick lets the guys out and meets me back on the rear patio where I am straightening the white gauze fabric we used for outdoor curtains. I gather the fabric in the middle and tie a black rope around it for decoration. Nick stands in the doorway, leaning against the frame.

"Heidi," he says simply, his tone commanding my attention.

Oh god. This is it. We're alone. The way my name rolls off his tongue sends shivers down my spine. I take a deep breath and turn to face him. His eyes are dark and his expression utterly serious.

"No more work." He slowly shakes his head as he directs me. "It's time to come inside."

CHAPTER TWENTY-NINE
Heidi

Nick takes my hand and leads me inside. "I want to take you on a tour," he says.

He leads me through the living room to a hallway. We see two guest bedrooms and a bath then we approach a third room in which the door is closed.

"What's in there?" I inquire.

Nick looks at the door briefly then looks back at me. "Just another bedroom. Nothing special," he dismisses the room altogether.

All the rooms are to one side of the hall with the exception of the bathroom, which is on the left. There is a very large mirror on the wall opposite the bedroom he didn't show me. I watch as he slides the mirror to one side, revealing a second, shorter hallway. *Clever.* Down the second hall are two rooms: a library and an office. These rooms have the same floor to ceiling windows with the same view of the lake as the kitchen, living, and dining rooms. We walk past the library, which also looks onto the front property, and into the office. Nick lets go of my hand and regards me as I give the room a quick once-over. There is a large dark walnut desk, facing the window, in the center of the room with folders and papers stacked neatly in one corner, a phone in the other, and a desk calendar with all sorts of markings on it in the middle. Behind the desk are three bookcases of the same walnut finish that stand about eight feet high and are filled with what looks like red and gold law encyclopedias. In front of his desk is a single cognac leather chair. To the left of the desk is a wall that houses framed photos of Nick in various baseball positions. I smile to myself. It figures he'd be athletic. He's probably good at everything he does.

There's a long narrow console table under the photos with various newspapers and magazines on it. I would assume they include articles about him inside. Why else would he keep them?

I'm looking out the window, resting my hip against the side of his desk, when he walks up behind me. He moves my hair to one side, draping it over my shoulder. Instinctively I move my head to that side, offering my now bare neck to him. He places soft kisses on my skin, beginning at the top of my shoulder and working his way up to the spot just below my ear. His hands grab my hips and move them away from the desk so he can slide my dress slowly up around my waist. He steers me around so I'm facing away from the window.

"Spread your legs baby," he says coolly.

I grab hold of each side of his desk and do as I'm told. He slides his hands up the side of my body and then places his palm flat at the top of my spine, right between my shoulder blades, and gently pushes me forward. I follow his lead and go the rest of the way until my breasts are pressing against the hard wood. I'm literally face down, ass up, bent over his desk. He brings his hand back down to my bottom, giving it a gentle rub and I wonder for a split second if he's going to spank me. I've always thought I'd laugh at a man for smacking my ass, but right now I find myself *wanting* it from him. I suppose he decided not to because his hand subtly moves between my thighs. He runs a finger along my dripping wet slit and groans as he drops to his knees and touches me again.

"I love you like this. So wet. So ready for me." He pulls my swollen clit into his mouth, drawing it in slowly, as if he's trying to stretch it as far as he can. Then he lets go of the hard nub and begins to flick his tongue back and forth on the same spot, slowly at first, lapping at it, then faster and more determined. And just as I am about to come undone, he stops and draws it back into his mouth once again. His tongue runs up one side of my opening and back down the other. Over and over again. Like an artist who has mastered his trade. I am moving with him, desperately trying to find my release. It feels *so* good. My insides are trembling and clenching. I can feel little pulses of pleasure rippling through me, getting more and more intense with every stroke of his magic tongue. And then everything goes black and all I know is what I'm feeling. Nothing else matters. Not the fact that I'm screaming his name. Or the fact that I've knocked the phone off the desk. Or that I'm frantically fucking his face right now. Just this feeling. This deep, deep, throbbing and wave of complete and utter bliss that is taking over from my core all the way to my toes. He sucks my clit into his mouth and grabs my hips to hold me still as I come. My body is still experiencing the aftershocks of my intense orgasm when he pulls me down onto his lap. I straddle him as he sits on the floor. He tucks a wild strand of hair behind my ear and studies my reaction.

"Holy shit Nick. Are you trying to kill me?" I tease, still breathless.

He smirks and thrusts his hips upward, reminding me of his erection.

"That's the plan. Death by orgasm." His smirk grows into an impish grin. I lick my lips and smile back.

"Well I can certainly think of worse ways to die," I reply as I rock back and forth on his lap, causing friction between his hard dick and my still throbbing clit.

He lifts his hips and pushes into me again. "Ready for more so soon?" His voice is strong yet laced with a hint of amusement. I unbutton his vest and slide it off him.

"Please Nick, don't make me wait again," I plead.

He brings his mouth to mine, stopping just centimeters from my lips. "Tell me what you want Heidi," he demands, speaking barely above a whisper. I begin undoing the buttons on his shirt, spreading it open as I make my way down. "You, Nick. I want you."

Despite the incredible orgasm he just gave me, my body still craves...*him*. I need to feel him. Completely. Not just his touch. Not just his words. Not even his tongue. *Him*. "I need you." The desperation I feel echoes in my voice.

I finally peel his shirt off and let it fall to the ground behind us. Then I reach between us and unbuckle his belt. I get the top button of his trousers undone before he stops me.

He places his hands on my hips and pulls me closer. "Come here baby," he says as he runs his hands up and down my back, soothing me. But I don't want him to soothe me. I want him to fuck me. "Here, come with me," Nick urges, using his hips to shift my body off his lap. He stands, extending his hand to help me up.

He leads me back down the hallways and up a set of stairs off the living room. At the top of the stairs there's a loft overlooking the living and dining rooms. Off of the loft there are two sets of double doors. He leads me through the set to the right. The room is large and open. Centered on one wall is a king size bed with four tall posts on each corner. The posts are square and thick at the bottom but taper in at the tops and there are rails connecting each post to the next, like a canopy bed, only masculine. I walk to the bed and hold onto one of the posts as I try to imagine him sleeping here. Nick comes up behind me and unzips the back of my dress. He slips the straps off my shoulders causing the material to fall to the floor in a puddle around my ankles. I stand silent and still as he unfastens my bra and slides it off as well. "Turn around," he says resolutely. I obey. I feel very self-conscious and on display. But only for a moment because now here I am, looking at him, shirtless, shoeless, with his pants unbuttoned and forget that I'm naked. His body looks as if it were carved in stone. Every inch, every crease, right down to that enticing little "V" that is my arrow to heaven, is perfectly precise. His skin is the most beautiful golden brown tone and is silky smooth to the touch. I run my hands across his broad shoulders down to his biceps that don't even need to be flexed for me to feel the solid muscle there. There's the lightest

166

dusting of hair on his chest. If I weren't so close I wouldn't have even seen it, but it adds to his masculinity. I trace a trail of figure eights with my fingertips from his chest down to his perfectly sculpted abs. The entire time I'm admiring him, he's gazing at me intently. "Fucking beautiful," he states simply. *That's exactly what I was thinking..*

Nick lifts me up and sets me on the bed. I scoot myself back and lie down. He pulls my legs up and removes my heels one at a time, then runs his hands along the back of my calves, massaging me. I pull my legs up and bend my knees so that my feet are flat on the bed. He is still standing, watching as I run my hands along the inside of my thighs, stopping just as I reach the apex. I slowly run a finger over the smooth, wet flesh there. Nick begins to remove his trousers and I remove my hand as I watch him. He takes my hand and places it back where it was. "No. Don't stop. Let me watch you." I obey, rubbing slow, wet circles over my swollen flesh.

Once his pants are off, he leans over me, and takes my nipple in his mouth. The warmth and wetness of his mouth on my breast combined with the quickening of my pace on my clit creates a surge of pleasure through my body. He's so close. I'm naked. He's naked. I can feel his erection on my thigh. I need more. I arch my back, offering him more of my breast. He licks the hard bud once more then pulls it into his mouth and clamps down on it with his teeth. Just hard enough to send tiny shock waves to my core. I moan. Damn, that felt really good. He does it once more. *Oh my god.* I thrust my hips up, seeking out the orgasm that is slowly building.

"That's it baby. Take the pleasure with the pain." I take a deep breath, begin to still my ever quickening fingers, and contain my orgasm for now. I'm not coming again unless he is inside of me.

I curl my fingers in his hair and pull his face to mine. After placing a slow seductive kiss on his full lips, I plead with him. "Please Nick." He teases me by rubbing the thick head of his cock along my slick entrance. I buck my hips, urging him inside.

"All of you. I want all of you."

Nick reaches between us and guides himself in. Achingly slow. He's fucking huge. I gasp as he fills me to the hilt. My body stretches to accommodate him as he holds himself in place for a moment. Good god. If he goes any further he's going to come back out my belly button. He fills me. Completely. He guides himself back out and in again a couple of times, allowing me to adjust. It feels so good. *He* feels so good. It's like he's completed a part of me that was missing. Like I've been walking around with no leg and now

I have a leg and I never want to be without my leg again. My body will never be the same after Nick.

"You feel so good inside," he groans. His voice echoes the way I feel. He locks his arms under my knees, lifting my ass off the bed as he pulls my knees toward my chest. He braces himself with his hands beside my head. Holy shit he feels even bigger this way. I can't move. He has me locked in place. He rocks slowly into me at first but quickly picks up his pace. Soon he's fucking me. Hard. I can't take it. I reach over my head and grab the headboard to steady myself. He hits that spot and my body goes haywire. "Right there Nick. Stay right fucking there," I moan. He continues pounding. The same spot. Over and over. Until for the second time today, my body trembles and quivers with the most intense orgasm I've ever had. I close my eyes and cry out as the waves crash over me. I re-open them just in time to witness the sexiest thing I've ever seen. Nick clenches his teeth together and sucks in a sharp breath before closing his eyes and shouting a gritty "Fuuuuuck." His lips are parted and I can see him taking in a breath and holding it for a second before exhaling it back out. My insides continue to clench around him as he fills me. When he opens his eyes, he finds me staring at him, biting my bottom lip. He backs off of me just enough to allow me to straighten my legs, which I quickly wrap around his. He's still inside of me. Half hard. I feel it flex and wonder if it's an involuntary thing or if he's doing that on purpose. The thought makes me smile. He narrows his eyes at me curiously and smiles back.

"Hey," he says merely.

"Hey," I say back. I feel it again. The pulse of his not fully erect dick inside of me sets off delicious sensations in my insides. My body reacts and my hips begin to move underneath him. He arches a brow and I blush and shrug, but continue to move against him. I find myself rocking back and forth underneath him, taking whatever of him I can get. He presses his pelvic bone into me. I didn't think I could come again but the pressure against my clit along with the feeling of having him inside of me has me right there. He's not even hard but just having him *there* feels so good. He's watching me as I greedily take more. I stare back at him, unable to look away. I moan softly as I come once more. It wasn't as intense this time but it leaves me feeling completely sated.

Nick's eyes are dark and full of want. "I could watch you come all day."

I feel my cheeks heat up. I'm sure it's not every day he has women giving themselves an orgasm by grinding his pelvic bone and fucking his semi. I couldn't help myself. It was the pulsing. He should have never started that penis flexing thing. He rolls off of me and lays on his side.

"You better eat your Wheaties if you plan on making that a new hobby, Senator," I tell him playfully.

He graces me with my favorite tilted smile. "If that's a challenge baby, consider it accepted," he says as he mindlessly trails his fingertips over my body, tracing circles around my nipples, then down my abdomen and across my hip bones. Maybe it's my body's reaction to the hyper-orgasms I just experienced, maybe it's the fact that I just shared a highly intimate moment with the possibly most perfect man in the universe, maybe it's fear of losing this feeling I've been waiting so long to finally find, or maybe my body is just happy it finally got what it's been craving since the first time Nick touched me, but my emotions are in overdrive and I have the overwhelming urge to cry. Not a sad cry. More like a happy cry, or a relieved cry. I don't cry. But I want to. Nick tucks a stray lock of hair behind my ear. "You're staring at me. Why?"

I take a moment to consider my words. I've never been one for serious. It's not my thing. But I want him to know how he makes me feel. "I feel like you've just given me the first hit of a drug I'm not gonna want to stop taking." He licks his lips and moves in to kiss me.

"Then it's a good thing I'm not going anywhere."

CHAPTER THIRTY
Nick

Sexy as hell. That's what she is. As many times as I've played this moment over in my head the past week, nothing compares to the reality of having Heidi here, in my arms, utterly sated. The way she fell apart for me has me wanting to keep her falling apart for me, every hour of every day. The way she parts her lips and holds her breath until the pleasure takes over and she can't help but to cry out. Then she licks her lips after, like she's just experienced an incredibly satisfying meal. But even sexier than that, is knowing that she's finished for any other man. That it's me she's addicted to now, me that she craves.

She's looking at me the way you look at someone when you have something to tell them but aren't quite sure how. And it scares the shit out of me. Does she regret this already? Did I fuck it up? That's all I could think until I find the courage to ask her. She tells me, in no certain terms, that she can't get enough of me. That she is, without a doubt, completely mine. *Thank fuck.* Because I'm in this thing. Balls deep.

I get out of bed and extend my hand to her. "Come with me."

She complies without question. No reservation. No disputing. She just...trusts me. And that fucking turns me on. We go into the bathroom where I start the shower. I lather her up with soap and rinse her off, paying special attention to every detail of her beautiful body. Then she drops to her knees and starts pumping my erection. She runs her tongue from my sac all the way up the length of me, circling my swollen head before working back down. Then she starts sucking. And pumping. And humming. *Fucking humming.* Or moaning. I don't even know but holy shit. It doesn't take long before her mouth and fist push me over the edge. *Mother fucker.* I have fantasized about that mouth. I've stared at it and wondered what it would feel like. But damn. Even my active imagination didn't see that one coming. And then she soaps me up and washes me off. Balls and all. And it feels like I'm coming all over again. Even though there's no physical evidence to show that I am.

Heidi looks pleased with herself as I dry her off and wrap her in my robe. Shit, she should be. Her mouth had me shooting off like a volcano. Damn she looks good in my robe. I throw on a pair of lounge pants while she brushes her hair. She walks out of the bathroom looking like my own personal angel wrapped in white. She rakes her teeth over her bottom lip and smiles shyly at me.

"Would you care for a drink?" I offer. *I know I need one.*

"A drink would be nice," she politely replies.

I chuckle to myself. No ma'am. This is no time for manners. I know how dirty that mouth really is. I take her hand and lead her downstairs. Built in to one wall of my kitchen is a wine cooler. It's about six feet high by four feet wide and houses wines from vineyards all over the world. As well as a couple of bottles of my favorite scotch. "Do you have a favorite?" I ask.

"Moscato. White or red. No pink," she replies quickly. So she likes the sweet stuff. I figured that.

She's leaning against the island with one hip propped against the edge. "So, do you always run around Washington DC with no underwear on?" she asks as I hand her a glass of white wine. Her expression is serious but her tone is light.

I knock back a stout sip of my scotch. This woman has my senses all fucked up and my nerves hyper-reactive. I can't think. I know she was attempting lighthearted conversation but I have other plans for her.

"No. That was strictly for your benefit," I explain as I step behind her. I lean forward and speak directly in her ear. "Just like you not wearing any is strictly for mine."

She sets her glass on the counter and tilts her head to one side. I wrap my arms around her waist and untie the robe. My hand makes its way inside, grazing the bottom of her full breast. I cup the whole thing and bring my fingers to her hard little nipple. She inhales a sharp breath. Then I pinch. And she moans. "See? If I want to do that, for example," I clarify. She likes when I pinch her here. She has no fucking idea. All the things I want to do to her. She wiggles her ass against me. Her body is begging for mine. My other hand snakes around her waist and down her stomach to find her wet slit. She's ready for me again already. *So wet.* I spread her juices over her swollen clit and whisper, "Or if I feel like doing this..." Now she's writhing as I touch her. My Heidi. So eager.

"Turn around baby," I tell her.

She abides. Her eyes are filled with lust as she looks up at me. I grab her by the hips and sit her up on the counter in front of me. The robe is split open, showing me only a small part of her breasts but her legs are spread, allowing me to admire the rest of her. I drop my pants to my ankles and scoot her to the edge. She wraps her legs around my waist and holds onto my biceps while I sink into her. She's so hot. So fucking hot. And she fits around my dick like her body was made just for me. Every time I thrust full force, I feel myself hitting the bottom. She squeezes my arm as I fuck her. The harder I fuck, the harder she squeezes. And that just encourages me to fuck her harder. She throws her head back and hugs her legs tighter around my waist. I know she's almost there so I lean forward and give her what I know she wants. I take her nipple in my mouth and bite down. *Jackpot.* Heidi bucks forward and clutches me tightly between her legs as she yells to the world that she's coming. I let up on her nipple, gently licking and kissing it while she rides out her orgasm. A few intense seconds later I'm right there with her. Mother fucker. I think my knees are going to give out.

We're both taking slow, deep breaths just trying to get everything back to normal. I can feel the sweat running down my back. Heidi is running her fingers through my damp hair. She has such a gentle touch. But I have a feeling she doesn't want to be touched gently. Not all the time anyway. I can tell by how excited she gets when I use my teeth. Or when I fuck the shit out of her. So many layers to this beautiful woman in front of me. And I plan on discovering them all, one at a time, until she is truly and completely mine.

The alarm beeps twice, indicating an outside door has been opened, and a voice echoes through the living room and kitchen. "Nick. I know you're home. I saw your..." *Fucking Monica.*

She stops short the second she steps into the kitchen. One day she'll learn to mind her own damn business. All the blood leaves Heidi's face, leaving her pale and obviously mortified. Me? I don't give a fuck. You walk in a man's home unexpected, you should be prepared for pretty much anything. Monica's been around a while. I'm sure she's seen worse. But Heidi. Heidi is not thrilled with the situation. She swiftly drops her hands from my head and pulls the robe tight around her body. I inhale a deep breath so I don't lose my shit, and pull my pants up before I turn to address Monica.

"Shit Nick! Since when do you...." She pauses to reconsider her words. "You know what? Nevermind." Monica closes her eyes and shakes her head like she's attempting to shake the image from her mind. She sets a plate covered with aluminum foil on the counter. "I brought you dinner." She's looking at me like it's *my* fault she walked in on what she just walked in on.

What the hell? What is she? My mother? I don't owe her any explanation. Heidi slides down from the counter and starts to leave the room. I grab her wrist and pull her next to me. I can feel her resistance to my touch even though she's trying not to make it obvious. My eyes search hers for a clue as to what she's thinking. She smiles up at me. It's weak and meant only to soothe me but it's her way of letting me know she's fine so I accept it and let her go.

"Just going to the bathroom," she assures me. Then she pops up on her tip toes and kisses my cheek before disappearing up the stairs.

I look over to Monica who is about to leave as well. "Thank you for the food."

I'm sure she's just as embarrassed, although she doesn't show it. She's tough. At least I came out of the whole Matthew/Elise thing with nothing but a bruised ego and fucked up opinion of love. She got all that plus one. Olivia is a beautiful little girl but I can't help but think she is a constant reminder of her father. And that can't be easy on Monica. I admire her for the mother she is. I see the struggle she has as a single parent.

My mind immediately shifts to Heidi and her son. I wonder if she has the same struggles. If his father is involved in their life. The thought sparks a twinge of jealousy that he shares something so intimate with her. That he is a permanent part of her life. I wonder if they still see each other.

There's so much more I want to know about her. I could spend an entire day listening to her tell me about herself. Except that when she's near me, I can't keep my hands off her so I doubt we'd get much talking done.

Monica interrupts my thoughts before they get too deep. "You're welcome. Sorry for....interrupting," she says. Her tone is not the usual badass, defense-mode tone I'm used to. It's almost apologetic. Meek. That's different.

"Don't worry about it. Make sure you have a nice dress for tomorrow night. I have some important people I want you to meet." She smiles and nods, but says nothing as she leaves.

Monica graduates nursing school soon and I plan on introducing her to some pretty influential people in the medical industry. I don't mind helping her out but she can't live in my pool house forever.

I spot Heidi beside my bed as I enter the bedroom. She is fully dressed and holding on to a bed post as she slips on her heels. Surely she's not leaving. I get that she's embarrassed but damn, there's no need to be hasty.

"Going somewhere?" I ask.

She smoothes her dress and looks at me thoughtfully. "You may not know this but I have a pretty big party tomorrow." Her eyes flash a hint of playfulness and I try to read whether or not she's upset.

"I may have heard something about it," I say as I continue moving toward her.

A stray piece of hair falls over her eye so I reach out and tuck it behind her ear. Her lips part as she sucks in a breath and closes her eyes. Seeing the way I affect her is intoxicating. She gives me a little taste of it and I get greedy and want more. So I keep touching her. Then I kiss her. Slowly. Softly. I want to savor every second of her.

"Have dinner with me." I give her a minute to reply. When she doesn't, I continue, "If you still want to go home afterwards, I will bring you. Promise." She looks up at me with those big green eyes and wets her lips. I swear when she looks at me like this I would do anything she asks.

She nods and replies, "Okay."

I hope my smile isn't too cocky. Fuck it. I'm pleased. She's not going home. Not if I can help it. Not tonight. Ten minutes later we're in my truck and on our way to Ruffino's.

CHAPTER THIRTY-ONE
Heidi

Nick has a way of convincing me, without words, to do whatever he wants without me ever knowing he dominated the situation. He's such a natural politician. The kitchen incident actually worked to my benefit. It gave me a minute to regroup. This whole thing was going way too fast. I had no intention of spending the night with Nick. Sure, the sex was amazing. Okay I take that back, I've had sex. What we had...was *not* sex. Someone needs to invent another word for it. What I had with Nick was an incredibly intense and almost surreal experience. He took my body to levels of pleasure it has never been before. It's like we were dipping into some crazy feeling people aren't meant to feel. You know, like how we only use a certain percent of our brains because it would make us crazy if we used the whole thing. It's like that. But with the senses. He's messing with me. From the inside out. I'm having a hard time separating the physical from the emotional. And I can't fall into that trap again.

My mind was made up. I was going home to regain my sanity before seeing him tomorrow night. And in he comes, with his smooth voice and silver tongue. So here we are, having dinner at some expensive restaurant on the river. He's just sipping his whiskey while he watches me eat. If I weren't so freaking hungry I may be a little uncomfortable with it but I'll save that drama for later. I'm starving. That stare though. God it's like he's sending Jedi mind sex from his head to mine. He's just sitting there, all crooked smile and seductive eyes, swishing the gold liquid around in his glass of ice before taking in a mouthful. I have to put down the fork and admire him for a moment. The Veal Michael is good but nothing is more satisfying than that look. "What?" I ask.

He takes another sip. "Just thinking."

I slide my plate to the side so it's not a distraction. "Oh? About what?" I make an attempt at imitating his sexy sip.

Nick sets his glass on the table, never moving his eyes from mine. "I don't want to go home alone," he states plainly.

Here we go. The moment of truth. If I tell him no, I risk upsetting him and give up another earth shattering round of sextasy. If I say yes, I risk falling for him. As if I haven't already done that. But at least I set up boundaries and stay in control. I take another sip. The red wine is tart and dry. Not what I'm used to. So it's not helping much. I set the glass down and try not to be serious with my reply.

"With that smile, I doubt you go home alone often," I tease.

He brings his elbow up to the table and rubs the stubble trail from his jaw line to his chin. He's choosing his words. Maybe I shouldn't have made a joke of it. "Let me say it another way then...I want you to come home with me."

Does he even know what he's asking? He may have random sleepovers all the time, but I try not to make it part of my routine. Sleeping with someone, in the literal sense, is a significant symbol of comfort and trust. You're entirely vulnerable when you sleep. And then there's the whole holding each other close...for hours..thing. Not to mention the drool. And you don't have the intermission period to collect your thoughts and remind yourself that this is temporary, a means to an end. It's incredibly intimate. He may not think much of it. But I do. He must sense my hesitation because he continues before I am able to object.

"I'm not asking for a kidney Heidi. I just want more time with you. Is that such a bad thing?" *I guess not.*

"No."

He smiles again. "I'm not ready to let you go yet. I don't know if I ever will be."

Oh god. Did he really just say that? I think my heart just stopped beating. You can't just go around looking like he does, saying things like *that* to women after you just gave them epic back to back orgasms. That sort of thing causes our brains to turn to mush. The waiter saves the day, coming to collect the check at that moment. Nick knows he threw me for a loop. He chuckles and reaches for my hand as he stands. "Let's go baby."

I persuade him to stop by my apartment so I can grab a toothbrush and some fresh clothes. I glance at him, leaning in the doorway while I pack my bag, taking in the way his jeans hug him in all the right places and the sleeves of his gray crew shirt fit snug around his biceps and across his toned chest. Everything he does is sexy. They could make a reality show called *The Senator* and just have cameras follow him around. Women around the world would DVR that shit just to sit around and watch Nick brush his teeth. True story.

When we get back to his house I drop my bag in his room and meet him back in the kitchen. Of course he's pouring another drink. I don't see how he still has a liver. But then here I am, right beside him, accepting another glass of wine. He leads me through the double glass doors into the backyard. The view of the river at night is beautiful. We walk down the hill to the pier and look at the reflection of the lights on the water. Nick is standing behind me with his arms wrapped around me. He leans his face in close to mine. His stubble tickles my shoulder and I can smell the scotch on his breath. This feeling right here. Absolute security in the arms of a completely masculine lover. It fills a void I didn't even know I had until now. I've always thought I could handle anything life threw at me. And I could handle it alone. I controlled my own future and I decided who, what, when, and where would be a part of it all. Nick has me questioning all of that. He has shown me what it feels like to have someone beside you. That it's okay to let someone else make the call once in a while. It's okay to let go and just *feel*.

He pulls me closer to his body, making me hyper aware of his arousal so I press my backside into him letting him know I like it. I hear him suck in the air through his teeth as he grinds himself into me in response. "You should know I'm insanely jealous right now."

Do what? Am I missing something? Did something happen that I don't know about?

"Jealous? Of what?" I ask. I try to turn to face him but he holds me in place.

His hands move to slide down the sides of my body until they reach the hem of my dress. His thumbs slide underneath, just barely as he whispers against my neck.

"For one, this dress. The way it covers your body. My hands want to do that."

Oh god. *Please keep talking.*

His fingers take the hem and pull the dress up my thighs to my waist. I never replaced the panties he ripped off me earlier so I'm bare from the waist down. The breeze kisses my hot skin, cooling me down. Nick wets his lips. His mouth is so incredibly close to my skin that I feel the kiss of his tongue against my flesh. I have goosebumps. The anticipation of his touch drives me insane. He takes the glass of wine from my hand and brings it to his mouth. "And this glass of wine. When it touches your lips. My mouth wants to be there."

He holds the glass of chilled liquid against my neck. It feels so good. My skin is scorching. He brings the glass to my lips and urges me to drink. As soon as the glass leaves my lips his mouth is on mine. The erotic sensation of the cool liquid combined with our hot mouths makes me moan. He pulls away and bites his bottom lip then nips my ear lobe.

"Spread your legs baby. Let me have you." My body obeys without question. One hand slides between my thighs, grazing the top of my mound before a single digit slips inside and discovers how wet he makes me. He slides the finger back and forth, spreading my wetness all over me.

I roll my hips against his hand, silently begging him for more. He slips the finger inside me again and my body quivers. He curls the tip and moves slowly. Holy shit I want to scream. He brings his finger back out and tugs on my swollen clit. It's so sensitive. Little shocks of pleasure shoot through my stomach. Then he starts rubbing it in slow, soothing circles. *Ohmigod.* His other hand slides up my throat and grabs my chin pulling my head back so I'm forced to look at him. His eyes are burning into mine. I open my mouth and pull the tip of one of his fingers inside. He moves the finger rubbing my clit back inside of me. It feels so good but my body is greedy. I want more. I want *him.* I grind against his hand, seeking out my pleasure. My hand makes its way behind my back to where his hardness is pressing into me. I stroke him through his jeans. *That.* That's what I want. I want to beg him to give it to me but I can't form a coherent sentence right now. His fingers have moved back to my clit and he's rubbing harder and faster now.

"Nick," I moan as I start to fumble with his belt. Shit. I'm going to come. I hold my breath and let the waves crash over me. His second hand moves from my chin to my hip to steady me. Thank goodness because I'm pretty sure I'd collapse without it. I arch my back and let the pleasure take over my body. Nick whispers against my ear. "That's it baby. Ride it out."

As I begin to come down, my body writhes and rolls with satisfaction. I lick my dry lips and catch my breath. "God you're fucking sexy," he tells me as he holds me.

The wine glass has long since fallen to the ground. I guess we'll get it tomorrow. Now that I have regained the feeling in my legs again, we head back up to the house. In the bedroom Nick inches up behind me and unzips my dress then slowly slides it off my shoulders, kissing my flesh as it's exposed. Once the fabric falls to the floor, I turn around and slip his shirt over his head then begin working on getting him out of those jeans. Nothing is rushed. And not much is said. Our bodies are saying things our words never could. I appreciate every inch of his body as I undress him. From his strong, broad shoulders to his surprisingly pretty feet. He is a thing of beauty.

Nick lays me on his bed and worships my body from head to toe. Not a single inch goes untouched by either his hands or his very talented mouth. We spend the next hour touching, teasing, licking, and kissing. I lose count of how many orgasms. Then he slides inside me, giving me what I have been craving since the minute he touched me outside. It's not the hardcore fucking from earlier. This is different. He holds my hands and takes his time. And when I come, he comes with me, kissing me with a passion as intense as my orgasm.

Friday, July 4

I don't think I even moved in my sleep last night. I fell asleep on my stomach to the feel of Nick's tender touch tickling my back. He was whispering things I probably would have liked to hear but I was too spent to recognize what they were. I don't know when he finally gave up on conversation and fell asleep too. No drool on my pillow. *Thank goodness.* But also no Nick. What time is it anyway? I get out of bed and dig my phone out of my bag so I can check the time. I have vendors meeting me here at ten o'clock and the last thing I need is to oversleep. It's only eight so I'm good. I do a quick scan through my emails to make sure there's nothing important. The venues I contacted about Hudson's fundraiser have all emailed me back. I cross my fingers and hope for good news. Apparently today is not the day for good news because all three venues are booked through the next year. Hudson needs surgery next month. Do the math. It's not happening. *Good morning Heidi. This is life. I'm here to completely screw up your day.* Newsflash life: You're a bitch. Today is mine.

CHAPTER THIRTY-TWO
Nick

My lungs are burning. My shirt is soaked. It's only seven thirty in the morning but it's already hot as hell. I usually start my morning run before the sun comes up. I usually wake up alone. Not this morning. This morning when I woke up, I saw it. Lying next to me. Peacefully breathing in and out. My saving grace. My Heidi.

She never moved as I moved her hair aside to get a better look at her face. She didn't budge when I trailed soft kisses across her bare shoulder blades. For fifteen minutes I marveled at my own personal piece of heaven. Last night was fucking perfect. I touched her like I've been waiting the past month and a half to touch her. I took my sweet time making sure she understands not one inch of her body isn't mine to touch. To taste. To have. I didn't want it to end. I could stay inside her forever.

And this morning, even though on the outside it may look like I'm in control, she's the one running the show. She calls all the shots. And she doesn't even know it. There's nothing I won't do for this woman. I've put so much energy into making her mine. I never even realized she has made me hers. Entirely, wholly, and absolutely hers.

When I get back from my run, Heidi is in the kitchen whipping egg whites and cutting vegetables. Her little white tank top hugs her curves just as tight as her black leggings do. That ass. Damn.

She smiles when she sees me. "Omelet?" That actually sounds amazing. My stomach is about to eat itself.

I move to stand behind her. She smells like peaches and flowers, like she just showered. "You didn't eat dinner. And you have lost a lot of fluid in the past twenty-four hours. I can't have you passing out on me you know." The lady's got a point.

"No. We definitely can't have that," I agree.

She turns around and wraps her arms around my neck, pulling me close to her. I'm sweaty. I'm positive I stink. But she kisses me anyway. I use all of my restraint to keep from having her ass right back on the counter like I did yesterday.

Her first vendor arrives just before ten. Heidi runs upstairs to put a second, slightly looser tank top on over the tight one. Which is probably a good thing. If I had caught the chef looking at her inappropriately I'd have had to kick his horny ass.

Heidi persuades me to leave her alone so she can focus on transforming my backyard and patio into a cocktail party paradise. Too bad my office has an entire wall of windows facing the exact area she happens to be working in. I make a few phone calls but couldn't tell you what we talked about. All I can concentrate on is watching her. The way she moves. The way she takes control. Her confidence. I'm not the only one captivated by Heidi. Out of the twenty or so people on the back lawn, the half of them that are male can't seem to get enough of her attention. Scrambling to help her move or lift something. Heidi is the poster child for independence however, so she's not having it. I laugh to myself. Those boys can't be a day over eighteen years old. They wouldn't know where to start with a woman like mine. I don't blame them for trying though.

The minute she's close enough, I knock on the glass to get her attention. When she looks my way I crook my finger motioning for her to come inside.

"You're supposed to be working, Senator," she says as she enters the room. She walks over to me, stopping in the space between the chair I'm sitting in and my desk.

"Everyone needs a break now and then," I tell her while taking her hands and pulling her onto my lap. Her legs are straddling mine and her breasts are in my face. My hands make their way under her shirt and up her back. Her skin is so soft. Her hair is pulled into a messy pile on top of her head, exposing her delicious neck to me. My mouth immediately goes for the skin there. Her fingers twist themselves into my hair and she grinds her core against my cock. She pulls her head back and then leans in to kiss me. Then she looks over her shoulder out the window to the group of people scrambling around the backyard. She slides off my lap and I grab her hips to keep her from going anywhere.

"Break's not over yet baby," I remind her. When she looks back at me she has a mischievous gleam in her eye and she's biting her lip.

She drops to her knees in front of me. I eye her curiously. "Lose an earring?"

Surely she's not going to...

And then here she is. Looking up at me with those eyes I can't say no to, and she says, "It's a fantasy Nick. Humor me." She then proceeds to unzip my jeans and slide them, along with my underwear, off my hips. And then my girl sucks my dick. Hidden from sight underneath my desk. In front of a window. In front of a yard full of people. Her tongue. Her mouth. Her hands. Good god. It's fucking phenomenal. I throw my head back and growl. She stops and looks up at me. "Ssshh. Don't let them see."

181

Fuck me. She wasn't shitting me about the fantasy. I watch her. I want to grab her hair and tangle my hands up in it. Instead I hold the edge of my desk. I want to grunt and groan. Instead I bite my lip. She goes steady until I can't take it anymore. One thrust. Two. And I'm shooting my load down her throat. "Fuck. Heidi. Shit," I say as she milks me dry then finishes off by licking me from root to tip. When she takes my balls into her hot mouth and moans, I swear I almost come again.

She wipes her mouth with her thumb and forefinger then licks her lips and smiles at me. I smile back at her and help her up. It could be the fan-fucking-tastic blow job I just got but I'm looking at her and thinking, *'How the hell did this happen? How did she pick me?'*

My girl feeds all her little helpers lunch and sends them off for the rest of the afternoon. I enjoy watching Heidi interact with the people she works with. She's not at all overbearing or pushy. It's more about knowing what she wants and making it happen. Maybe that's why they all seem to love her.

We have four hours until the party officially begins but I have a meeting with the guest of honor, Daniel Chastain, in about three. We have a few things to iron out before we get out there with all the deep pockets. I need to make sure we're on the same page on certain issues. I'll be damned if I advocate a candidate who's just going to end up being a pain in my ass.

I meet Heidi in the kitchen where she's stuffing the leftover sandwiches and fruit into Ziploc bags. I can't take my eyes off her. It's impossible to be in the same room with her and not have the urge to touch her. Is this shit normal? It's not normal for me, I know that much. I ease my way over to the sink and help her rinse the plastic serving trays. The sooner she finishes up here, the sooner I can get her back upstairs.

"Shit!" she shouts out of nowhere. My first thought is to see if she's hurt herself somehow. I grab her waist and turn her to face me, cupping her cheek with my other hand.

"What? What happened?" I ask. I don't see blood. How bad can it be? Heidi smiles and leans into the hand that caresses her face. "Nothing. I just remembered I still have to pick up my dress."

That's it? A dress? I'm sure we could work out some other form of clothing. Or she can hide in my room naked. I'm okay either way.

"Tell me where and I'll have it brought over," I offer. No need for her to stress over something as simple as picking up a dress. I forget shit all the time. Improvising is a way of life. In true Heidi fashion, she declines my offer, telling me she needs to stop by her store for a minute anyway. As much as I want to argue with her for the sake of keeping her here, I have to remind myself that she is the same woman I met a little over a month ago. The woman who carves her own path and makes her own way. Going caveman on her probably won't impress her much. So I let her go. This is fucking ridiculous. I'm sitting in my office not getting any work done because my sorry ass is staring out the window. Remembering the way Heidi looked this morning while I watched her get ready for the party. Thinking about the way she held my dick in her mouth. Pouting because she left. I'm a grown ass man. I can survive a couple of hours without my girlfriend. *Wait. What?* Girlfriend? Since when? She spent one night. That doesn't make her my girlfriend. Do I even want a girlfriend? *Only if it's her.*

Well damn. What have I gotten myself into? I have to be back in Washington on Tuesday. What are you going to do then, Nick? Make her come with you? Shit. *I have to be in Washington on Tuesday.* And I haven't gotten shit done. I guess it's time to stop acting like a pussy and do my job.

Two hours later Heidi is back and I have returned all my phone calls and emails, the ones that matter anyway, and conducted two radio interviews. Pretty productive afternoon if you ask me. Chastain will be here in less than an hour so I guess I should make myself presentable. It's been a good sixteen hours since I've been inside of Heidi and I am without any doubt frustrated right now. She greets me with a kiss and follows me upstairs. We make small talk about work while I pull my tux together. She watches with hungry eyes as I get undressed. If she only knew I want her just as badly. Well, the hard on I'm sporting probably gives it away.

Heidi approaches as I start to unfasten the button on my jeans. She moves my hand and takes over, unbuttoning and unzipping me. Her hand slips inside my jeans and rubs my cock. She strokes me a couple of times before reaching down and cupping my balls. A growl escapes my throat and I push myself into her hand. She looks up at me with a sly smile. "Miss me?" she prods.

"A little."

She strokes me once more. "Just a little? Feels like a lot."

Her tone is playful but her eyes are full of fire. I reach across and pull her tank tops over her head, one at a time, until she is standing in front of me with bare breasts and perky nipples. All this time she's been walking around with no bra. I'm incredibly jealous and turned on at the same time. No wonder those kids were following her around with their tongues hanging out. I unknowingly lick my lips at the sight, my mouth silently begging to latch on to the temptation before me. Heidi moves her hands around to my ass. She reaches down and grabs a handful, pulling me against her body as she gropes. I grab a fistful of her hair and pull her head back so I can taste her. I don't fuck around with the kiss. It's straight to the point. She responds with the same passion I come at her with. I lift her up until she wraps her legs around my waist and I carry her into the bathroom. I don't let her go while I reach in and start the shower. I sit her ass on the counter next to the sink while the water warms up. Her hands fumble around until she has my jeans pulled down from my hips then she uses her feet to push them down my legs. *So eager.* I pull on the piece of fabric holding her hair on top of her head and her long curls fall down over her shoulders. "Tell me what you want baby."

Heidi grabs my head and puts it in front of her heaving chest. "I want your mouth," she pulls my face to her breast, "right here." *Gladly.*

Then she pulls my underwear down and wraps her fingers around my dick. "And I want you," she squeezes, "inside me." *You don't have to ask me twice.*

She leans back, arching her back enough to grant me access to her full breasts. I take one in my mouth and she moans. Besides hearing her scream my name, it's the sexiest sound I know. Followed by the most annoying sound I can think of at the moment. The doorbell rings. Not once. But twice. Mother fucking Chastain is here. And he's about fifteen minutes too early. He loses points for that. Heidi snaps out of her pleasure induced reverie. "Nick. Someone's here." *Don't remind me.*

"Forget him. He can wait." I go back to kissing her neck, shoulders, and make my way back to her breast. I slide her off the counter so I can pull her pants off. She's standing in front of me in nothing but a thong and I swear if I don't get inside of her soon I'm going to go ape shit. And now my phone is ringing. Thanks for spoiling the moment, fucker.

Heidi pulls away from me. "Someone wants you almost as much as I do." I don't give a shit. This whole mother fucker could go up in flames and I will. not. stop.

I take her by the hips and hook my fingers in the sides of her panties. "Turn around."

She complies. And I slip the thin lacy fabric off her hips and down her legs. My hands automatically knead her firm little cheeks. I have an overwhelming urge to smack her ass but I'll save that for another time.

"Look in the mirror baby. I want you to see how sexy you are Heidi. I want you to see what I see." Her eyes meet mine in the glass in front of us. She immediately looks away when she realizes the view before her. I wish she knew how beautiful she is. How amazing she is. My fingers make quick work of making sure she's ready for me. She's so wet. As if I had any doubts. Then I fuck her. Like I've been waiting sixteen hours to fuck her. And when she's about to come, I grab her chin and make her watch herself in the mirror. Then I let her watch me.

The aggravating piece of shit I'm having this party for has managed to ring the doorbell three more times and call my phone twice. By now I'm sure the water running in the shower is cold but I step in anyway. I don't bother with fixing my hair or putting on a tie. I just throw on my suit pants and shirt and let Heidi know I'll only be a few minutes. She tells me she has people coming soon so I shouldn't hurry.

Daniel and I meet in my office and go over things like the health care act and his views on opening up a new pipeline for drilling. Once in a while I catch a glimpse of Heidi directing traffic outside and it makes me smile. Until I see her with the chef. They're laughing and she's got her hand on his shoulder. She's pointing at my boat. A million different scenarios are playing in my head right now. Most all of them end with me going out there and fucking the shit out of her right in front of him. I wonder if she showered. I'm hoping she didn't so he can smell me on her. Okay that's some crazy shit. Why the hell am I so jealous?

I focus on keeping on topic with Daniel and staying away from small talk. We have all night for that. I'm ready to get out of this office. By the time we wrap things up and I make it outside, Heidi has gone upstairs to finish getting ready.

I walk in the room just as she's zipping up her dress. She takes my breath away. Her hair is pulled up off her neck but a few unruly curls fall around her face. Her dress. Dammit her dress. It's black and gray and shows her bare shoulders. The top part is a see thru gray material with black lace creeping up to cup her breasts. The lace continues down and comes to a "V" just above her belly button but the entire back is just the see thru gray. It reminds me of a sexy corset. Which sparks a desire to go lingerie shopping. I imagine her walking around my house in nothing but some seriously sexy shit.

From her hips down to her feet the material is a darker gray with an almost metallic look to it. And the whole damn thing fits her like a glove.

Every inch, every curve, and just the suggestion of exposed flesh, right here on display for me.

She catches me staring and smiles. "You like the dress?"

I move closer to where she stands. "I like you wearing the dress."

"I like you liking me wearing the dress," she tells me as she traces her fingers along the collar of my shirt. We won't make it to the party if she keeps this up.

"That doesn't mean I'm opposed to you taking it off." My fingertip runs along the seam of her dress, softly tracing the tops of her breasts, plump and begging to be touched. Her hands move from my collar to the back of my head, where her fingers wrap around my hair and tug. "Nick," she says, her voice not much more than a whisper. It would be so easy to just unzip her dress and spend the rest of the night locked in this room with her. It wouldn't bother me in the least, but this is a perfect opportunity for Heidi to get her business' name out there. And there's Daniel. This is a big night for him. So I decide to keep my dick in my pants. For now.

I place my hand on top of hers and gently bring it to my lips. I place a kiss on her knuckles and smile. "We'll get to that baby. I promise." With my other hand I brush a loose curl back. "I'm ready to go show you off."

Her cheeks flush. It's not something she does often, but it's sexy when it happens. I pull out my bow tie and when I move to put it on she stops me. "Let me," she requests. Her touch is so gentle and studious. I could easily get used to this.

When we finally make it outside, most of the attendants she hired are already here. Including the chef, who is staring at Heidi like he's an inmate on death row and she's his last meal. I intentionally place a hand on the small of her back and draw her nearer to me. She inhales sharply at my touch. Seeing the way I affect her excites me. She never makes it obvious though. She remains focused on scanning the area for any adjustments to be made. Apparently she found some because she plants a kiss on my cheek and lets me know she'll be back soon. While she's tweaking and perfecting, I grab a drink and mentally whip the piss out of Chef boy-I'm-horny.

CHAPTER THIRTY-THREE
Heidi

The place is absolutely beautiful. In place of the usual tents, we constructed four white pergolas wrapped in vines and covered in lights. Under each pergola are four round tables with white table cloths and wooden chairs. Each table is decorated with a variety of different sized candles and colorful floral arrangements. Sprinkled throughout the grounds are three wine stations, each with its own server. Each station consists of three wine barrels. On one barrel are trays of glasses and on the second barrel is a selection of grapes, cheeses, and fresh bread. Under the patio is the serving station for the food, four cabaret tables, and a lighted bar for anyone who isn't a fan of wine. In the center of it all is a large white fabric gazebo set up with a dance floor and stage for the band and DJ. On one corner outside of each pergola is a large display of lanterns on barrels and greenery. Facing the water are three seating areas with a bench under a smaller wooden pergola. Lighted cylinder-shaped paper lanterns hang from the top of the pergola, which is also wrapped in vines. All in all, I'd say it's not too shabby.

Nick looks delicious in his black tux. All I need is a corsage and a back seat and it's the perfect prom date. It's scary how comfortable I feel with this man. Literally. I am scared to death. I am falling way too fast for Nick Knight and that is not good news. I had to take a time out this morning before I started acting like an idiot. As usual, Shelly was no help. Her advice was *"Good sex is hard to find. You better get it while you can."* Thank goodness for Hannah, who decided to drop a bomb on me this morning. She was supposed to be here to help me with all of this but apparently her boyfriend and his damn job obligations got in the way. He starts work in Houston on Monday and she is going with him. So not only am I losing my best event planner, I'm losing an even better friend. Needless to say, my haywire hormones take a backburner to dealing with Hudson's surgery and losing Hannah.

Joel is showing me a couple of additions to the menu for the evening when I spot Nick. With *her.* I should have known she was going to be here. Why wouldn't she be? Taylor Montgomery is dressed to kill in her painted on, bright red, bandage dress. It's short but not blatantly so. Her lipstick is bright red and her platinum hair falls around her face in vintage Hollywood style. She is fondling Nick's bow tie and laughing at something he obviously said. I just fixed that tie! And why is he letting her do that?

He just keeps talking like it's no big deal that she has her trashy little hands all over him. Joel chuckles and puts an arm around my shoulders. "She just wants the attention darling. You out class her ten to one," he tells me. It's not very reassuring but I smile and thank him anyway.

Right then Nick and his guest approach us at the food table. "Taylor, you remember Heidi?" Is he seriously introducing his booty calls to each other? This guy has some serious balls. If looks could kill, the laser beams I'm shooting him with would have him in a body bag in a minute. Joel squeezes my shoulder to calm me.

Taylor squints her eyes as if she's trying to figure something out. Maybe she doesn't remember the first time we saw each other. I do. It was the first time I saw Nick outside of the office. When I thought she was his girlfriend. The night I went home with Alex. She looks at Joel, then back at me. Then she says, "I knew you two looked familiar! Jackson Street Pub. A couple of weeks ago. You really make a beautiful couple."

No freaking way. She did not just do that. I can't see myself but I'm sure if I could, the look on my face would resemble something between complete horror and sheer anger.

"Oh, we're not...No...Not a couple....Not at all," I stutter. Nick is standing with his hands in his pockets, head cocked to one side, and his jaw is twitching. I know what he's thinking and I immediately want to defend myself. But then I remember, he just walked up here with a woman he's screwing and introduced us like we're going to be best friends or something. And if he thinks I'm into that threesome crap, he has definitely misread me. Not happening buddy. I'll see your death glare and raise you one of my own, mister.

Taylor smirks and moves her eyes to Joel's hand on my shoulder. "Hmm, well that's too bad. You look really good together." Then she looks at Nick and tugs on his arm. "Coming?" she asks.

Nick's eyes never leave mine. Like he's sending me some mental reprimand. It's intimidating but I'll be damned if I let him know that. I raise my chin and take in a deep breath, but never look away. I never even notice when Joel drops his arm from my shoulder. Nick doesn't acknowledge Taylor's question. Instead he clenches his jaw one more time, asking me, "Got a minute?"

I narrow my eyes and turn the one corner of my mouth up. "Of course." Without a response, Nick turns and walks into the house. I guess I'm supposed to follow him. I look at Joel and let out a huff as I square my shoulders and prepare for the stand-off. As I walk past Taylor I stop and say, "You know, for a reporter, you don't seem to be very good with the facts." She rolls her eyes and walks away.

Nick is leaning against the island with his back to me when I walk in. Flashbacks of yesterday and what happened on that counter take over my thoughts. I wonder if he is thinking of it too. Suddenly I'm not angry anymore. Irritated, yes. But not angry. I lean against the counter beside him. We both spend a minute just staring ahead. "Are you fucking him?" he finally asks. His posture never changes and he continues looking in front of him. Like he's worried my answer will affect him and he doesn't want me to see.

I swallow hard. "No," I answer truthfully. "How many times are you going to ask me that?"

He turns to look at me. "Until you tell me the truth."

Seriously? Double standard much?

"That is the truth. Your turn. Anything you want to tell me about Taylor?" My tone is clipped and we're in the middle of the stare down of the year, but I'm not backing down from this one. He is not going to jump my shit for something I'm not even doing when his little afternoon delight is right outside that door.

Nick moves to stand in front of me, just inches from my face. He places his hands on the countertop on either side of my body, holding me in my place. "I don't give a fuck about Taylor. Is *he* why didn't you answer my calls that Saturday? Or most of Sunday for that matter?"

"I was hung over. It was a long week. I needed a friend and a drink."

"And all of your female friends were conveniently unavailable?"

"Yes, actually. We had just finished a wedding. He was already there. I'm not fucking him Nick. Never have been. Never will be. Unlike you and her. Right?"

He doesn't answer. Which ironically *is* my answer.

"I don't like the way he looks at you. Or the way he touches you. You aren't his to touch," he says.

I know he's saying something I should reply to but I'm having a really hard time ignoring the huge lump in my throat. Shake it off Heidi. Do *not* cry. He's still screwing her. And he won't even deny it. God I wish he would. Even if it's just a lie meant to make me feel better. It's like I had built up this picture perfect relationship between us in my mind and now it's coming apart in shreds and blowing away in the wind. This is exactly why I don't do this shit. This feeling in the pit of my stomach right now. *He's still screwing her.* The way he screwed me. Just last night. Oh god. I need to throw up. I need him to get away from him. I push against his chest but he doesn't budge. I can't breathe. I need a drink. "Move," I tell him.

He narrows his eyes and twitches his lips. Is this asshole really about to smile at me? Fine. He wants truth. I'll let him have it.

"Don't you get it Nick? I'm yours. Only yours. Since the first time I walked in your office, before I even knew I would belong to you, I was yours. You have me. Body and soul." I fight back tears. I hate this. Hurting. Talking about emotions. Feeling this way.

Nick closes his eyes and lays his forehead against mine. "It drives me crazy to think of another man touching you. Tasting you."

I bring my hand to the sides of his face and bring his head up so I can see his eyes. I need him to know I'm telling the truth. "No one has done any of that. Not since the night you kissed me."

He interrupts me by placing an index finger on my lips before I can say any more. "Don't," he says.

"Don't what?"

"Don't put a time stamp on it. You accused me of not getting it, but I don't think you get it either. You do things to me Heidi. Crazy things. It doesn't matter if it was last night or last year, the fact you were with someone else, anyone else, drives me fucking nuts."

My thoughts wander to Alex and how Nick would react if he ever found out. If he feels for me half of what I feel for him, it would crush him. Or really piss him off. I'm not sure I can predict which just yet.

He glances over my shoulder and chuckles. I love his face when he's smiling. I love it when he's serious. And when he's horny. It's pretty safe to say I just love his face. "We have quite the crowd out there," he says with a smirk.

"Yea, we should probably get going," I reply. He's not moving though. His smile fades and he looks at me with those intense golden brown eyes.

"We will. There's just one more thing." My hands have fallen down by my waist. My heart is pounding, either from the adrenaline of being so upset or from the closeness of him. I nervously shift my weight from one foot to the other. The air feels too thick to breathe and I'm worried about what is coming. Nick

traces a finger down the side of my neck and over my collarbone and I immediately get goosebumps. "I'm not fucking her," he affirms. "It is true that if she had her way, that wouldn't be the case. But you have ruined me for any other woman."

He kisses me softly and sweetly. He tastes like cinnamon and scotch. He always tastes like cinnamon and scotch. It's my new favorite flavor. "I am yours Heidi."

All the nervousness disappears, replaced by total elation. I don't think I could be any happier at this moment. He takes my hand and leads me back outside where Joel has pretty much saved my ass and taken the lead. I'll have to be sure to make it up to him somehow. Maybe I can get him a date with Miss Montgomery. I laugh to myself. That's more of a *screw you* than a *thank you*. I'll think of something.

Nick is shaking hands and kissing babies. Okay he's not actually kissing babies but you get the point. I get the band set up and make sure all of the attendants have everything they need for this thing to run smoothly. I feel a hand on my back and freeze. I know it's not Nick because I'm watching him have an intense conversation with two gentlemen in tuxedos. The tall one is not bad on the eyes. The short bald one looks like he's a bit constipated. A little less cheese, a little more grapes buddy. He kind of reminds me of Elmer Fudd. Back to the hand on my back. I turn to see who is touching me, silently hoping it's not Joel. I take that back. When I see who it is, I'd almost rather it were Joel. "Absolutely stunning," Alex says in my ear.

I swallow anxiously and step away, hoping it appears more like I'm turning to face him than shying away from his touch. "Thank you. We've all worked hard making sure it's perfect."

His eyes roam my body. "I wasn't speaking of the décor, but you're right. It is perfect." Alex takes a sip of the gold liquid that fills the glass of ice. He must sense my anxiety because he leans in and whispers, "No worries love. He's occupied for the night." Alex stands up straight and takes another sip. "The only thing Nick loves more than sex is politics. It makes sense if you think about it. Either way, he's screwing someone," he adds with a chuckle. *Well that wasn't very nice.*

"And I guess as an attorney you never do that?" I arch my eyebrows at him, challenging him to disagree.

He graces me with a wide grin. I didn't realize I had missed seeing that grin until now. "There had to be a reason we're best friends, right?"

Best friends. Alex and Nick are best friends. And I have been naked with both of them. I am trash. I might as well have screwed brothers. There's no way this can end well. I decide it's better to just change the subject. "So who is he talking to anyway? He looks familiar."

"Graham Batiste. Owner of BKG, the big bad wolf who's huffing and puffing and blowing your house down," Alex informs me. His tone almost sounds regretful. He nudges my shoulder with his. "Would you like me to introduce you so you can kick him in the balls?"

I look up at him, feigning shock. "Alex! I'm a lady. I would never do that. In public." Then I nudge him back and smile.

He places a hand on the small of my back and leads me over to where Nick is now laughing at whatever Elmer just said. They all turn to look at us as we approach.

"Pardon the interruption. Mind if we join you?" Alex asks. The man I now know as the bully on the playground moves his bright blue eyes over my body before locking gazes with me.

"Nice going Alexander. Who's your friend?" Graham questions. He's speaking to Alex but keeps his eyes on me. *Nice going?* Like Alex just made three shots in a row and won the big stuffed dog at the carnival. The guy is super hot but I have a serious hunch he's a complete douchebag. Maybe it's the fact that he thinks he can run around with his big ole checkbook and take whatever he wants from whomever he feels like. Or maybe it's the fact that he's taking something from *me.* Either way, I'm not a fan.

Alex looks at Graham, then back at me. He pulls me a little closer. I'm guessing this is pure instinct and he has forgotten that Nick is not even three feet away right now. "This is…" he begins when Nick interrupts. Nick extends his hand to me and I take it. "Actually, she's with me." His hand slides around my waist then down my hip to skim my behind as if he's staking some sort of claim. *Men.*

"Graham, this is Heidi Lemaire. Heidi, Graham Batiste." He nods his head at each of us as he makes the introduction.

I didn't think he had it in him, but Mr. Batiste actually looks a little surprised. "Heidi Lemaire in the flesh. Well I can certainly see what all the fuss is about," he says as he shoots Nick a cocky grin. "Please don't take it personal. Business is business. You understand, don't you?"

I understand you're a dick.

I remember I'm a lady and fake a smile. "Of course," is all I care to reply. He reaches in his suit jacket and pulls out a card. Handing it to me, he says, "Here's my cell. If you need *anything*, call. Anytime."

Didn't Nick just say I was with him? This guy has balls of steel.

If he thinks I'm playing his game, he's got the wrong girl. I don't want your number Casanova. Just write me a check so I can move on with my life. I feel Nick tighten his grip around my waist as he takes a slight step forward. "My needs are currently all taken care of. But thank you for the offer," I reply with a smile. Hey, I'm being polite. Alex snorts then plays it off by downing the rest of his drink and scanning the crowd.

"Keep the card. You never know when things could change," Graham says with a wink. Then he looks back at Nick. "Just a bit of advice: A woman like that should never be left alone at a party like this." He plasters a cocky grin on his handsome face and looks back and forth between me and Alex. "Someone might see it as an opportunity to steal her." And with that he shakes Nick's hand and moves on to the next group of well-dressed, affluential men.

What. The. Fuck. I fight back the urge to trip him as he walks away. But I am thinking of having Joel put Visine in his food. A good case of raging diarrhea never hurt anybody. *I'm kidding.* A little.

"Well he's a keeper," I say sarcastically.

Nick laughs and pulls me closer. "He's a man used to getting what he wants and you are making that difficult for him. In more ways than one," he explains. He's wearing that irresistible crooked grin. That grin makes me want to do unspeakable things to his body.

It's a good time for Alex to excuse himself to grab another drink. Nick informs me he needs a refill as well so we make our way over to the bar. It only takes four interruptions from partygoers craving Nick's attention til we get there. It amazes me the amount of effort people put in to getting him to notice them. Although, it doesn't surprise me. He's magnetic.

Nick is ordering his drink when I spot Monica just a few feet away. I'm still embarrassed about what she walked in on yesterday. But deep down in the pit of my stomach I think I am more bothered by the look on her face when she spotted us. She looked like a kid who just found out Santa isn't real. The pain was so blatantly obvious and I can't help but wonder if there is more to their relationship than I originally thought. I know if I had to live fifty feet from Nick Knight, a strictly platonic relationship would be a full-fledged miracle.

She looks gorgeous. Her long dark hair falls around her shoulders in silky curls. She's wearing a strapless navy blue dress with a fitted bodice covered in sequins. About mid-thigh the sequins end and the rest of the material is see-thru chiffon. She catches me looking at her and smiles politely. I wrap myself in my shawl of confidence and walk over to where she stands. "Your dress is beautiful," I tell her.

Her smile becomes a little less fake and a little more genuine at my compliment. "Thank you. So is yours." It's a safe and typical response and I'm not surprised she chose it.

Nick approaches before we have to have an actual conversation. I'm all about being nice, but I don't think either one of us has had enough drinks yet to get chatty so I'm thankful for the interruption. He makes small talk for a minute then offers to introduce her to a few people. He tells me he's trying to help her land a good job. I tell him he doesn't have to explain. Then I send him out into the playground of the rich and powerful with a beautiful woman. God I'm an idiot.

'It could be worse,' I tell myself. He could be out there with Taylor Montgomery. I make a round to make sure none of the attendants needs anything, picking up empty glasses and plates on my route. Then I decide it's time to head to the bar and have a few drinks of my own.

CHAPTER THIRTY-FOUR

Nick

Graham-fucking-Batiste. Asshole extraordinaire. I'm glad my business with him is done for the night. I should kick his conceited ass for talking to Heidi like he did. But she held her own against him and I swear I could have kissed her smart little mouth right then and there. Ever since the confrontation in the kitchen, I have wanted nothing more than to take her inside and fuck her stupid. Instead I'm out here pushing my way through conversations with people and trying like hell to get to the bar. Heidi is the perfect companion, though. She stands graciously beside me and smiles her beautiful smile, hypnotizing everyone she meets. And when I finally get my drink, I am surprised to find her talking to Monica. Actually, I'm quickly learning Heidi is full of surprises. There's nothing predictable about her and I love it. She's so far removed from any other woman I've ever known. Including Elise. Which kind of scares the shit out of me and excites me at the same time.

Monica really outdid herself with the dress this time. If that doesn't impress these horny bastards, I don't know what will. I figure I'll take advantage of her boldness and go ahead and introduce her. I waited for Heidi's reaction to see if there were any hints of the jealousy from before. Nothing. I have to say, I'm a little disappointed. Seeing her jealous kind of turned me on. I'm a sick fuck, I know. But I just see it as motivation to show her exactly who I belong to and all the reasons I'm not going anywhere.

The first one I introduce Monica to is Gabriel Broussard, President of administration at Tulane. We go over proposed plans for the year ahead and then I fill him in on Monica's credentials. They hit it off great so I leave it at that and go to find Heidi, who coincidentally happens to be at the bar.

I sneak up and wrap my arms around her from behind. I feel her body tense for a split second before relaxing again. I place my mouth right against her ear. "What would you say if I told you I want to peel this dress off and taste every inch of your delicious body? Right here. Right now." I feel her take a deep breath but she doesn't move. She doesn't even turn to look at me when she responds.

"I would say, 'The zipper's in the back, Senator.' Have your way." There's that mouth again. Heidi has a way of challenging me with her dirty little words. It's like her own personal way of teasing me. Tempting me. And it makes me fucking crazy.

I'm always up for a good challenge so I inch my mouth down to her bare neck and blow, slowly and deliberately. Then I bring my lips to her throat and hold them there for just a second before nipping her hot flesh with my teeth. Not hard. Just a graze. Then I place a gentle kiss there. I know I've hit my mark when I see goosebumps appear. I inch my mouth down and begin the process over again in the new spot. This time I use my tongue instead of my teeth. "Nick," she whines, and I know I've got her right where I want her.

She apparently regains her composure because she straightens up and turns to face me. She places her hands on the sides of my face and looks me in the eye. "It's time for your speech."

Are you fucking kidding me? I'm trying to take a dip and she's worried about my speech. All I can do is smile and shake my head. My Heidi. So unpredictable.

"Yes ma'am," I tell her with a nod. Then I give her a quick kiss before I make my way to a stage in the tent located in the center of the property.

"Good evening ladies and gentlemen. What a beautiful night for a party huh?" I'm greeted with claps and "hell yeahs."

"First things first, I would like to thank the beautiful Heidi Lemaire for putting together such an amazing event on such short notice. I think I may have given her less than a month. And she definitely pulled it off." More clapping and a few high pitched whistles.

I search the crowd for her until I finally spot her to the right of the stage. She's standing next to Nate. I remember them walking up together earlier and wonder if she's with him on purpose or just by chance. She smiles and waves and those thoughts disappear. I continue with my speech, aiming to keep it short and sweet. Whether she's next to him by accident or not, I don't like the feeling I have about Heidi spending so much time with my best friend. That shit brings back bad memories.

"Next, I would like to thank you all for coming out and supporting my good friend and your next candidate for State Senator, Daniel Chastain." Again with the clapping. "Every year, each one of you plays an active role in making these fundraisers a huge success and I hope this year proves to be no different. We are all here to work together to achieve the same goal. And that goal is to attain the betterment of the state of Louisiana. Now I'll stop wasting your time and let the real star of the show take it from here." I point at Daniel and motion for him to join me on stage so he can give his speech. I can't hand him the microphone fast enough.

Heidi is laughing at something Nate just said when I find them. I place a kiss on her cheek and an arm around her waist. "Nice speech, Senator," she tells me. One corner of her mouth turns up, accentuating a cute little dimple.

"Eh, it was okay. I can think of other things I would have rather been doing, but my coordinator is a stickler for schedules," I reply with a cocky grin and a wink to let her know I'm just giving her a hard time. I know she likes when I look at her that way, so I make sure I do it often.

"Thank you for keeping her company," I say to Nate, who is busy sipping his whiskey.

"I'm quite sure it was the other way around. She's a very…fascinating woman," he informs me. As if I didn't already know this. "Feel free to go rub noses and make more money. I'll make sure she enjoys the party." His tone is sarcastic and snarky. He tips his glass to me and then takes a long sip. The air is suddenly thick with tension and my mind is going a mile a minute trying to figure out why. Is he drunk already?

"I've done all the business I plan on doing for the night," I tell him. Then I look over at Heidi, who looks a bit nervous. *Why?* "I'm all yours."

Heidi grabs my hand and squeezes. She looks up at me with reassuring eyes, as if she knows I need it. "Dance with me?" she asks, recapturing my attention.

"Anything you want baby." I lead her to the dance floor where she moves with a smooth, seductive grace. Her body follows mine step for step. My hands wander from her back to her hips and then back up. I bring her body close to mine as we sway to the bluesy beat of the music. Her hands make their way into my hair. Damn I love it when she does that. "Are you enjoying yourself?"

She wets her lips and smiles up at me. "I am now."

I want to kiss her. Badly. But I know I won't want to stop there so I settle for nuzzling my face in her neck and inhaling her sweet scent. I nudge my leg a little further between her thighs as our hips sway. She has one hand wrapped in my hair and the other entwined in mine and she's watching me watch her move. Every once in a while she smiles to herself then glances across the dance floor like she's nervous about our audience, even though I know Heidi is far from shy. I stop moving my feet so that we now just remain in the same spot, staring at each other, swaying back and forth. The rest of the world doesn't exist in this moment. There's just me and her and the music. I trace a finger tip across her cheekbone and she closes her eyes, savoring my touch. I am about three seconds from kissing her when the music comes to a stop and the band begins to play a faster song. I take her hand and lead her off the dance floor. Thankfully, we're only stopped once before we get to an uncrowded area.

"I'm sorry I haven't been much of a date," I tell her. I should have known that though. Every time I go to one of these things, much less host one, I have people pulling at me from all sides. They're either asking for favors, or telling me how to vote during the next session, or complaining about some bullshit. Once in a while I get lucky and acquire an offer to help fund my campaign. Most of the time it's in exchange for favors but anyone with a brain knows that's pretty much how politics work. I just make sure the "favors" don't do any major damage to anyone in the process and we're all good. I'm good as long as we stick to things like leasing land or approving permits, pushing deadlines up, or back, whichever the case may call for. Take Heidi's case for example. BKG is a huge financial backer of mine. Graham wanted her property. Sure, I could have stopped it. We could have gone to court and drawn it out. I would have won. But that wouldn't have benefitted anyone. The casino creates more revenue and more jobs for the city. BKG remains happy. And in turn, I made damn sure Heidi will be very well taken care of in the process. It's a win-win. Though I'm not sure Heidi would see it that way. She would probably say I'm just saving my own ass at the expense of her business. Which is exactly why I'm not discussing it with her anymore. I sent Nate all the paperwork yesterday. I am about to hand him a check for $100,000 to give to Heidi, and my role in this whole thing is complete. What? Come on. It's not a dick move. She's being more than compensated for her loss. We're giving her $100,000 cash and taking care of all of her relocation expenses. She gets to start over. With what she wants instead of just what she can afford.

So I apologize for leaving her alone most of the evening. Being the amazing woman that she is, she thinks nothing of it. "Don't apologize for doing your job Nick. You forget I'm working tonight too."

I take her other hand in mine and wrap her arms around my waist. "Well I happen to have some pull with the man who hired you and I think I can get you a break."

She laughs at my remark. "Come with me. I want to show you off," I insist before she has time to argue. I've seen the way these mother fuckers are looking at her and I want to make it crystal clear she's not just here for the drinks.

"You should have picked a better date if you wanted a trophy on your arm."

Is she kidding me? Surely she's kidding me. She has to know she's beautiful. But just in case she's serious, I decide to let her know it.

"You are the most beautiful woman here and I want everyone to know you're here with me."

She squeezes my butt and smiles up at me. "There's no need for flattery. You're already getting laid. I'm a sure thing." She crinkles up her nose and nods her head up and down in confirmation.

Absolutely fucking adorable. I can't wait to get her inside and let her make good on that promise. "No flattery. Just truth." I pull myself from her and offer her my arm. "Ready?" I ask.

"Set, go," she responds as she loops her arm in mine.

I introduce her to a few judges, an ex-governor, the current governor, and a few state senators. She is her usual charming self and they are all soon just as much under her spell as I am. She has such poise and grace. And confidence. Whether it's real or just for show, it's like she's been doing this all her life. Although I suppose she is no stranger to social gatherings and people skills is pretty much a job requirement for her, so it shouldn't surprise me that she fits right in. When we meet up with the CFO of Halliburton, he brings forward a proposition that we should discuss somewhere more private.

"Go get 'em tiger," Heidi whispers to me as she plucks a kiss on my cheek. "My break's over anyway. Time to make another round."

"I'm sure your assistant can handle it baby."

"I'm sure she could too. If she hadn't quit this morning."

Damn it. Why didn't she tell me this earlier? Because she's stubborn and thinks she can handle everything on her own, that's why. *Mental note: Show Heidi she can depend on you.*

She must see the hesitation in my expression. Halliburton can wait until normal business hours. If Heidi needs me to help her now, that's what I will do.

"Go," she commands with a shoo of her hands. "I've got it all under control. The hard part's over. It's all downhill from here," she assures me. Though I'm not sure if she's lying or not since I've never organized one of these things myself.

"I'm sorry," is all I manage to say. I know she has to be upset even though she would never let it show.

"It's okay. You can make it up to me later. Go make your money," she says with a wink. I take her hint and bring the meeting inside to my office where we go over specs and set up a formal meeting at my downtown office Monday morning.

Thirty minutes later I've covered all the ground outside and still there's no sign of Heidi. I decide to take the opportunity to track down Nate and handle this check business. Oddly, I don't find him either. He probably had a few too many and found someone hot, willing, and ready to drive him home. Damn. I'll catch him later I guess. Right now, I am wondering where the hell Heidi is. I carry my search inside the house. Voices upstairs catch my attention. I stop just outside my bedroom to get a closer listen.

"We're not talking about this Alex. Just unzip the damn dress so I can get this over with," I hear Heidi say. *Alex?* That's what everyone calls Nate. Well, everyone but me. Is she talking to Nate? Why the fuck is she telling him to unzip her dress?

"I have a right to know if you're fucking him, love. I think I at least deserve the truth here. Even though it's pretty fucking obvious. I want to hear you say it."

What the fuck? It is Nate. Why in the hell does he give a shit who she's fucking? And what makes him think he deserves anything? Who the fuck does he think he is? Wait. *Love.* Did he just call her *love*?

"You're drunk," she tells him.

I'm not going to keep standing here like a fucking pussy. I walk in the room. Heidi is standing by the bed and Nate has his hands on her. His fucking hands on her. Her back is to him and he is standing right behind her, positioned to unzip her dress. He's leaning forward and "ssshhh-ing" her in her ear. The room disappears and all I see is red. I don't see Nate. I don't see Heidi. I just see red. This isn't happening. I grab Nate by the back of the shirt and slam him against the nearest wall, face first.

Heidi turns around, eyes wide and jaw dropped. "Nick! Stop! Ohmigod!" Nate turns to swing at me but I get him first. I'm pretty sure I busted his mouth. That's it. I'm done. I turn to Heidi who has lost all color from her face. I think she may even be crying but I'm too fucking mad to care. I approach her slowly, cautiously. She doesn't move. She stands completely still. Breathing slow, calculated breaths. She's afraid of me. It's written all over her face. I wipe a tear from her cheek then place my hand on her shoulder, rubbing circles there with my thumb. God, even as angry as I am, I still can't help myself from touching her. I look her deep in the eyes. She meets my intense gaze, never faltering as I inch closer to her. "Get your things and get the fuck out of my house." My voice is surprisingly calm. Stern. Cold.

She reaches out to touch me and I grab her wrist. "Nick it's not what you…" she starts to explain.

"I'm only going to ask this once Heidi. So be very careful how you answer." I silently debate on whether or not to move forward with my questioning. I'm not sure I want to know the answer. "Did you fuck him?" My words are slow and deliberate.

She swallows hard as she looks up at me. Our entire future dissolves right there in her eyes. She lets a few tears fall freely then starts to cry harder. So there's my answer. And here I thought it was the chef I had to be worried about. Joke's on me. "I believe I asked you to get out," I repeat.

"Nick, please," she pleads. I can't look at her. I can't touch her. I can't talk to her. I'll give in. I know it. And I'll be damned if I let this happen again. I turn my back and walk out of the room. I hear her sobs as I continue down the hallway to the stairs. At least she's smart enough not to chase after me. I just hope she's smart enough to get the fuck out. And take her boyfriend with her.

I spend the rest of the night on my boat. With Johnnie. I'm not in the mood to bullshit and I'm certainly not in the mood to stay sober. I'll sort through all the shit running in my head tomorrow. But tonight, tonight I curse the day I ever met Heidi Lemaire.

ALEX

I had three different plans for how this evening should go. Plan A: I bring a date, hoping Heidi is at least a little bit jealous, and then get too shitfaced to really care. Plan B: I continue to pretend that the whole fucked up situation doesn't exist. And then get too shitfaced to care that it actually does. And Plan C: I fake food poisoning and skip the entire thing altogether. I go with Plan B. Probably wasn't the best of the three, being that the "getting shitfaced" part of the plan backfired. Instead of making me numb, it brought everything I've been feeling for the past weeks to the surface.

Then I see Heidi. She is breathtaking. She had me interested, in yoga pants and tank tops. In this dress, I'm downright bewitched. I spent most of the sober part of the evening just watching her. The way she confidently smiles at all these people she's probably never seen before. The way she graciously picks up empty glasses and refills the buffet pans. Like she's part of the serving staff instead of the one signing their checks. Nick is doing what he does best. Charming the pants off everyone in sight. He has a gift for that. You almost can't help but be drawn to him. Too bad he is completely impervious. I have to admit he's different with Heidi though. But I suspect most people are.

Somewhere around my third drink in, I get the courage to approach her. She is visibly on edge. Almost as if she's afraid to be talking to me. I let her know the coast is clear. Strictly for her benefit. At this point I don't care if Nick sees us or not. She wants to know about Graham Batiste. So I introduce them. Or at least attempt to. My good friend Nick has to stake his claim and make it clear the prize is all his. We don't compete for women. We may have shared one or two but all in all, it's never been an issue. I have my type. Nick has his. And Heidi is surprisingly not his normal type. He usually prefers them shallow, weak, and plastic. He calls them disposable. Heidi is none of those things. She is however, every bit my type. She had me hook, line, and sinker from the moment she talked back to me in my class. I knew her little agreement was shit when we made it but if it was the only way to get my foot in her door, then I say what the hell. Every time I think of her, which is pretty much daily, I wonder what would have happened had I not convinced her to choose him. Would she have chosen me? Would things be different?

And now he's parading Monica around like she's his prize. Idiot. He doesn't ever say much about her but I do know that they swapped bodily fluids right after the big blow up with Elise and Matthew. Coping mechanism I suppose. Since then he has this overwhelming sense of obligation to take care of her. Whether or not they're still banging, I don't know. Never cared. Until now. For once, I agree with Graham. How do you leave a woman like Heidi alone? Unless they're still trying to figure things out. Maybe she's having second thoughts.

No sooner am I thinking he's a prick for abandoning his date for another woman, than I see him approach Heidi near the bar. His hands and mouth are all over her, sparking intense emotions inside of me. His actions are far too intimate for someone trying to figure things out. I should have gone with Plan C.

I'm on drink five, I think, when I hear her voice behind me. "There you are. I've been looking for you," Heidi says. My expression must give away the fact that I'm completely blindsided by her statement.

"Nick is busy and this isn't my usual crowd." She scans the groups of people around us. I follow her lead and have a look myself.

"So you decided to slum it over here with me?" I ask, amused.

She nudges me with her shoulder. "Stop it," she says. Her eyes move from my face down to my feet and back up again. She arches a brow and smiles seductively at me. "You know, you clean up pretty nice."

"I doubt your date would approve of you flirting with me ma'am." I'm mostly joking but there is a hint of sarcasm in my voice.

"Not flirting. Observing." She pops up on her tip toes to whisper in my ear. "This is where you say thank you."

I respond to her observation with a grin. "In that case, may I *observe* that you look beautiful?"

Her cheeks flush at the compliment. She has no idea how stunning she really is. "You may," she says. "And thank you."

Nick begins his speech, commending Heidi, deterring her attention from me. It isn't long before he's finished and headed our way. I can't say I blame him. I wouldn't want to share her either. As a matter of fact, I *don't* want to share her. Why does he get to win anyway? Just because he got screwed over once. I've been screwed over. We've all been screwed over. Heidi wasn't even given the chance to choose. I forced her decision. And now I want her to have it back.

She must notice the tension in the air because she puts distance between us by luring Nick to the dance floor. If I have learned one thing about Heidi, it's that she doesn't like anger and she doesn't like conflict. The way the two of them mold together on the dance floor, it looks like she's succeeded. When the dance is over, Nick spends a little time introducing her while I work on drink number six.

Halfway through she's dragging me by the arm into the kitchen. "I really need your help right now Alex," she commands, her voice frantic and agitated. She lets go of my arm once we're inside and growls. "I can't believe that bitch! God I hate her!" She's really cute when she's mad. I stifle back a laugh. I assume my role as her assistant and wait politely for my orders. But I can't hold back my smile. "It's not funny!" she shrieks. "She tore my dress," she says as she turns around to show me the huge rip in the skirt of her gown. She rolls her eyes and shakes her head. "And I know it wasn't an accident. You don't just step on someone's dress with five inch heels." She growls again and I chuckle.

"Come on love, it's just a dress," I tell her. Although I have to admit I'm mentally replaying the incident in my head, trying to figure out how the rip got so large. She's still irritated so I continue, "Tell me what happened."

"Taylor Montgomery. That's what happened." She pauses to take a deep breath before continuing. *Ohh.* I get it now. Taylor would obviously be a sore spot for Heidi considering...well...you know.

"She's standing behind me being obnoxious and when I decide to walk away, she accidentally lands her heel on the hem of my dress. Well of course she doesn't pick up her foot, so the more I move, the more it tears. And now this," she says, pointing angrily at the big hole.

"And now you want me to help you pick her up and throw her in the river?"

She shoots me a confused look. "What? No. I need you to unzip me so I can change," she explains. I guess she didn't find my comment amusing. She grabs my hand and leads me to the stairs. "Hurry, before Nick comes. I don't want him to think I'm just being dramatic."

What the hell. Me. Heidi. Unzipping clothing. I'm in. Doesn't matter the cause. Hold on. How does she know where his bedroom is? Why are her things here? Has she spent the night here? *Is* she spending the night here? Breaking her rules already. With him. "Planning a sleepover? So soon?" I ask. My tone is condescending and I'm positive she knows where I'm going with this.

"We're not talking about this Alex. Just unzip the damn dress so I can get this over with," she tells me. She never has been one for talking. The alcohol makes me forget about being a gentleman.

"I have a right to know if you're fucking him, love. I think I at least deserve the truth here. Even though it's pretty fucking obvious. I want to hear you say it." This is it. The final nail in the coffin. The moment I've spent the past two and a half weeks dreading. Nick is my best friend and I want this

204

for him. He deserves it. I just wish it didn't have to be *her*. No matter what I told her, a small part of me wishes she would tell me I made a mistake pushing her to be with Nick. That she was mine first. But I see the way she looks at him. The way they look at each other. And I know whatever we had is gone. It was exactly what she told me it was going to be. She never lied or made false promises. Casual sex between two people. Nothing more. But *they* have more. Anyone with eyes can see that. I'm just hardheaded and need to hear it for myself.

"You're drunk," she dismisses.

I lean in to convince her to disregard my mental state and hear me out anyway.

In a split second all I see is black. And suddenly there's a throbbing pain right by my temple. I hear Heidi yell but am not quick enough to see what or whom she's yelling for. Instinct kicks in and I swing but miss my target. Then I'm on the ground and the entire side of my face is stinging from the impact of someone's fist. What the fuck? I open my eyes and the floor is blurry. Blood drips from my brow and there's immediately a bitter copper taste in my mouth. Shit. I blink to focus.

Nick. His voice is cold and hard. I can't make out what he's saying but I can imagine. Depending on what part of the conversation he walked in on and how things looked from his angle. Okay so I deserve this ass kicking. I should have left it alone. Now Heidi is crying and he is gone. I know what he must be thinking. I know what I would be thinking if I were in his place. I also know he won't be coming back for an explanation. No. He's got way too much pride for that. All I can do now is help Heidi pick up the broken pieces and hope like hell he changes his stubborn mind. She deserves a man who can realize exactly what she's worth. Maybe that man can still be me.

To be continued…

Thank you for reading! I really hope you enjoyed my debut. Nick and Heidi's story continues in part two: A Man's World, which is available NOW!!!

I also have two other works in progress. Sin With Me is set to release late Summer 2016 and Amesbury Park is set to release Fall 2016.

I've included a little excerpt of part two for your reading pleasure. Enjoy!

A Man's World

Part two of A Woman's Touch series

By Delaney Foster

CHAPTER ONE
Heidi

You know when you're watching a movie and you know something bad is about to happen but there's nothing you can do about it? So you just sit there on the edge of the sofa and wait for it to be over. Yeah. That's pretty much how I would describe what just happened.

Taylor Montgomery was determined to make sure Nick wanted nothing to do with me. Well, she got her wish. Although I bet she never thought this would be how it played out. I knew when Alex followed me upstairs after she tore my dress nothing good would come of the situation. I am just too stupid to connect my thoughts with my vocal chords. I should have told him to go back downstairs. I should have told him I had it handled. And I never should have asked him to help unzip my dress. Another stupid move. In my defense, it's not like I asked him to take it off or anything. As a matter of fact, I remember specifically telling him to unzip and leave. That's when I realized how drunk he was. And how hurt.

Alex is a really good guy. We had a good thing. Until I met Nick Knight. Nick is like gravity to me. I am pulled to him. Whether I want to be or not. I don't have a choice. I'm not sure I ever did. It's been one month since Nick came into my world and flipped it upside down. And now he's gone. Alex is bruised and bloody. And I am standing here in a $1200 dress that looks like a family of rats got a hold of it. Not exactly the way I had imagined this evening going.

I am a whirlwind of emotions right now. Surprise turns to worry. Worry to afraid. Afraid to want. Want to need. Need to pain. The look in Nick's eyes when he walked in the room was like nothing I had ever witnessed. Not when Trey would get angry and flip shit. Not even when I told Cole I was leaving. This was different. This was deeper. Darker. Some crazy combination of emotions I've never seen before. When he approached me after wailing on Alex. So slowly, so calm, it was all I could do to just stand and wait for him to make his move. I wanted to reach out and touch him. Soothe him. I need to tell him he's thinking some really crazy shit right now. Beg him to listen. But one look, one touch, and I knew that would be pointless. He needs time. So I watch the man I don't think I can live without walk out of this room. Without asking him to stay. Without following him. I don't think my heart can take hearing him tell me it's over before it's really only just begun. I lean my head back against the thick post and slide my way down until my butt hits the floor.

Alex coughs and pulls me out of my trance. Oh god. He looks horrible. Why didn't he fight back?

It's not like he doesn't know how. I have watched him beat shit up every Tuesday night for the past three months. "Ohmigod Alex!" My eyes pop open and my hands fly to my mouth when he turns to face me. There's blood spilling off the top of his right brow where the skin is split open and he has a nasty cut and there's some decent size swelling going on right at his cheekbone. His lip is busted and bleeding.

"Come on, love. It's not that bad," he says, attempting to smile. He winces at the action so I'm guessing it *is* that bad. He scoots toward me and leans against the side of the bed, letting the mattress support his weight.

"You keep telling yourself that, champ."

Alex makes another attempt at smiling. It hurts me to look at him. "Come here. Let me look at that."

He does as I ask and scoots closer to where I am sitting. I lean in and inspect the damage. It's hard to tell if he needs stitches or not because there's so much blood. I move to get a closer look. Our faces are just centimeters apart and he's giving me this intense look. I've seen that look before. God, what have I done? "Alex, I'm so sorry." He brings his hand to my face in an attempt to comfort me. The gesture is gentle. Sweet. I can't do this. Instinctively, I look over my shoulder at the door.

"He's not coming back Heidi," Alex tells me, his expression apologetic.

"I know." And I do. As much as I want him to barge back in here and admit he overreacted. To hold me and kiss me and tell me we'll work through this. I know he's caught in a place somewhere between hurt and anger. I've been in that place. And even though being there alone probably isn't the best route to take, it's the one way to ensure things aren't said. Things that will be regretted later. Things that emotions can disguise as truth.

I stand and reach for Alex's hand. "Come on. Let's get you cleaned up."

To be continued...

48844307R00119

Made in the USA
San Bernardino, CA
07 May 2017